DOG TRAINING
THE
AMERICAN MALE

L. A. Knight

WJM BOOKS
AN IMPRINT OF A&M PUBLISHING
FLORIDA

DOG TRAINING THE AMERICAN MALE
Published by WJM Books
An imprint of A&M Publishing, L.L.C.
West Palm Beach, FL. 33411
www.AMPublishers.com

ISBN: 978-1-943957-00-2

Printed in the United States of America

ACKNOWLEDGMENTS

It is with great pride and appreciation that I acknowledge those who contributed to the completion of Dog Training the American Male.

First and foremost, many thanks to the great team at WJM Books/A&M Publishing—editors Tim Schulte and the amazing Barbara Becker, marketing guru Michelle Colon-Johnson and publicist Lissy Peace, as well as Trish Stevens at Ascot Media Group. Special thanks to Mark Maller and Belle Avery, as well as our amazing webmasters, Doug & Lisa McEntyre at Millennium Technology Resources.

This novel (loosely based on actual events and dog training episodes with our first German Shepherd and her wacky trainers) is dedicated to two wonderful people who left us way too early. The first is my father, Lawrence, our Knight in shining armor who believed that laughter was the best medicine. The second is Mark's oldest son, Wade, a friend to all. This imprint is named in his honor.

Blessings,
L.A. Knight

You can contact L.A. Knight by email at:
LAK82159@aol.com
Visit L.A.'s website:
http://laknightentertainment.com/

1

Nancy

NANCY BEACH'S HAZEL eyes snapped open in panic, her heart pounding as if it was chugging blood from a water cooler. *You fell asleep! What time is it? Did you miss the interview?*

She nearly lost her breakfast when she saw the credits rolling on the greenroom's flat-screen television. Then she saw the digital clock.

Nine fifty-seven. Oh, God ... thank you. Thank you, thank you, thank you.

She realized she was no longer alone in *The Today Show* guest waiting room. An angelic little girl with blonde curls occupied the chair to her left. The eight-year-old's feet dangled over a cushion as she read the *Wall Street Journal*.

Impressed, Nancy asked, "Are you really reading that?"

"The future looks bleak. Mother says I need to

1

be prepared. Why is that disgusting man staring at you?"

Nancy turned to her right where a one-legged Hell's Angels biker was gazing at her from across the fake-glass coffee table like a Rottweiler in heat. In return, she offered a polite smile. "Is there something on your mind?"

The biker grinned, continuing to stare at the perky mounds of flesh pressing against her cream-colored blouse.

"*Kathie Lee & Hoda* starts in one minute. Do you really think it's necessary to make me feel so uncomfortable before my interview?"

The little girl folded back her page, glancing at the Fortune 500 stocks. "He can't make you feel anything. Why are you giving him all your power?"

"I'm not. I'm just trying to reason—"

"He's a mongrel. He doesn't possess the social capabilities to reason."

Nancy whispered, "But he only has one leg."

"Yes, and he's mentally raping you with the one on the right. Tell him he either takes a hike, or you'll punt his frank and beans up his asshole with your size-eight Pradas."

The biker's smug smile evaporated. Struggling to stand using his crutch, he hobbled into the corridor, grumbling to himself.

Nancy's flesh tingled as the theme music for *The Today Show with Kathie Lee & Hoda* pumped out of the flat-screen television.

The little girl continued to scan the stock index while offering advice. "Predators sense fear. Are you really ready for your interview? Those two bitches will eat you alive if you don't bring you're a-game."

"I'm ready."

"You'd better be more than ready. Your Arbitron ratings are in the toilet. *The Today Show* booking is manna from heaven—a make-it-or-break-it moment."

"I prepped for weeks. I've got my six success points down pat and two really amusing anecdotal stories—one for single women, one for married ladies. I'm just not sure how to get the men interested."

"I suppose you could flash them your tits. It's keeping them interested that always gets you in trouble."

"Excuse me?"

"Dark clouds are forming on your horizon. Sorry, just reading your horoscope. You're a Libra, yes? I saw it on your Facebook bio. Uh-oh." The child pointed to the television, where Hoda and Kathie Lee were taste-testing wine with their first guest, a French chef.

Nancy watched, horrified. "Look at them! They're sucking down Château Margaux like it was drawn from the Fountain of Youth. They'll be toasted by the time—"

"Mrs. Beach, we're ready for you." The associate producer, a black woman in a navy collared shirt, khaki pants, headphones and sneakers entered the greenroom.

"It's Dr. Beach, actually. I have a doctorate and an MBA. It should be in my intro."

"Got it right here. If you'll follow me, and watch your step."

"Dead woman walking," muttered the blonde-haired eight-year-old, turning another page.

Nancy followed the associate producer down a restricted-access corridor past the make-up room. "That little girl—who is she?"

"Just another child prodigy destined for mediocrity." The producer stopped at the stage-right entrance of Studio A. "Wait here."

A sound man joined them, clipping the business end of a pencil eraser–sized microphone to the collar of Nancy's blouse and the battery pack to the back of her charcoal-gray skirt.

Through a maze of booms, bright lights and mobile cameras trailing thick black power cords, she spotted her quarry. Kathie Lee Gifford and Hoda

Kotb were "in commercial," while an assistant prepped them for their next segment.

Nancy closed her eyes and mentally recited her radio-host mantra like it was the Lord's Prayer: *I am the keeper of my own fate, emancipating myself from the self-imposed bonds of my gender. I am the keeper of my own fate, emancipating myself from the self-imposed bonds of my gender. I am the keeper of my own fate.*

"And we're back. Hoda, I just love Miami, I wish we could stay here more than a week. Do you love Miami as much as I do?"

"Absolutely. But do you know what I love more than Miami, Kathie Lee? Thursdays. And today is Thursday, which means it's time for 'Okay—Not Okay.'"

"Right you are, Rooda woman … oops. Did I just say Rooda?"

"You called me rude!"

"It was the wine. My lips are numb. You know I'd never call you rude, unless of course you made a comment about my belly flab."

Nancy's pulse ticked upward. *Come on, ladies. I'm losing precious seconds of air time.*

"Anyway, Ho-down, this morning we're going to be discussing relationships."

"Which brings us to our next guest, a relation-ship counselor who hosts a local radio show in West

Palm Beach called *Love's a Beach*. Let's welcome … Dr. Nancy Beach."

The producer gestured.

Nancy walked into the blinding lights and audience applause. She waved to no one in particular then took the vacant stool on Kathie Lee's left, her eyes straying to the two teleprompters.

"*Love's a Beach*—I love that, don't you, Hoda?"

"It's perky. She's perky. How old are you, fifteen?"

Nancy maintained her grin until her cheeks twitched, waiting for the audience's laughter to subside. "Actually, I'm twenty-six, with a doctorate degree from Penn."

Education established. First success point down. Five to go.

Kathie Lee looked impressed. "Penn, wow. Were you called in to console those poor victims assaulted by that creepy football coach, Jerry Sandusky?"

"That was Penn *State*, Kathie Lee."

"Okay. So were you?"

"No. I'm actually a relationship and intimacy specialist. My radio show, which airs on WOWF 1160 AM weekdays from noon 'til three, counsels women to better empower them in their business and personal relationships with the Y chromosome: *men*."

Points two and three down. Three to go.

Hoda nodded to the audience. "Empowering women in their relationships with the Ys; that really is so important."

Kathie Lee smirked. "Believe me, I ask myself why all the time. Why, Regis? Why? Why? Why?"

"Dr. Beach, how many years have you been married?"

"Oh, I'm not married."

"Engaged?" asked Kathie Lee.

Nancy's pulse pumped faster. "I *was* engaged. Twice. Suffice it to say neither relationship worked out."

"Sounds to me like you could have used a relationship and intimacy counselor. Am I right?" Hoda turned to the audience for support.

The audience applauded.

"Oh, stop it, Ho-woman. I'm sure Dr. Bitch … oops. Did I really just say that? I meant Dr. Beach—"

"Were they sleeping around on you?"

"Huh?"

"Your two fiancés," Hoda asked, continuing her cross-examination. "Did they cheat?"

"Been there, sister," Kathie Lee chimed in. "Of course, you don't toss the baby out with the bath water. Not if you really love one another."

"Or if you're planning someday to run for president," Hoda added with a snarky smirk.

Nancy casually dispersed a sweat bead touring her right cheekbone. "It's funny you should mention that. In my women's counseling seminars—"

Kathie Lee interrupted point four. "Are you dating anyone special now?"

"Dating? No. I'm sort of between boyfriends."

"Oh. What about women? Ever think about playing for the home team?"

"No. But my older sister, Lana—"

"Forget your lesbian sister," said Hoda, cutting her off. "How long since *you* had any?"

"Since I had any what?

"Sex. And no counting vibrators or dildos."

"Oh, they never count vibrators or dildos," Kathie Lee chirped, addressing the studio audience. "Why is that, I wonder? And who exactly is *they*?"

"Shh, I want to hear her answer. C'mon, Dr. Beach, when's the last time you felt a man's sausage squeezed between those silky twenty-six-year-old gymnast thighs?"

Nancy's pulse danced along her neck, her rattled psyche seconds from a full-blown meltdown. *How would Hillary Clinton handle this assault? Would Sheryl Sandberg dignify this inquisition with a response?* "Hoda, for now I've chosen to prioritize my career over my social life."

"Don't avoid the question; just give us a time

frame. Six months?"

"I, uh—"

"Longer?"

"I don't know … maybe a year."

Kathie Lee's eyes widened. "A year? You're twenty-six, and you haven't had sex in a year? Good God, did you join a convent?"

The audience roared, encouraging another assault by Hoda. "Listen, sweetie, take some advice—use it or lose it. Youth is like a man who has hit thirty—it only comes around once. Before you know it, you'll be forty and injecting Botox like it was heroin. Then you'll hit fifty, and you'll be waking up every hour with night sweats and hot flashes. Am I right, Kathie Lee, or am I right?"

Kathie Lee nodded. "Menopause—they should call it women-opause."

"Wait, wait, I just realized something," Hoda said, facing her audience. "How can a talk-show radio therapist advise her callers about marriage when she's never been married, relationships when she isn't in one, or sex when she isn't getting laid? That seem strange to you, Kathie Lee?"

"Like a three-input ding-dong … can you imagine? Hey sex doctor, my birth canal is a two-lane highway compared to your unused twat."

Nancy's retort caught a dry spot in her throat,

and suddenly she couldn't speak.

"Good one, Kathie Lee. I bet blondie's vag is so tight, she uses it to store loose change."

"Unlike you, Ho-Ho. You could hold two Gucci purses and a Dooney and Bourke handbag in that man cave of yours. Oh hell, I just peed my pants."

"Aaaaahhhh!"

❧ ❧ ❧

Nancy Beach shot up in bed, her heart pounding, her Penn Quaker Athletics tee-shirt soaked in sweat. Hyperventilating, it took her a full thirty seconds to realize that she was in bed in her sister's apartment, that it was all just a dream.

Wow.

The emerald glow from the digital alarm clock read 5:13 a.m. Reaching for a clothing drawer, she pulled out a clean tee-shirt, stripped and changed, and then resettled herself beneath the quilt, her "inner Freud" providing a post-game analysis of her dream.

The blonde kid, obviously that was me—a child prodigy destined for mediocrity. And Hoda and Kathie Lee, their barbed responses—a window into my own neurosis. The biker—another man waiting to take advantage of my kindness ... Unless it was Dad? The eight-year-old me telling the adult me to kick him in the balls, to take control of my life. I really had it together when I was a kid. God, what the hell happened to me?

Stop!

That's victim-speak. So you went through a few bad relationships—big deal. You're focusing on your career now. It's definitely needed. Only my career as a radio host and relationship counselor deals with relationships, rendering my advice more theoretical, rather than organic—which is why my ratings suck.

Stop!

You're a Penn graduate, a qualified psychologist with an MBA. You don't need a Y in your life to teach women how to secure a place for themselves at the workplace table. You don't need to be groped on a blind date by a junior partner in a law firm in order to teach women how to speak up more in board meetings. And who the hell names their kid Hoda anyway?

It took ten minutes before Nancy's toxic thoughts yielded to exhaustion, her breathing settling into a soothing rhythm.

The heart-stopping *whrrrrrrr* of a blender violated the early morning silence, reigniting her pulse. Eyes wide open, she stared at the ceiling, her blood simmering as she waited for the cursed blender to cease. When it continued into a second minute, Nancy kicked off the blanket and leaped out of bed. Striding barefoot toward the door, her right foot planted itself firmly in the plastic container of kitty litter, a gravel-coated nugget squeezing between her toes like silly putty.

She looked up at God, exasperated. "All right already, I get it. Enough with the stupid metaphors!"

Her sister's tabby poked its head inside the tiny bedroom, the cat's audible protest obliterated by the blender.

"I hate you too, Madonna."

Walking to the bathroom on her heel, she stepped inside the bathtub and rinsed the cat turd from between her toes. She dried her foot and headed for the kitchen, intent on silencing the annoying blender.

Poised before Nancy was the back of a shirtless bodybuilder possessing the deeply tanned, steroid-enhanced posterior physique of a young Arnold Schwarzenegger. The top of the bodybuilder's red unitard remained rolled down around the sculpted hourglass waist to the matching sweatpants. Power-ful rear deltoids rippled as the Adonis's arms swung back in a slow stretch, causing the wing-like latissimus dorsi to dance.

"Jeanne?"

No response.

"Jeanne!"

The athlete-in-training turned, revealing a pair of naked, surgically-enhanced breasts—two pale-white silicon grapefruits dangling from the trunk of the wrong tree.

The female bodybuilder shut off the blender. "Morning, Nance. Did I wake you?"

"You woke half of Boca." Nancy attempted to focus on the woman's chestnut-brown eyes, but the boobs were bobbing and weaving above the six-pack abs like two mutant glands in a bad horror movie. "Jeanne, no offense, but do you think you could sling the twins?"

"Why? Do my tits make you nervous?"

"Your camel toe makes me nervous; the rest I don't want to think about. I mean, you are my sister's … you know."

"Come on, you can say it … *lover*." Jeanne pulled the top of the unitard up over her breasts. "You've shared our apartment for over a year now, and you still can't accept that."

"I accept it. I just don't want to see you naked."

"See who naked?" The bedroom door across the hall opened, and Lana joined them. The thirty-one-year-old brunette wore only a towel. Nancy's big sister snuggled in Jeanne's massive arms, her hands reaching around to grope her lover's buns of steel.

"Eww, so hard. Like tortoise shells. Am I the luckiest bitch in Boca?"

"No, I am."

"Unh unh, baby, I am."

"No, I am."

"Will you two shut up!"

Lana winked at Jeanne. "Looks like somebody got up on the wrong side of the bed."

"Up? This isn't up. This is me sleepwalking with menstrual cramps. It's 5:40 in the morning."

"Damn, I'm gonna be late for my *Sand and Six-Packs at Sunrise* class. Gotta run, sweet cakes." Jeanne poured the blender's green sludge into a thirty-two-ounce cup and then offered Lana a passionate good-bye kiss from her sun-chapped lips.

"Baby, don't forget your doctor's appointment."

"Aw, Lana, you know how I hate going to the gynecologist. They look at me like I'm some kind of freak."

"Please, baby. This one comes highly recommended. Dr. Vincent Cope—I texted you his address. Be there by 9:15."

"I'll do it for you." Jeanne grabbed her car keys from a peg and bounded out the front door of the apartment like Hercules's twin sister.

Nancy locked the door behind her. "We need to talk."

Lana turned on the coffee maker, filling the glass pot with water. "I told you about Jeanne's new training schedule, so don't start complaining."

"I'm not complaining. Okay, I am complaining. I'm exhausted, Lana. These walls are paper-thin, and the two of you go at it every night like a bad episode of something on Animal Planet."

"Can I help it if we're back in the honeymoon stage?"

"It's not normal."

"Who cares about normal? We're in love. And since when did you become the standard bearer of normal—the relationship counselor who no longer believes in relationships?"

"On that note, I'm going back to bed." Nancy escaped to her bedroom, Lana in pursuit.

"Don't just walk away—hey, what happened to Madonna's litter box?"

"I stepped in it … again. Can't you find a better place for it than in my bedroom?"

"Technically, it's Madonna's bedroom; she was here first."

"Madonna doesn't pay a third of the rent; I do. Then again, I'd rather smell cat shit than your girl-friend's yeast-infected thongs." Nancy climbed back in bed.

"Aw, poor little victim. Why don't we talk about what's really bugging you."

"My ratings will climb. I've been working my ass off to build an audience."

"I'm not talking about your radio show, Nancy. You have no social life. It's been fourteen months and three Adele CDs since Sebastian cheated on you."

"It's been fourteen months since I *caught* Sebastian cheating on me. The little bastard was banging my roommate right up until her second trimester. And leave Adele out of this; the woman's a saint."

"Yeah, the patron saint of misery. Enough with the cry-fests. Get back in the game."

"What? Dating? How many times must I tell you? I'm in career-building mode. I don't have time to devote to a relationship."

"Then how about a few one-night stands, just to keep the vag from sealing up? Just make sure he wears a rubber, and don't give him the password to your computer."

"I never gave Dan my password. Okay, I sort of gave it to him when his computer went down. I never thought he'd access my online banking and steal Dad's inheritance."

"Maybe you're just sick of the male form. Don't look at me like that. It happens. Being bi-curious was the best thing to happen to me."

"I'm not into women, Lana. And seriously, Jeanne's got more testosterone in her than half the Miami Dolphins."

"Don't let those muscles fool you. Jeanne's all woman where it counts. She thinks like a woman, she loves like a woman—"

"And she screws like a teamster."

"Listen to you. You are so angry. Jeanne makes me happy. Remember happy? You haven't smiled since Dad died."

"Don't go there."

Lana sat on the edge of Nancy's bed and brushed her sister's blonde hair with her fingertips. "I miss him, too. As for your two loser fiancés, learn from your mistakes and move on. Next time around, don't lose your emotional compass. You did the same thing with Fred."

"Fred?" Nancy rolled over to face her sister. "Fred was our dog. All he ever did was bite me."

"That's because you used to hug him so tight around his neck he couldn't breathe. You may be a relationship therapist, but you know dick about men. Guys are like dogs, Nancy. They need to learn the rules when they're puppies. You went from zero to sixty with Dan. You practically put Sea Bass through law school. Next time you fall for a guy, instead of jumping up and down on Oprah's sofa like Tom Cruise trying to convince the world he's not gay, teach that dog not to get up on the sofa. Set some boundaries; house train the little prick."

17

2

Jacob

THE THIRTY-ONE-YEAR-OLD man with the reddish-brown mop of hair, unkempt matching beard, and sleepy hazel eyes rested naked on his back in the queen-size sofa bed, staring down at his belly. "I need to lose weight. From this angle, I can't even see my dick."

"Maybe you just need a bigger dick?"

Jacob Cope turned to the nude Asian female sharing his bed. "You're complaining about my dick? Ten minutes ago you were moaning so loud I was afraid my brother could hear us from his house."

"You were the one moaning. If you recall, my mouth was full."

"Oh yeah." Jacob sighed. "Part of me suspects I'm a loser; the other part thinks I'm God Almighty."

"Go with the loser."

"Why do you have to be so nasty?"

"You want nasty? Smell my breath. And enough with the John Lennon quotes. You're worse than a Trekkie."

"John Lennon was much more than a Beatle; he was the voice of a generation. The guy actually helped stop the war in Vietnam by having a bed-in for peace."

"Hey, I was there, remember? You weren't even a glint in your father's eye."

"Still, I've always felt like a child of the '60s." Jacob watched the ceiling fan's revolving wicker blades. "I'd love to do something great like that. Can you imagine me and you staging a bed-in to stop the war in Afghanistan? Better yet, what if we could organize a nationwide sleep-in to reverse *Citizens United*, get the money out of politics? You may say I'm a dreamer, but I'm not the only one."

"Instead of dreaming, why don't you wake up and get a decent job? You've been living in your brother's guest house for nine months. You haven't brought home a real paycheck since Lehman Brothers shit-canned you."

"It wasn't my fault they went belly-up. Bastards ran the stock down to nothing. I lost millions."

"You made them millions. It's been years since you testified against them. Go back to Wall Street."

"Forget it. Wall Street is my Vietnam, my

Apocalypse Now. My computer programs and algorithms were used to hurt people. Now I just want to make people laugh. Practicing my act with you—it's the best part of my day."

"You know what the best part of my day is? The best part of my day is the garden hose in my mouth."

Jacob's heart skipped a beat as he heard footsteps approaching outside on the concrete stoop, his eyes focusing on the unbolted front door. "Oh, shit—Vin, don't come in!"

His older brother keyed in, the door swinging open. "Jake, we need to—holy shit, what the hell is this?"

"It's not what you think!" Jacob leaped off the sofa bed, rummaging through a pile of fast-food garbage for his SpongeBob boxer shorts.

"This is what you've been doing every day—in my man cave?"

"It's completely consensual. Can you just get out?"

"No, I can't get out. Helen was right. You need serious help." Vin approached the life-size naked Asian rubber sex doll lying spreadeagle across the bed. "Is that Yoko Ono?"

"It is. I happen to be a big fan of John Lennon."

"So you're paying tribute to him by screwing a plastic version of his wife?"

"Synthetic rubber. And so what?"

"Jacob, this is just weird. Can you imagine what Ma would say?"

"Ma hated all of my girlfriends. I fail to see the problem here."

"Have you given up on real women?"

"No, but I have urges."

"And Yoko fills them?"

"You jack off into a towel. I use a sexy receptacle. Either way, it's just an expulsion of bodily fluids."

"Yeah, but I don't lie around and talk to the towel afterward."

"I was practicing my ventriloquism."

"With your dick in her mouth? That's one hell of an act. Where do you even get something like this?"

"Celebrity Sex Dolls. I had to special order her."

"She does have nice hooters. Three inputs?"

"It's standard."

"Is she shaved down there, or is her bush big and matted like a Zulu warrior?"

"What is it you want, Vincent?"

"Bad news: Helen's mother's visiting in January and will be with us through Passover. I've been ordered to deliver your thirty-day eviction notice."

"It's a big guest house; I don't see a problem. Why do I need to leave?"

"Are you mental?"

"I happen to like Helen's mother."

"Listen, space cadet, you, Yoko and my mother-in-law playing Three's Company in my guest house—it ain't gonna happen. And don't you have to be at work?"

"I'm on the twelve-to-six shift. Don't *you* have to be at work?"

"I'm a gynecologist and my own boss. I don't punch a clock; I am the clock."

"I am the walrus, goo goo g'joob."

"You're an idiot. Clean this place up. It looks like a crime scene. And hide that stupid doll. I don't want my sons seeing it. Wade's just hitting puberty. It could ruin him. Back in my day, all I had to get off with were dad's old *National Geographics*."

3

Vinnie

THE BLACK 2002 FORD EXPLORER headed south on State Road 7. Its driver handled the wheel with her left hand while her right thumb dug into her neoprene shorts, desperate to scratch the incessant itch originating from her crotch. *Lana was right. I should have taken care of this long ago.*

Glancing out the passenger window, Jeanne Pratt searched the odd-numbered addresses, locating the South Florida Gynecology Center on the southwest corner of Palmetto Park Road, directly across from a Hooters restaurant.

Hooters and cooters. Cute.

Jeanne parked the vehicle and climbed out, checking the leather seat for stains.

Bypassing his reserved spot, Dr. Vincent Cope parked his Lexus in back of the one-story brick building two spaces from the trash dumpster. For several minutes, the forty-one-year-old father of three closed his eyes and listened to Howard Stern on his Sirius radio.

Helen was right. Jacob had become a squatter in their guest house. But what his wife refused to understand was that his kid brother had been through hell.

Helen had put Vincent through his own hell over breakfast.

"We've been married, what, seventeen years? And in those seventeen years, Vincent, how many times have you allowed one of my relatives to use our guest house?"

"*Our* guest house? If you recall, it was supposed to be my office—my man cave—until you put up curtains and added a sofa bed."

"When my Aunt Milly's condo was being fumigated for roaches and she needed a place to stay for seventy-two hours, do you remember what you told her? I'll tell you what you told her. You told her the local YWCA had cots, served a great lentil soup, and, if she wanted, you'd be happy to arrange free water aerobics classes."

"The woman told me she likes a good lentil soup."

"Shut up. Last year, when my mother wanted to visit during the Christmas holidays, you decided to renovate the guest house bathroom. Wade's Bar Mitzvah? New wallpaper. My sister's wedding? You had to have wood floors put in. But when your mother demands you take in your younger brother, suddenly my guest house becomes the home for wayward derelicts!"

"Helen, Jake's not a derelict. He's gifted."

"He's a mental patient!"

"True, but he's a gifted mental patient. I mean, come on, the guy was recruited by Lehman Brothers when he was nineteen. Six-figure bonuses, the 401K —it was all tied up in stock. It's not his fault the company went bankrupt."

"We're going bankrupt supporting him!"

"Not true. Jacob's working now."

"Yeah, part time. What does he do all day alone out there, other than order fast-food delivery on your credit card?"

Vincent powered off the Lexus. He had opened his gynecology practice fifteen years before when real estate was worth something and the mortgage rates were low. Then the economy had tanked, and it seemed as if the insurance companies fought every patient claim. Many of his colleagues had dropped their medical malpractice insurance, getting patients

to sign waiver forms; others ran strictly cash busi-
nesses. Vin had fought going that route, taking on
extra hours to run weight-loss clinics two nights a
week, but the new schedule was exhausting. Plus he
coached Wade's Little League baseball team. Helen
had to drive Dylan to hockey practice, and Austin
had Tae Kwon Do. By the time he got home and
crawled into bed, Helen was asleep.

What kept Vincent Cope up late at night were
not the two mortgages, his ever-increasing overhead,
or chasing after insurance companies; it was the
expenses looming ahead. Wade was fourteen, Dylan
twelve and Austin ten. When the boys' hit adolescent years, there'd be drivers' licenses and auto
insurance premiums that would add up to another
three to four thousand dollars a year per teen driver,
not to mention college tuitions.

Vincent Cope laid his head back on the leather
upholstery. *God help me if they get into an Ivy League
school. I wonder if I can charge Helen's mother to rent our
guest house.*

*Or maybe I'll just clear out half of my closet so she'll have
a place to hang upside-down and sleep.*

Dismissing the idea, the gynecologist exited the
car as a black cat scurried by and leaped into an
open steel dumpster, its actions igniting a chorus of
angry hisses and feline protests from within.

"Stupid cats. Quit digging through my trash. That's not fish you smell!" He kicked the side of the bin then headed for the employee entrance located on the south side of the building.

His nurse practitioner, Wanda Jackson, greeted him with his white lab coat and a sarcastic, "After-noon, Dr. Cope."

"Don't exaggerate. It's only 9:20."

"Your first appointment was at eight."

"Mrs. Kleinhenz. What'd you tell her?"

"Same thing I told all the patients you blew off: that you had emergency surgery. I rescheduled Mrs. Wishnov and Mrs. Goldfarb for this afternoon during your lunch break."

"Wanda, I need my lunch break."

"Well too bad."

"Wanda, I'm a forty-year-old man and your employer. If I say I need my lunch break, then I need my lunch break."

"And I'm a forty-three-year-old divorced black woman with two kids and bunions, and I say have a protein bar and an orange juice and watch your damn Internet porn later."

"All right, just keep your voice down. So how are little Trixie and Dixie?"

"Trevor's a junior in high school and Danielle just got the lead in her sixth-grade musical."

"I'm sure you're very proud."

"Oh yeah. Now I get to lay out sixty bucks a week for private singing lessons, and ya'll know my ex ain't gonna help. You and me seriously need to discuss my raise."

"Sure thing. Let's do it today during lunch." Vincent patted her on the shoulder and headed to the nurse's station. "Okay ladies, the muffin king is here. Where's my first patient?"

Nurse Kim and Nurse Dawn look at one another, covering up their giggles.

"What?"

"Room 2. A new patient. Chart's on the door."

"Oh ... kay." Vin walked down the hall to the exam room, casually checking his pants zipper.

Removing the chart from the bin outside the door, he scanned the information. *Jeanne Pratt, age thirty-two. Yeast infection.* He knocked and entered. "Ms. Pratt, I'm Dr. Cope—holy Lou Ferrigno."

A naked bodybuilder with a deep tan and florescent-pink toenails was sitting up on the exam table, the dressing gown draped over his—*her*—chest.

"Sorry, Doc. The exam gown didn't fit over my deltoids."

"That's because they're made for—I mean, no worries, as long as you're not cold. Would you excuse me for just one moment?"

Vin ducked out the door and into the corridor, where his two nurses were eavesdropping. "Is this a joke? Did Dr. Berkowitz set this up?"

Nurse Kim shook her head. "So? Does she have the doughnut or the hole?"

"A hole, obviously, or she'd be seeing Berkowitz. Send Wanda in. And quit congregating."

Vin reentered the exam room. "Sorry. Since this is your first visit, I asked one of my nurses to join us. It's standard procedure. So, what kind of work do you do?"

"When I'm not competing, I run a moving company with two other female bodybuilders. Pratt, Morrison, and Shear—PMS Movers."

"Cute. Do you have a card? I may need to hire you to move someone in about a month."

"Business or domestic?"

"Domestic. My kid brother. He's been living in my guest house."

"I hear you. My girlfriend's younger sister moved in with us over a year ago. What a pain in the ass. Hey, maybe we should fix them up?"

The door opened, and Wanda entered. "Eww. Smells like somethin' up and died in here. Mother Mary, will you look at you."

"Nurse Wanda, this is Ms. Pratt. Ms. Pratt is a female bodybuilder."

"Guess ya'll needed to have gone to medical school to figure that one out. Hey, Ms. Pratt, go on and flex. Let's see what you look like angry."

"Wanda!" Vincent glared from across the room. "My apologies, Ms. Pratt. Nurse Wanda was raised by wolves. We're still breaking her in domestically."

"I don't mind. And call me Jeanne."

Wanda wrapped both hands around the naked woman's flexed right arm. "Feels like a baseball in there. I bet Dr. Cope wishes he had guns like yours."

Vin looked up from working a pair of rubber gloves over his fingers. "For your information, Wanda, I used to have arms like that. I had a choice: keep lifting or maintain the dexterity necessary to perform life-saving surgery."

"Right. Cause ya'll need skinny arms to lance hemorrhoids." Wanda adjusted the exam table's stirrups, allowing the patient to rest her bare feet in the supports. The metal housing creaked beneath the weight of her muscular outspread legs. "Jeanne, can I hire ya'll to beat the shit outta my ex-husband?"

"Hey, Whoopie Goldberg, enough." Dr. Cope adjusted his mask and leaned in. "Been fermenting a while, I see. Why is it that women who work out think they can remain in their sweaty clothes for hours at a time without risking infection?"

"Guilty as charged."

"I don't want to use a speculum. The fungus has caused some inflammation around the labia."

"It itches bad."

Wanda snuck a peek. "Yeech. Looks like bologna and mayo."

"I'm going to write you a prescription for pills and an ointment you'll use three times a day. If you have time, I'd also recommend a Gynnie Gusher."

"What's that?"

"It's a special bidet I invented. It allows for a deep vaginal cleansing using a scented medicated flush. My patients swear by them. The gusher comes in wintergreen, peppermint, midnight cool and baby's breath."

Wanda nodded. "With all the Cheese Whiz down there, I'd go with the peppermint."

"Set it up. Hey, Doc, what about that blind date with your brother?"

Wanda stifled a laugh. "Ya'll want to set Jacob up with Jeanne? She'll crush his head like a walnut."

"Not Jeanne. Her girlfriend's sister. Do you have a picture of her?"

"Wanda, hand me my fanny pack." Jeanne fished through the leather bag. Pulling out her iPhone, she quickly scrolled through a dozen photos. "Here she is. Nancy Beach. She hosts a radio show in West Palm."

31

Wanda inspected the image of the petite blonde woman in the Santa hat. "She's cute."

Vinnie took a look. "She is cute. Too bad she's not Asian."

"What?"

"Huh?"

"Why she gotta be Asian?"

"I said too bad she's *Caucasian*. Jacob's always had a crush on you, Wanda."

"Are we talkin' about the same brother?"

"Never mind."

"The Wall Street hippy?"

"I was kidding. So Nancy's a radio host, huh?"

"She's a psychologist-turned-relationship-radio-host. She talks the talk but never walks the walk, if you know what I mean."

"My brother's a hypochondriac. It's a match made in heaven."

Wanda nudged him. "Go on and show her his picture. Maybe her girlfriend's sister would prefer an Asian too."

"Don't be a wise ass." Vinnie scrolled through his iPhone. "Here's one we took with the boys at Disney World."

Jeanne looked at the photo. "It's hard to tell what he looks like with his face all squished up in Mickey Mouse's headlock."

"That was a terrible misunderstanding. At the time, Jacob suffered from musophobia—a fear of rodents. He's completely over that now."

"Nancy's no gem either. She's still carrying chips on her shoulders from two bad engagements. Problem is she's sort of sworn off dating. She does like to bowl. Maybe if we go as a group—"

"Perfect. How about we meet you at the alley in East Boca tonight, say around eight? I'll bring my wife and Jacob. You bring your girlfriend and her sister."

"Done deal." Jeanne held her hand out to shake, and her gown fell away, exposing her breasts.

Wanda's eyes widened. "Damn. I need to get to the gym."

4

The Sunshine Hour

THE LIFESTYLE REVOLUTION INC. offices occupied the entire mezzanine and first three floors of a high-rise office building in downtown West Palm Beach. The facility, designed by Olivia Cabot, eldest daughter of millionaire and retired investment banker Truman Cabot, featured a women-only gym, a health spa, a vegan restaurant, a liposuction clinic, three classroom suites and the offices and broadcast facilities of AM radio station WOWF.

Olivia's plan was to use the station's on-air hosts to bring clients to the facility, where their physical, mental and spiritual needs could be met. Each radio personality offered workshops and weekly group sessions—the higher their ratings, the better the attendance.

Nancy called her sessions "The Sunshine Hour."

At precisely 8:45, Nancy Beach slid her passkey through the security slot and entered the double glass doors of Lifestyle Revolution. *Fifteen minutes early, what Dad called Vince Lombardi time. "Set your watch to Lombardi time, and you'll never be late."*

Seated before her at the central kiosk was Lynnie Ruffington, a rotund, tough-as-nails transplant from Mountain Home, Arkansas, a small town she described as "Mayberry, only with trailer parks and booze."

"Good morning, Lynnie. Where's my Sunshine Hour?"

"I had to put you in the Hillary suite."

"Lynnie, you know I hate the Hillary suite. It's always so cold. What about the Lady Gaga suite. Better yet, the Liza."

"The Liza suite is reserved for Dr. Porter's menopause class, and Lady Gaga's back door is still jammed open from those construction workers. By the way, congrats." Lynnie reached beneath her desk, retrieving a walnut plaque featuring a large brass vulva. "*The Vagina Monologues* named you one of their Florida Vagina Warriors. Guess all those letters and emails finally paid off."

Nancy took the award from her and read the inscription. "'Dr. Nancy Beach: A vagina-friendly person who embodies the spirit of equality and empowerment.' Vagina friendly? It makes me sound like a lesbian."

"You're not, are you? I'm only asking because I happen to know a young single entrepreneur stud who'd be perfect for you."

"Is he rich?"

"Does it matter?"

"No, of course not. It's just the way you made it sound. So he's a stud, huh?"

"Put it this way: he's the Mexican twin of the guy who played Gilligan on *Gilligan's Island*. That's right, sister. He's quite the looker."

"That's … wow." *Nod politely and start walking away.*

"Okay, he's our lawn guy. And believe me, the only reason Arnoldo is still on the market is because he's an illegal immigrant. Guy's always smiling—got a head full of teeth. Can't understand much English, but, hey, with a man that can be a plus, right? Here's the kicker: if you marry him, me and mom get free lawn care for the next ten years. Of course, you would too. Back in Mountain Home, we call that a perk. Arnoldo's got lots of perks us ladies fancy."

Point to your watch, mumble something about being late, and—

"You ever see a lawn guy's fingers, Dr. Nancy? They're thick and calloused from pulling weeds. We're talking breakfast-sausage thick. Back home, we call 'em Jimmy Deans." Lynnie winked. "Yeah girlfriend. I think we're on the same page."

"Okay then. Anything else?"

"Oh yeah, *The Today Show* called. Something about a guest appearance."

Nancy's heart raced. "*The Today Show*? Really?"

"Nah, I'm just fucking with you, but your sister called. She said it was urgent."

Nancy strode down the classroom corridor, her blood still boiling over the receptionist's little joke. *How can I succeed when I'm in an environment surrounded by Neanderthals? I share a producer with three other hosts and office space with fifteen other radio personalities, all of us trying to build a following with little to no publicity, no budget and a new program director who's out to change everything around here just to make a name for himself. We're like a nest of newborn sea turtles, everyone struggling to make it across the beach to open water while seagulls swoop down from the sky trying to eat us.*

She passed a pair of construction workers replacing the emergency fire-exit door of a lecture hall. She paused outside the door of the Liza Minnelli suite, eavesdropping on a heated conversation between Dr. Nell Porter and one of her patients.

"So I told the filthy son of a bitch that if he stuck that thing in my mouth one more time, I'd bite

37

it off and wrap it around his goddam neck!"

"Gertrude, remember the hot-flash exercises we went over last week?"

"Doctor Nell, how am I supposed to take slow, deep breaths with his thing in my mouth? For Pete's sake, it was dripping down my chin!"

"Gertrude, he's your dentist. The suction tube removes excess saliva from your mouth so you don't have to continuously spit."

Nancy felt a surge of jealousy. Dr. Porter handled the menopause crowd. She had found her niche and her practice—and her ratings were thriving.

I need to find my own niche, something trendy.

Remembering Lana, she speed-dialed her sister's number on her cell phone.

"Hello?"

"Lana? It's me. What's wrong?"

"Nothing's wrong. I just wanted to make sure you were free tonight."

"Why?"

"Date night, little sister. You, me and Jeanne are going bowling with another couple and the guy's single brother."

"A blind date? That was the emergency?"

"Yes, and you're going. There's no pressure here. If you like him, great; if not, we'll kick some ass and go home."

"What time?"

"Eight o'clock."

"Let me think about it."

"Nancy—"

"I'm late for my seminar. Call you in an hour."
She hung up, mentally searching through her menu
of excuses. *I started having menstrual cramps earlier this
morning, and you know my first day is always the heaviest.
Nah, she'll know. Wait until after five then call and tell her
the new programming guy scheduled an after-hours meeting.*

Powering off her cell phone, she said a quick
prayer (please God, let there be standing room only
inside) then entered the Hillary Clinton suite, a small
auditorium with theater-style seating for two hundred.

Seated in the front row were four women—three
Sunshine Hour regulars and a newbie.

Laticia was a mocha-skin black woman in her
late thirties. The security guard worked nights at a
gated community in Delray Beach and suffered from
anger management issues stemming from an abusive
first marriage.

Bonnie was white, single and in her late twenties
—an elementary school cafeteria worker fighting an
obesity problem she blamed on a domineering mother.

Sophia was the youngest at nineteen years old
and Hispanic. The community college student's arms
were covered in tattoos displaying her eighteen-

month-old daughter's name and image. She had not seen the child's biological father since the night he impregnated her in the high school's boys' locker room.

The short white woman in her mid-sixties was new.

Either a recent divorcée or a widow, Nancy surmised. *Stay positive. Four is 25 percent better than three.* "Good morning, ladies, and welcome to the Sunshine Hour, a free weekly seminar for women, sponsored by my radio show, *Love's a Beach with Nancy Beach*. Before we begin, would everyone stand please and recite the pledge?"

The three returnees stood, joining their leader: "I am the keeper of my own fate, emancipating myself from the self-imposed bonds of my gender."

"Excellent. I see we have a newbie. Please, tell us about yourself and describe the Y chromosome in your life."

"The Y who?"

"The man in your life, assuming it's a challenging relationship with the opposite sex that brought you here."

"Well … my name is Edna Dombrowski. I'm sixty-three years old, originally from New York. The Y chromosome in my life is—was—my ex-husband, Walter."

The other women chanted, "Why, Y, do you make us cry?"

"Did Walter make you cry, Edna?"

"Sometimes. After all, we were married thirty-six years. We had good times, some ehh, but we stayed together. Mostly for the kids."

"What went wrong?" asked Bonnie. The weight-challenged attendee spewed remnants from her last bite of doughnut.

"The trouble began about a year ago when we stopped having … relations. Walter claimed he couldn't get it up because of a swollen prostate. Well, he sure got it up for his secretary, Claudia."

Laticia shook her head. "Girlfriend, if some Y did that to me, I'd have gone Lorena Bobbitt all over the mother fucker."

"I'm sorry?"

"I'd have cut off his pecker." Laticia mimed slicing off a man's penis.

Nancy cringed. "Laticia, we can't go around castrating every Y who hurts us. We're here to help Edna gain a new perspective about what happened so she can prevent the situation from occurring in her next relationship."

Sophia turned to Edna, her words slightly garbled by her tongue piercing. "Was you there for him sexually?"

"I thought I was. Thirty-six years, I don't ever recall him complaining."

"But was you *really* there? Did you just lie there and stare at the ceiling fan, or did you make him feel like a Aztec God?"

"Aztec God? Walter? The man laid down, and I climbed on. He had a chronic bad back."

"I ain't sayin' you should'a hurt him. I just know the guys I been with over the last like ten years go crazy whenever I talk nasty to them."

"You've been sexually active for ten years? How old are you?"

"Nineteen. Okay, eight years. Anyways, next time you is with a man of the opposite sex, try this: 'Oh God, Walter! Oh God, you are so big. Bury that dagger in my pussy. Sacrifice me to the gods!'" Sophia high-fived Laticia. "Trust me, girlfriend. Once you go Hispanic, ain't no need to be romantic."

Edna's complexion paled. "I'm a sixty-three-year-old Jew from the Bronx. When I was your age, I was still a virgin. I birthed three kids and had a hysterectomy, and in all those years I never referred to my personal area as anything but my personal area. If I moaned like that, Walter would have had a heart attack."

Nancy held up her hand, cutting off Sophia's retort. "Edna, I think Sophia's point is that we can empower ourselves by using certain tools that feed our Y's ego while allowing us to establish a sense of equality in the relationship."

"What for? So I can compete with some young *shiksa* like yourself? See how your husband feels about you in thirty years when your boobs start sagging and your pubic hair turns gray."

"Oh, Dr. Beach isn't married," said Bonnie, draining her Diet Coke.

Laticia shrugged. "The lady don't even got a boyfriend."

"That's not true," Nancy snapped. "I mean, I was engaged ... twice. I decided to break things off for a variety of reasons, some similar to Edna's."

"Yeah, but that was like decades ago."

Edna's face flushed pink. "Dr. Beach, I thought you were a relationship counselor?"

"I am. If you'd like to see my degrees—"

"Who cares about a degree? When I read the Lifestyle Revolution brochure, I had no idea you were so young. How could you possibly know what I'm going through? And not to be dating, with your looks ... the Puerto Rican slut knows more about relationships than you do."

"Got dat right."

"You're right, Edna. When it comes to relationships, my own personal experiences are somewhat limited. But don't discount my education. Tapping into my wealth of knowledge, we can craft the tools you need to work on you."

"Know what, Dr. Beach? Maybe you ought to work on yourself."

Nancy watched, feeling helpless as Edna gathered her belongings and left.

The phone rang twice before Lana answered. "Nance?"

"Pick me up at the apartment at 7:30. I'm in."

5

Always Be Polite

THE INFORMATION TECHNOLOGY company, I-Guru USA, was located on the first floor of the building formerly owned by American Media Inc., publisher of the *National Enquirer*. AMI moved out in the wake of the 2001 anthrax attacks that contaminated the building and killed one of the tabloid's photo editors. The new owners had the property decontaminated, but there was no rush to rent space. I-Guru set up shop three years later under a heavily discounted long-term lease. Despite the savings, the IT company's Boca Raton overhead remained considerably higher than its corporate offices in Bangalore, India, where 95 percent of its customer calls were routed.

The company's lone US satellite office (a requirement for certain clientele) was limited to the manager's office, a small kitchen, supply room and the phone room where a dozen semi-soundproof cubicles housed I-Guru's IT techs. Eleven of the cubicles were manned by graduate or postgraduate students from India. Each man wore dark slacks, white button-down shirts, dress shoes and matching black ties. Their work cubicles were organized and kept immaculate. A sign, "Always Be Polite," was thumb-tacked to their otherwise vacant corkboards. Each man spoke with a Zen-like calm into a headset:

"I am so sorry you are experiencing these difficulties, Mr. Hollander."

"Thank you for your patience, Mrs. Angsten. If you don't mind, we will begin to address your problem by restarting your computer."

"Again, I apologize, Mr. Gelet. Since the last attempt did not resolve the problem, we shall try something else. I am certain this will work."

The twelfth man, occupying the last booth, was wearing a soda-stained Miami Dolphins tee-shirt, Bermuda shorts, sunglasses and thong sandals. His bare feet were propped up on the desk. A Miami Dolphins cheerleader calendar hung crooked from his corkboard, along with a variety of pictures that included John Lennon, the Three Stooges and Pamela Anderson from her glory years on *Baywatch*. His desk was littered with files, and the floor beneath his cubicle with fast-food wrappers.

Jacob Cope scratched his auburn beard and then let out a carbonated burp. "Sorry, it's these damn Big Gulps. Let's try this again, Mrs. Badcock, only this time click on the right side of the gerbil. Yes, I know it's called a mouse, but when you abuse it like you have. … No, ma'am, that's the left side again. Honestly, I have no clue why your husband told you that. … Well, you married him, dear."

Sanjay Patel, the floor manager whose cubicle was located to the left of Jacob's workplace leaned back into his neighbor's sight line and desperately signaled him to be polite.

Jacob Cope offered Sanjay a thumbs-up. "My apologies, Mrs. Badcock, I'm sure your husband is—" He listened to her gruff reply. "No ma'am. I said Babcock." He lowered the volume on his headphones as the woman's rants grew louder. "Ma'am— excuse me—I understand. It was an honest mistake. But seriously, either way, there's still a cock in your name. That's not my doing. Hello? Hello? Geez, some people get so touchy."

Sanjay stared at him, slack jawed. "Jacob, these are paying clients. You cannot treat them in this manner."

"Some people, no matter what you do, they're gonna hate you. And another thing, all this apologizing—it's un-American. Believe me, my people don't like it. It makes us feel uneasy. We're calling to

47

get our computer running again, and some foreign guy I don't even know keeps apologizing. For what? True story: Back in Manhattan some chick gave me crabs and never apologized, and I had to shave my balls. First time you do that, it's scary as shit. I still dated her, though. Damn, she was hot."

"Jacob, being polite is simply a means of showing respect to our—"

"Hold that thought." Jacob's cell phone vibrated in his pants pocket. He waited until the second tingle before answering it. "What's up, big brother?"

"Listen carefully, and tonight you could be balls-deep inside something with a pulse. Her name's Nancy, and she's the sister of one of my patients. I mean, she's the girlfriend's sister—anyway, she's very cute, and we're all going bowling tonight at eight. Go home, shower, trim the bird's nest you've got growing on your face, and then pick me up at my office at 7:30 in your van, and we'll ride over to the bowling alley together."

"Vin, you hate my van. You won't even let me park it in the driveway."

"Shut up and pay attention. Helen's meeting us at the bowling alley in her car. If things go well, I'll drive home with Helen and you can give Nancy a ride back to her place in the Scooby-Doo van. Get it?"

"Got it. Wait, who's Nancy?"

"Your date."

"I don't know, Vin. It sounds great and all, but according to my horoscope, the timing's not good. Plus, my online therapist just diagnosed me with cainophobia."

"What are you afraid of now? The bible? "

"Cainophobia is a fear of newness. Maybe if we waited a few more weeks?"

"No way, Sigmund Freud. It's gotta be tonight."

"Can I at least bring Dubuya?"

"Dubuya?"

"My George Bush dummy. I could practice my act."

"No! No puppets. No sex dolls. Just you. See you at 7:30."

6

First Impressions

VINCENT COPE PACED beneath the green and white awning of his medical center, his eyes focused on the parking lot entrance from State Road 7. *It's 7:43. Where the hell is he?*

Ten minutes passed before the 1976 Volkswagen van with the two-tone white and tangerine-orange paint turned into the medical center parking lot, its rotting dual tail pipes belching fumes.

Vin yanked open the passenger door, the rusted hinges squealing in protest. Stepping on an empty McDonald's cup, he climbed up into the vehicle and situated himself on the torn plastic upholstered seat. "You're late."

"Sorry. I was at the retirement home visiting our mother. Ma's very upset with you, Vincent."

"Ma's been upset at me since my second year at med school when I decided to become a gynecologist instead of a brain surgeon."

"She says you haven't visited her since April."

"We had her over for Thanksgiving. Doesn't that count?"

"She said it's not the same thing."

"Listen, little brother. I visit our mother and the dentist twice a year. That's all the pain one man can endure. Anyway, forget Ma. I need you focused on Nancy."

"Who's Nancy?"

"Your date for this evening!"

"The Hooters waitress?"

"She's not a Hooters waitress. She's a psychologist. I may have texted she has nice hooters. Jesus, try to stay focused."

"Please don't call me Jesus. I may be a miracle of creation, but I can't perform miracles."

"You can move out of my guest house; that would be a miracle." Vin winced as the heel of his right shoe caught something beneath the seat. Reaching between his legs, he dragged out a Jet Blue Airlines inflatable life jacket. "Expecting turbulence?"

"You know I suffer from severe hydrophobia."

"Don't tell me this hunk of rust you're driving is amphibious?"

"Don't you ever read the news? People die in canals every day. Florida's a virtual death trap."

"Jacob, you're my kid brother, and I love you.

But you need serious help."

"Is that why you set me up with a shrink?"

"She's cute, and my patient assures me she's nice. Why don't you give her a chance?"

"If she's so nice, how come she's not married?"

"As a matter of fact, she was engaged twice."

Jacob jammed on the brakes, sending Vinnie's forehead slamming into the glove box.

"Ow, fuck! Are you crazy?" Vin leaned over and punched his brother in the arm.

"Ow."

"Drive the car, you lunatic."

"Two broken engagements are a red flag. My spidey sense detects a severe case of androphobia."

"What the hell are you talking about?"

"The Hooters waitress has trust issues."

"Psychologist!"

"Take it from an expert. Trust issues are nearly as difficult to overcome as apotemnophobia, and that took me three years."

"What's that? A fear of being normal?"

"It happens to be a fear of amputees. Some doctor you are."

Nancy Beach followed her sister and Jeanne through the east entrance of the bowling alley, her ears assaulted by the echoes of rolling balls and crashing pins, her nose by the overpowering scent of industrial cleaner mixed with cheap buttered popcorn and overcooked pizza. "I can't believe I actually let you talk me into this."

Lana reached back and pulled her sister by the crook of her elbow so she was walking between herself and Jeanne. "Don't even think of running. And try to smile; it's not an execution."

"There they are." Jeanne waved in the direction of the west entrance where Vincent and Jacob Cope were making their way across the worn scarlet and violet carpet, the taller brother intercepted by a perky brunette in a black and rose-colored bowling shirt and matching skirt.

"He's too tall for me."

"That's his brother, my new goolie doctor. Jacob's the guy in the beard."

"He's sort of cute, in a Danny DeVito meets Woodstock kind of way."

Across the room, Jacob eyed the three women. "I thought you said she was cute. She looks like The Rock with tits."

"That's my patient. Nancy's the blonde in the middle."

"Oh. Hey, she really is cute." Jacob checked his breath. "Damn burritos. Quick, I need gum!"

Helen fished through her purse, locating a breath mint. "Here, suck on this."

Jacob popped the white tablet in his mouth as the two trios met at center court.

Jeanne handled the introductions. "Dr. Cope, this is my sweetheart, Lana Beach—"

Jacob laughed, launching the breath mint from his mouth, striking Nancy in the face. "Oh, God, I'm sorry."

Vin rolled his eyes. "And this is my little brother, Jacob."

Jacob shot him a look.

"Sorry. I meant younger. He's not little. None of the Cope men are little."

Helen smirked. "Guess you must have been adopted. Hi, I'm Helen, Vinnie's wife."

"Looks like the missus bowls a little, Doc" Jeanne said. "What do you say, shall we make things interesting?"

Vinnie switched to his poker face. "I don't know, Jeanne. What do you have in mind?"

"Three couples, three games. The winning couple collects twenty dollars apiece from the losers—forty bucks a game."

"You're on."

Vin retrieved his bowling ball, waiting for the pins to reset. Jeanne and Lana had won the first match by nine pins over him and his wife—thirty-one pins over Jacob and Nancy's combined score. Going into this, the tenth and final frame of the second match, he and Helen held a slim six-pin lead.

Okay, V.C., you let Conannie and her lover steal game one. Game two is yours.

Eyes focused, back muscles taut, Vincent Cope moved like a cat as he strode into his approach and released the ball.

The bowling ball rolled straight and true, striking the head pin and setting off an avalanche of ivory, leaving in its wake the infamous seven-ten split.

"Suck balls, not again!"

Jeanne high-fived Lana.

Helen shook her head. "How many times must I tell you? Don't aim for the head pin."

"I didn't aim for the damn head pin. I hit the head pin. I didn't aim for it."

"You never listen. I carry a 184 league average, and you never listen."

"You also carry a lower center of gravity and child-bearing hips to keep you balanced. I'm lanky. Plus I'm fighting the effects of a devastating football injury that ended my collegiate career."

"What collegiate career? You played one year on

the practice squad."

"Exactly. We battled the ones every day! You saw Rudy. You saw what that poor kid had to endure. There are pieces of me scattered across every inch of turf at Wellington Business School. Thank God I was blessed with a mind as well as athletic talent. Thank God."

Helen rolled her eyes.

Jeanne called out, "Hey, Doc, I'll give you three-to-one odds on one of those mint cleansings of yours if you nail the split."

"You're on!"

Having forfeited the competition, Jacob and Nancy were seated next to each other at the end of the wrap-around bench, engrossed in conversation.

"Is Jeanne always this competitive?"

"Always," Nancy said.

"Vince too. It gets obnoxious after a while."

"I suppose everyone has their baggage to carry." Glancing at Jacob's wristwatch, she noticed it was a dive watch. "Are you certified?"

"Did Vince tell you that? Sure, I have a few phobias, but I've never been committed."

"No … no, not certifiable—*certified*, as in diving." She pointed to his wrist. "That is a dive watch, right?"

"Oh, yeah, I guess it is."

"How often do you dive?"

"Oh, I've never been diving. The watch was a gift from one of the managers at Lehman Brothers."

"The investment firm?"

"Yeah. I designed a lot of their software. I had no idea they were using my programming to camouflage their accounting gimmicks. Bastards went bankrupt owing me millions in stock options and bonuses."

"That's terrible."

"Tell me about it. I had to testify before a Congressional committee. It was around that time when a lot of my phobias started coming out." Jacob looked up as Vinnie yelled, "Suck balls!" as he missed the spare.

"Jacob, have you ever had therapy?"

"Mostly just online chat rooms. It helps."

"What about therapy from a real professional?"

"When I was younger. My mother sort of screwed me up at an early age."

"What happened?"

"It's a little embarrassing."

"I'm a psychologist. I seriously doubt you could shock me."

"My father was in the armed forces. He committed suicide when I was six."

"I'm sorry. Posttraumatic stress?"

"Yeah. Anyway, Ma was pretty upset by the whole thing, so she made up this convoluted story about Dad being killed in a horrible accident. It really screwed with my head."

"What did she tell you?"

Jacob blushed. "I can't. It's too embarrassing."

Nancy smiled. "Oh, come on. How bad can it be?"

"Pretty damn bad."

Nancy hesitated, then leaned in and kissed him, her tongue swirling around his before slowly pulling out.

Jacob opened his eyes. "Wow."

"I have trust issues, Jacob. Men who are vulnerable are easier for me to trust."

"I'm your man. That's definitely me."

"Then take a chance and trust me. Tell me what your mother told you about your father's death that screwed you up so badly."

Jacob hesitated and then smirked. "She told me our last name had been Riesfeldt; she changed it to Cope after Dad's death so that we could cope with the accident that killed him. She said my father, Friedrich Riesfeldt, was a famous zookeeper and that he was needed in Germany to help a very sick elephant that was constipated. She said Dad got drunk on the plane ride over and ended up giving the elephant too much animal laxative. Dad passed out, and the animal let loose, burying my father beneath two hundred pounds of pachyderm poop."

"Oh my." Nancy covered her mouth, hiding her grin. "And you believed her?"

"I was young. Plus the story was all over the Internet. She showed me the picture." Jacob took out his iPhone and did a quick search for zookeeper Friedrich Riesfeldt.

Sure enough, dozens of reference articles appeared, several under the "Darwin Awards," a spoof award presented to those suffering the dumbest deaths imaginable.

(*Paderborn, Germany*) Overzealous zookeeper Friedrich Riesfeldt fed his constipated elephant Stefan 22 doses of animal laxative and more than a bushel of berries, figs and prunes before the plugged-up pachyderm finally let fly—and suffocated the keeper under 200 pounds of poop! Investigators say ill-fated Friedrich, 46, was at tempting to give the ailing elephant an olive oil enema when the relieved beast unloaded on him like a dump truck full of mud. "The sheer force of the elephant's unexpected defecation knocked Mr. Riesfeldt to the ground, where he struck his head on a rock and lay unconscious as the elephant continued to evacuate his bowels on top of him," said flabbergasted Paderborn police detective Erik Dern. "With no one there to help him, he lay under all that dung for at least an hour before a watchman came along, and during that time he suffocated. It seems to be just one of those freak accidents that happen."

"Oh my God, the woman's diabolical. But Jacob, you do know the story's not real."

"I was a kid. You see the name and the photo and your father's gone and what was I supposed to believe? Vin waited two years before letting me know my mother had made the whole thing up. Of course, by that time you can imagine how screwed up I was. To this day, I still can't go to the circus or zoo. I only started voting Democrat two presidential elections ago."

"Because of the elephant symbol?"

"Because of Sarah Palin. The woman's bat-shit crazy."

"Palin or your mother? Sorry, I shouldn't judge."

"Ma was hurting. I found out years later that my father had been having an affair. I guess she wanted to taint my memory of him. Hell hath no fury like a pissed-off Jewish mother."

Nancy reached out and held Jacob's hand. "Thank you for sharing your story with me. One day, if I get over my own fears, I may share my own father's story with you."

"Did he molest you or something?"

"Nothing like that."

"Was he a zookeeper?"

"No, and stop guessing. After you lost your job with Lehman Brothers, what did you do?"

Jacob exhaled. "Boy, that's a long story. Right now, I'm working as an IT tech in Boca. It's just a filler job. I've been training for a far more lucrative career."

"Programming analyst for the CIA?"

"Close. Ventriloquist."

Nancy laughed. "I'm sorry. I've never actually met a ventriloquist before. Show me some ventriloquism."

"I can't. Not without my dummy."

"I'll be your dummy." She scooted next to him, resting her legs over his thighs. "There. Now slide your hand behind my neck, and I'll mouth your words."

Jacob slipped his right hand beneath her blonde hair. His eyes focused on her tight jeans and exposed thong panties. "Normally I'd have my George Bush dummy on my lap, so pretend you're President Bush. So, President Bush, can you tell us any personal details about your two terms in office?"

Jacob maneuvered Nancy's jaw as he threw his voice, imitating the former president. "Heck yeah, Jacob. One time, me, Vice and Rummy got snowed in on a hunting trip and had to sleep together in the same tent. Naturally, as the decider, I decided to take the middle where it was warmest. Anyway, about three in the morning Rummy and Vice start moaning, waking me up. So I said, 'Hey Cheney, what gives?' Dick says, 'Mr. President, I just had a wet dream. I dreamt I was getting a hand job from a beautiful psychologist.' Rummy says, 'That's amazing, Mr. President. I just had the same wet dream.' Then I said, 'Heck, fellas, you two sure are lucky. All I dreamed about was skiing.' See, he was gripping the poles …"

Nancy laughed, hysterical. "You're really good. A beautiful psychologist, huh?"

"Yes, and no amputees—all four limbs intact."

"My four limbs are intact." Reaching between her legs, she rubbed his inner thigh. "So, how did you know I like skiing?"

Vin watched nervously as Jeanne prepared to take her approach. "Money shot, Jeanne. Try to focus. By the way, how's the yeast infection holding up? Hope you're not chafing."

"Thanks to you, she's minty fresh," Lana answered.

Jeanne unleashed her shot like a Greek god hurtling hail at a cluster of frightened mortals, the ball skimming the slick wood surface before blasting the pins into an orifice of fallen ivory.

"Game, strike and match. Let's see if I can bake this turkey in the oven."

"Hey, Vin, we're going to go."

The two couples turned to find Jacob and Nancy wearing their street shoes, ready to leave.

"Jacob's going to drive me home," Nancy announced.

"You go, girl." Lana hugged her sister.

Vince exchanged a fist bump with his younger brother. "Whatever gets you through the night, John Lennon."

Jacob nodded then led his date outside where his chariot awaited.

Thirty days later . . .

7

WOWF-AM

"I NEED YOUR HELP, LISTENERS. As you know, I have a new man in my life—George. George and I met on a blind date about a month ago at a bowling alley, and we've been seeing each other pretty steadily ever since. Well, George's sublet is up, and he needs to move out. And I've been sharing an apartment with my sister and her significant other, and I need to move. So naturally George and I have been talking about possibly moving in together into a two bedroom rental. Is it too soon? Call in and tell me what you think. Our land line is 561-222-WOWF, or you can text star-WOWF on your mobile phone."

Nancy glanced across her radio booth at Patricia Kieras. Situated behind glass in the control room, her producer's face was buried behind a paperback copy of *Fifty Shades of Gray*. "I see my producer, Trish, is signaling me that we have open lines. Did I mention that my boyfriend is an adult entertainer? Wait, that sounded bad. What I meant is that he's an up-and-coming comedian, but his humor is geared more for adults."

A yellow light illuminated on the control board. Without moving her book, Trish took the call, wrote something on a flash card, then held it up against the glass partition: "LINE 1. BOYNTON—RACHEL."

"And we have our first caller: Rachel from Boynton Beach. Good afternoon, Rachel, and welcome to the show."

"Yeah, I think you should dump this loser, George, and go out with a real man. I know this guy, Arnoldo. He's got his own trailer out in Loxahatchee by the sugar fields and—"

"Thank you, Rachel." Nancy hung up on Lynnie and took the next call. "Christine, from West Palm, welcome to *Love's a Beach*."

"Hi, Dr. Beach. Weren't you living with a guy who cheated on you?"

"My fiancé, Sebastian. He was sleeping with my roommate, Carol. What's your point? You think it's too soon? Sebastian and I dated for eight months, and we never lived together."

"My point is, if you live in sin, then you'll pay the price. My advice is to pray to the Holy Trinity and wait until you're married to share your bed with a man."

"Thank you, Christine. Our next caller is from Boca. Hi, caller, to whom am I speaking?"

"It's your mother. Who's this George? I thought you were seeing Jacob?"

The blood drained from Nancy's face. "Thank you, Mother. Yes, listeners, my boyfriend's name is really Jacob. I was just trying to be discrete—"

"Your sister tells me he's a Jew."

Oh, God. "Yes, Mom. Is that a problem?"

"It wouldn't be my first choice, but I suppose it could be worse—look at your sister, for heaven's sake. Actually, I prefer a Jew over your last boyfriend. ... What was the little Spanish prick's name?"

"Sebastian, and let's keep it clean."

"If you recall, I warned you about him. He had a wandering eye. The Jew, he's not a doctor, is he?"

"No, Mother."

"Too bad. I'm leaving on a cruise and need a prescription called in."

"Thanks for checking in, Mom, but we have other callers waiting—"

"Your father was circumcised. Did you know that?"

Nancy disconnected the call. "Mary from Boynton Beach, bless you for calling."

"Yeah, Dr. Beach, I think the listeners wanna hear more about this Arnoldo fella from Loxahatchee."

"Good-bye, Lynnie!"

67

8

Mother Cope

THE RECREATION ROOM at the Shusterman Retirement Home was bright and airy—but not too bright because the visually impaired residents complained that they had difficulty seeing the ceiling-mounted televisions and not too airy because the draft could cause a chill, which is why the air-conditioning was set at a balmy seventy-seven degrees.

There were several cliques of seniors in the rec room—the card players and the mahjong crowd, the kibitzers offering their unwanted advice, and the yentas gossiping about it. The TV groupies were divided among the serious viewers (*Matlock* and *Jeopardy!* being reserved time slots) and the drifters—those who drifted off into their afternoon catnaps. Snorers were relegated to the chairs along the shuffleboard patio.

To the outsider, living out one's days in a retirement home may have seemed like a slow, regimented death march to the grave, but for the active senior, there were numerous opportunities to explore their heterosexual "urges" thanks to the miracle of impotency drugs.

For seventy-two-year-old Carmella Cope, winter romances were something akin to a game of musical chairs. In the last four years the feisty widow had buried three of her last five lovers, earning the nickname C.C. Rider.

Morty Goldman had been eyeing Carmella ever since he had seen the big-breasted woman during water aerobics. When her companion of eighteen months, Sheldon Finklestein, succumbed to colon cancer, Morty had made his intentions known. He and C.C. had eaten lunch together every day that week (except for Tuesday, when Morty had his urologist appointment) and the last two dinners. That afternoon, Carmella had invited the former manager at Levitz Furniture to join her for the *Jeopardy!* hour—a prelude to dinner in her room.

Morty's plan was simple: he'd impress the seductress with his razor-sharp wit and then pop the Viagra right before the start of the Double Jeopardy round.

All was going according to plan until Carmella's younger son showed up unexpectedly, throwing the widower off his game.

"You're moving in with a whore?"

"Ma, Nancy's not a whore."

"If she's screwing you to cover her share of the rent, she's a whore."

"She'll be paying her half. And my boss upped my hours, so I'll be paying mine. I think I love her, Ma."

"Love? Jacob, you have no idea what love is."

"Shush!" Morty pointed to the television as Alex Trebek read the next question: "Definitions for one hundred: It's a four-letter word for deep personal affection."

"What is *anal*?"

Mother Cope whacked Morty Goldman across his shoulder with her gripper. "Watch your language around my son. And just so you don't get any ideas, I'm not a three-input gal."

"Geez, Ma."

"As for you, Jacob, I don't want you living in sin with this whore."

"It's my decision. And stop calling her a whore. Who knows? If our living arrangement works out, one day I could marry her."

"Marry her? *Oy gevalt!* This is all your brother's fault. He's kicking you out, isn't he? That ungrateful son of a bitch."

Morty chuckled. "Carm, I think you just insulted yourself."

Carmella whacked the old man again with her gripper.

"It's not Vin's fault. Helen's mother's coming to visit. So, yes, I needed to find a place to stay. But Vin and Helen let me use the guest house for over a year. The house we're renting is affordable, and it's on a month-to-month lease. So there's not a whole lot of risk. Plus Nancy and I need some privacy."

"You want affordable? I have a better solution. We'll buy you a cheap air mattress; you'll move in with me!"

9

Moving Day

THE SINGLE-FAMILY HOME was a one-story, two-bedroom dwelling located in a lower-middle-class neighborhood in Deerfield Beach. Helen, who worked part time as a realtor, had negotiated the lease, the first and last months' rent and security deposit guaranteeing occupancy throughout the time her mother would be staying in their guest house.

It took most of Saturday morning for Jeanne and her two female bodybuilding training partners to move Nancy's bedroom furniture and the rest of her stored belongings into the new house.

It took Jacob less than half an hour to toss his belongings in the back of his van.

By noon, Helen Cope had a cleaning crew stripping the linens and removing the furnishings to disinfect the entire guest house. The painters would arrive by three.

The orange and white Volkswagen van rumbled its way east on Hillsboro Boulevard, its driver lost in a whirlwind of thought. Neighborhoods in South Florida can change from one mile to the next—from million-dollar homes with plush golf courses for backyards to low income dwellings with barred windows, the stucco walls perpetually stained with rust from iron-infested water supplies feeding the sprinklers.

Jacob Cope had experienced both income extremes, and worse.

An introvert lacking his older brother's confidence, Jacob went through his early childhood years as the quiet, pale kid with the curly brown "Jew 'fro." By middle school, his peers had become the "geeksquaders," a group of video game junkies who escaped the pressures of adolescence in the library's computer lab. It was here that Jacob discovered a talent for writing algorithms, and by his senior year of high school, "the Copemeister" was engineering programs on par with developers at MIT.

Unfortunately, Jacob's grade point average was not on par with the admission requirements of a major university. With few options (attending a community college in Palm Beach County while living at his mother's home coming in just above suicide), he enrolled as a part-time student at New

York's City College, where he earned just enough money setting up accounting programs for a small investment firm to afford a rat-infested basement apartment in Chinatown.

It was in the spring of 2001 during Jacob's sophomore year that Lehman Brothers came calling, the talented undergrad's work having caught the attention of the Wall Street giant. A two-week interview process led to a six-figure salary offer and bonus plan to pay the nineteen-year-old whiz kid to develop a series of new accounting programs at the investment firm. A week later, Jacob withdrew from City College and moved to the Upper West Side, where the rats had to scale twenty-three floors in order to visit. And visit they did, sometimes in the middle of the night, carrying ledgers and requests to "disappear" deficits with algorithmic solutions that, to their naïve young superstar, made no sense.

Encouraged by the real estate market, with no federal regulations to fret over, Lehman and other investment firms continued buying, slicing, dicing, repackaging and reselling residential mortgages while raking in billions of dollars in profits. Jacob's stock bonuses continued piling higher. On paper he was a multimillionaire, and his bosses and new peers gleefully taught him how to leverage his assets to attract women. Suddenly, the social dweeb was styling in Armani suits, a new haircut and hot ladies vying to be his permanent arm candy to sleep with.

By early 2006, the programming whiz kid was suddenly struggling just to sleep alone. Despite the juggling of accounts, it appeared to Jacob and a handful of other junior executives that Lehman had leveraged more than twenty times its own net worth. When Jacob tried to point out the potential dangers of this six-hundred-billion-dollar deficit, he was ignored. When he attempted to sell his stock, he was delayed, bullied and ultimately denied.

Two years later the housing bubble officially burst, and Lehman's death spiral was complete, dragging Jacob Cope's net worth with it. Within days he had lost his job, his stock, his pension, his corporate Mercedes, and his corporate-leased apartment. With the other big investment firms and banks entrenched in their own bailouts and mergers, there were no jobs to be had, Wall Street shedding its work force by the thousands.

Waiting for the economy to recover, Jacob sublet a one-bedroom apartment in Brooklyn and looked for work. He attempted to finish his degree, but his rise and fall had been so harsh that he couldn't stay focused.

Two years passed. He moved to Trenton, New Jersey, and worked the grill at a local burger joint.

He purchased the Volkswagen van from his boss, not because he liked the way it ran (which was rare) but because he feared that one day he might actually need to use the vehicle as his residence.

Depressed, he drank—a lot.

When he spent his rent money on booze, he was forced to move into a homeless shelter. The shelters wanted him sober; his mind, wracked in fear, wanted him inebriated.

In April of 2011, the van became his home, his self-fulfilling prophecy complete.

🐾 🐾 🐾

Turning off the main strip, Jacob followed 52nd Street into a lower-middle-class neighborhood. The house he and Nancy were renting was two blocks down on the left, the driveway occupied by a PMS Movers truck. Two scantily clad female bodybuilders were seated on the open tailgate of the vehicle, neither of them Jeanne.

Jacob parked by the curb and climbed out. In the back of his van were two suitcases, his George W. Bush ventriloquist dummy, and a heavy cardboard box that held the Yoko doll. Vinnie had urged him to get rid of the lifelike sex toy. In the end Jacob had decided to bring her along—not for sex (after all, he had Nancy for that) but because he was feeling anxious about the move and found he could talk to Yoko to alleviate his fears.

I get by with a little help from my friends.

Glancing over his shoulder at the two muscular females, he quickly decided it was best to leave the heavy box inside the van until later when he could store the Yoko doll in the garage in privacy. Removing one of his suitcases, he tucked the ventriloquist dummy in the crook of his right arm and walked up the driveway, drawing the attention of the two female bodybuilders.

Jamie Morrison competed as a middle weight. Although the ebony-skinned woman was lankier than Jeanne, she was no less intimidating. Her training partner, Stacy Shear, was a heavyweight, her bulging flesh lathered in cocoa butter, her wavy brown hair bound in a ponytail that fell to the small of her sculpted back. Both bodybuilders wore red muscle tees with "PMS Movers" emblazoned across the chest. Having finished unloading Nancy's belongings, they were alternating sets using a Shake Weight dumbbell while they waited for Jeanne.

Jacob entered their aura like a skirt-clad businesswoman walking by a construction site.

Jamie smiled, pursing her lips. "Hey tough guy, need a hand with your doll collection?"

Jacob avoided eye contact with the Nubian

goliath. "No thank you. I think I can manage."

Stacy blocked his way. "Bet those chicken arms of yours couldn't manage thirty seconds on the Shaker." She grabbed the dumbbell in one hand and violently shook it, her right arm and upper body muscles reverberating, spraying him with sweat. "Try that, Doll Man."

"Yeah, Doll Man, show us your guns."

"Guns? Oh, you mean my biceps. Gee, I don't know if I should. Let me ask my friend." Jacob turned to the George Bush dummy, his right hand discreetly sliding into position beneath the doll's shirt. "Mr. President, you're the decider. Help me out here."

Jacob animated the doll, throwing his voice. "Jakester, are you seriously asking me if you should jerk off a dumbbell? That's just D-U-M, dumb."

Stacy pointed. "Hey, the little man talks."

"You must be the brains of the outfit. Sweet Jesus, Jacob, check out the size of Godzilla's camel toe. If it snows later we can all go skiing."

Stacy's smile disappeared.

"Seriously Jacob, if Rumsfeld's dick was that big, we'd have never invaded Iraq. Hey, Tarzan, be honest. Do you and Cheetah over there pee standing up?"

Jamie shoved her index finger in the dummy's face. "Keep talking, Mini-Me, and the next thing you'll be peeing is my fist down your throat."

"Just wash it off first. I hate the taste of man-gina in the morning. Hey, what's the PMS stand for? Preposterous Mood Swings or Permissible Man Slaughter?"

🐾 🐾 🐾

Jacob entered the house, the dummy's head twisted backward. "I tried to warn you, Mr. President."

"Maybe I misunderestimated them."

Hearing voices, he headed to the kitchen, where he found Lana and Jeanne putting away dishes from cardboard boxes. A gray cat was nuzzling their ankles.

"Welcome to your new home, Jacob."

"Thanks. Where's your sister?"

"Making a coffee run. Jeanne, better take Madonna out back before she shits all over the carpet."

Jeanne picked up the cat and nuzzled it against her neck. "Madonna's a good pussy. Yes you are."

Jacob watched Jeanne exit out the back patio sliding door with the tabby. "Jeanne sure does love her cat."

"Jeanne's pussy saved our relationship."

"Right, because she's—wait, what are we talking about?"

"Jeanne and I had a rough time when we first moved in together. I never thought we'd make it through the first month."

"Why? What happened?"

"Things changed. When you're dating someone new you're always on your best behavior. A month after we moved in together, the honeymoon was over. Sure, there's always sex, but how many different ways can you strap your partner to the bedpost?"

"I don't know. Three?"

"Jeanne saved our relationship when she bought Madonna. Instead of just being house mates, we became a family."

"I see. Then you're suggesting I buy Nancy a cat."

"No, Nancy's not into pussies."

"Right … because she's straight."

"No. Because my sister loves little white foofie dogs. We had a Bichon when Nancy was little. The pup ran off one day and broke her heart. Now you're going to get her another one."

"I am?"

"Jacob, do you want this living arrangement to work or not?"

"I do. But a dog's a big commitment."

"So is moving in with your girlfriend. Trust me. When my little sister's doubled over with menstrual cramps, you're going to need something to change

Mrs. Hyde back into Dr. Jekyll."

"I think we can manage without a dog."

"Really?" Reaching down, Lana grabbed Jacob's testicles, squeezing them.

"Ahh! Let go!"

"You think Hootie and the Blowfish here are going to tame my sister's menstrual cycle?"

"Meds … I'll get her meds!"

"Wrong answer. Try again."

"White foofie dog … white foofie dog!"

"There's a good boy. See, Jeanne and I really want this to work out. My sister likes you. Most important, she trusts you. So don't screw this up."

"White foofie dog. Got it."

10

Living Together
Phase One: Nesting

A NEW HOME IS a blank canvas waiting to be painted with the history of its occupants.

Having spent the majority of her last eight years living in pre-furnished dorm rooms and college apartments, Nancy's contributions to her first coed living arrangement included a queen-size bed, end tables, a quilt, several black-and-white framed Ansel Adams photos, a set of dishes, fast-food cups, mugs, a coffee maker, an alarm clock, a blender, a set of pots and pans, silverware for three people, a half-dozen cardboard boxes filled with books, a twenty-inch flat-screen television, and four powder-blue bath towels.

The impressive furnishings Jacob had purchased for his Manhattan apartment had been sold off years ago when his life had gone into a tailspin. Besides his clothes, shoes, personal hygiene bag and two cardboard boxes of "personal belongings," his domestic contributions amounted to little more than an air mattress, a zipper-challenged sleeping bag and a five-hundred-dollar gift certificate from Bed Bath & Beyond—the latter a housewarming gift from Vinnie's wife, Helen.

Other than Nancy's bed, there was nothing to sit on. There were no groceries to eat. None of that mattered to the young couple, who spent their first night in their new home eating pizza and making love in the master bedroom, before cuddling together to watch a repeat of *Saturday Night Live*.

Sunday was a bit more sobering. The sun awoke them at seven in the morning, its unfiltered morning rays blinding the sleeping couple from a multitude of bare windows.

Within the hour, Nancy had organized their day. With Bed Bath & Beyond not opening until ten, their morning would begin with a quick trip to the local supermarket to stock up on groceries for the week.

With that came their first dilemma: Were Nancy and Jacob roommates or a couple living together?

Roommates was a term that divided the home into his and hers, as in his and her bedroom, his and her bathroom and his and her groceries. A couple that lived together shared these expenses.

Nancy broached the subject on the ride to the grocery store. "When it comes to the rent, electric bill, water and cable, we split everything, right?"

"Right."

"What about groceries?"

"Split it," said Jacob.

"Good. I'll keep a monthly ledger—unless you'd rather create a computer program?"

"Pass. Wait, why do we need a ledger?"

"To keep track of expenses. Let's say you go grocery shopping and spend fifty dollars. That goes into the ledger, along with the receipt. At the end of the month we add up our expenses and settle out."

"What about tampons?"

"What about them?"

"Are we splitting them?"

"I don't know. Are we splitting your jock-itch powder?"

"I don't use jock-itch powder, or make-up, or razors for that matter."

"Fine. When it comes to groceries, you pay for your stuff and I'll pay for mine. Just make sure you buy detergent; I doubt Helen will be doing your laundry anymore."

"You, uh, can't do mine when you do yours?"

"I don't wash my roommate's clothes. I don't

cook or clean for my roommate either."

"What about sex?"

"I have sex with my boyfriend. So are we a couple or roommates?"

"Definitely a couple." Jacob turned into the Publix supermarket parking lot. "Hey, did I tell you that I love you."

"Aw, I love you too."

The shopping cart was three-quarters full by aisle four.

Jacob waited, helpless, while Nancy compared prices on two different dishwasher detergents. After a minute, she placed one inside the cart then moved on to the liquid dish soap.

"Nance, you just bought dishwasher detergent. Why do you need dish soap?"

"You can't wash everything in the dishwasher; some things you have to wash by hand." She grabbed a bottle of dish soap, moving on to the bathroom tile cleaners, then the glass cleaners, oven mitts, scrubbing sponges, laundry detergent, bleach.

Jacob exercised his veto power at the toilet paper. "I like Scotts. No dingleberries."

"What are dingleberries?"

"You know, those little wads of toilet paper that

get stuck in your ass hairs."

"I don't have that problem. You get your sand paper. I'll get my soft stuff."

"I thought we were sharing a bathroom?"

"We are, but we'll stock the powder room with the dingleberry-free toilet paper."

And it was on to aisle five.

Forty minutes and a second shopping cart later, Jacob stood at the checkout counter, sweat beads forming on his forehead. *Stay calm. It's not going to be like this every week. Most of these things are one-time expenses. A kitchen trash can? We needed that. Oven mitts and ice trays? Sure. Aluminum foil? Who uses 175 feet of aluminum foil? You could wrap the space shuttle in that much foil and save on the heat tiles. Freezer bags and trash bags? They'll last a while. Shampoo and conditioner? Okay, but why does she need the expensive stuff? I could use bar soap and be happy.*

Nancy's eyes watched the clerk as he loaded the three six packs of beer and four two-liter bottles of soda into the cart. *So much sugar—all those empty calories. And why must he drink so much beer? If I could get him to switch to bottled water and a cereal that doesn't have a cartoon character on the box, he'd probably lose twenty pounds.*

The cashier pressed the total. "Three hundred and seventy-seven, ninety-six. Any cash back?"

Nancy turned to Jacob. "Baby, did you want

cash back?"

Jacob looked at Nancy. "Sweetie, why don't you pay for this, and I'll cover the towels and curtains with my gift certificate at Bed Bath & Beyond."

"I already have towels."

"What about curtains?"

"Fine." Nancy fished her debit card out of her purse, her eyes furious.

"Are you mad?"

"Of course not. Why would I be mad? I just thought the BB&B certificate was a housewarming gift."

"It was. From my brother."

"Really?" She swiped her debit card, nearly generating sparks. "Because Helen told me it was a gift for the two of us."

The female cashier raised her eyebrows.

Jacob twitched a smile. "Well, of course it is. You just save that receipt for your ledger, and I'll handle the next big ticket item. Okay?"

"Okay. Where are you going?"

"Need air. Meet you outside."

Nancy smiled at the cashier. "We just moved in together."

"Honey, you don't have to explain. Before we got married, my husband did all his grocery shopping at the 7-Eleven."

11

Living Together
Phase Two: Routine

NANCY ENTERED HER HOME carrying two plastic Target shopping bags. She kicked off her shoes and left her car keys on the book shelf by the hall mirror. Oozing pride, she walked down the hallway past the powder room now decorated in violet hand towels, a turquoise rug and a gold-plated towel rack with a matching soap dispenser. Entering the kitchen, she gazed lovingly at the new oval glass table and four black leather chairs then entered the den to admire her new black leather sofa and beige La-Z-Boy chair, the copper and black area rug beneath the granite coffee table matching the two throw pillows, and the smart-looking saber-gray Venetian blinds complimenting the room.

Amazing what you can buy on interest-only payments for three years with 20 percent down. Of course, the two fake palm trees came a week late—they simply make the room, she thought.

She set the two bags on the glass table. From one, she removed a large box containing a wall clock, the face featuring an adorable white foofie dog. She popped in a double-A battery and set the time then fished through a kitchen drawer until she located a screwdriver and screw.

She had mounted the clock and was changing out of her work clothes in the master bedroom when she heard the Volkswagen's muffler backfire in the driveway.

Jacob entered his home carrying the newspaper, which he deposited on the bookshelf by the hall mirror. His bladder full, he hustled down the hallway, entered the powder room and let loose a stream of urine that splattered the rim of the bowl. He shook himself twice (more than twice and you're playing with it), flushed, then rinsed off his hands, drying them with one of the violet hand towels, which he left in a ball on the sink.

Entering the kitchen, he saw the two Target bags on the new oval glass table and rolled his eyes. He entered the den looking for Nancy finding only the new black leather sofa and La-Z-Boy chair, the area rug and granite coffee table and the saber-gray Venetian blinds.

What good were interest-only payments for three years if I had to put 20 percent down? Even upping my hours at work to forty a week only covered 30 percent of that nut. And did she really need the two fake trees?

Seeking solace, he popped a John Lennon CD into the CD player and headed for the fridge to grab a beer.

Nancy entered from the bedroom hall. "Hey, you. How was work?"

"Work sucked. I hate stupid people. The worst problem with being stupid is that stupid is forever. Next week they'll call me back to walk them through the same problem. How was your radio show?"

"Good," she lied. "I'm getting edgier. I think I need that, don't you?"

"Edgy's good. What's for dinner?"

"Burgers. Can you fire up the grill?"

"If I fire up the grill, then I'm the one cooking dinner."

"No you're not. You're turning on the gas, plopping three patties on the grill, and checking on them ten minutes later. I'm making fries and a salad. Jacob, your sandals—you're tracking dirt all over my clean floor!"

"Sorry."

"Can you take them off?"

"Then I have to put them on again to start the

grill."

"So?"

"So then I have to take them off again to come inside, then on again to flip the burgers, then off again to come back inside, then on again to get the burgers. That's a lot of work. All you're doing is popping the frozen fries in the oven and dumping some lettuce in a bowl."

"Fine. Take off those smelly shoes and bang the dirt off the tread, and I'll cook the burgers and do the fries and salad. But you're cleaning up dinner, and that includes the grill."

"I can't clean up dinner. I have to practice my act."

Nancy gritted her teeth. "Can't you practice your act while you cook the burgers?"

"How do I do that? Pretend the bun is the dummy's mouth?"

"Fine. I'll do dinner and clean up. You go practice your act."

"Thanks, Nance. Oh, remember, I like mine well-done." Jacob headed off to the garage to get the George Bush dummy.

"Take off your shoes!"

12

Living Together
Phase Three: When Does
That Lease Expire?

NANCY HAD INTENDED to celebrate her first month living with Jacob by serving her boyfriend breakfast in bed. That plan went awry when she woke up Sunday morning with menstrual cramps. Seated at the kitchen table, she downed her last aspirin with her morning coffee. Still in pain, she opened her laptop to check her email.

Jacob staggered into the kitchen in his boxer shorts and Miami Dolphins hooded sweatshirt at eleven o'clock. Heading straight for the oven, he cranked the dial up to 425 degrees then opened the freezer door and removed a frozen pizza.

Nancy looked up from her laptop. "Pizza for

breakfast?"

Jacob placed the frozen pie on an aluminum tray and shoved it inside the oven. "Call it an early lunch." Opening the refrigerator, he grabbed a beer.

"Jacob, it's eleven in the morning."

"It's light beer—half the calories." Jacob shuffled to the chair opposite her to read the morning paper.

"I got an email this morning from my producer—the quarterly Arbitron ratings. I'm drowning, Jacob."

"You'll figure it out." He glanced at the front page of the newspaper. "Did you see this? It says a Deerfield Beach woman was raped and assaulted last night. That neighborhood's not far from here."

"You know what I think? I think I need to do something completely off the wall to generate ratings. Maybe I should simulcast my broadcasts on the Internet topless?"

"Maybe you should run on a treadmill."

Nancy looked up from her laptop. "How will that improve my ratings?"

Jacob lowered the newspaper. "How will what improve your ratings?"

"Running on a treadmill."

"I meant instead of jogging in our neighbor-hood. Nance, this guy raped a woman not far from here. It's not safe."

"I'm fine. Although I wonder ... if I was

assaulted, I bet that would get listeners to tune in to me."

"Come on in the bedroom and let's see if it works."

"Forget it. I just started my period."

"Would that prevent a rape? Wouldn't that be cool if they invented a tampon with a spike in it? That would teach these maniacs."

"Maybe I should do a week interviewing rape victims? Or I could bring in a few martial-arts guys as guests—teach women how to defend themselves. What do you think?"

Jacob expelled a colon-reverberating belch. "Sorry."

"That's disgusting."

"It's all in the diaphragm. I could teach you. Then you could teach your listeners."

"I wish I could teach you to put the damn toilet seat down after you pee. I almost broke my back last night."

"Anyways, I don't get the whole toilet seat thing. Why is it that a woman can open and close a refrigerator and a car door but a two pound toilet seat in the up-position confuses the hell out of you. Do you shut your eyes and blindly butt-leap onto the toilet seat?"

"It was the middle of the night. I didn't want to

disturb you by turning on the bathroom light. This is the thanks I get."

"Sorry."

"Sorry, sorry, sorry. You're sorry when you track dirt in my clean house. You're sorry when you destroy the powder room hand towels. You're sorry when you leave your clothes all over the bathroom floor. And when are you going to settle up on this month's rent? Or pay for groceries again?"

"I told you. My extended hours are two weeks behind."

"It didn't stop you from playing poker Thursday night with your brother and his depraved doctor friends. How much did you lose?"

"I don't know. Not that much."

"Was it more than you spend on beer every week? Or should I say more than I spend on your beer!"

"What about those two trees in the den?"

"It's interest-only for three years!"

Jacob was about to respond when the oven timer went off. Using his sweatshirt as an oven mitt, he removed the hot tray and slid it onto the counter. "Want some?"

"God no. What I want is more aspirin. There's another bottle in the den."

Jacob left the kitchen and searched the den, his

eyes momentarily locking onto the front cover of the *Good Housekeeping* magazine lying on the coffee table. The photo featured a white foofie puppy curled up by a fireplace.

He located the aspirin by the television remote and returned to the kitchen. For the first time he noticed the face of the wall clock featured a tail-wagging white Bichon Frise.

Nancy snatched the bottle of aspirin out of his hand and staggered into the den. "The smell of that pizza's making me sick. I'm going to lie down—dammit!"

"What? What's wrong now?"

"The bottle's empty! Think you could run down to the store and get me some?"

"Sure, only the NFL pregame show comes on in ten minutes. Can it wait until halftime of the Dolphins-Eagles game?"

She teared up, her emotions lost in a tempest sea. "Do you ever think of anyone but yourself? Just once I'd love to see you make the bed or throw your dirty clothes in the hamper. Or fold a load of laundry … or wash a dish!"

"Okay, okay, I'll get you some aspirin, geez."

"Make it Advil. And a box of tampons."

"Aw, come on!"

"What's the problem?"

"I'm a man. It's embarrassing."

"Tampons, not maxi pads. Get the ones that say 'super absorbent.'"

"All right already, geez." Jacob grabbed his van keys from a hook and exited through the kitchen door leading out into the garage. *Why do women wait until their period comes to buy tampons? It's like waiting until you have to take a shit to buy toilet paper.*

He recalled Lana's words the day he and Nancy moved in together. *"Trust me, when my little sister's doubled over with menstrual cramps, you're going to need something to change Mrs. Hyde back into Dr. Jekyll."*

He paused a moment to stare at the large cardboard box containing his sex doll.

Yoko never needed me to buy her tampons. Or aspirin. Or a white foofie dog.

13

Foofie

JACOB TURNED INTO the drugstore parking lot, his nerves shot. For several minutes he listened to John Lennon sing "Mind Games" on his 8-track cassette deck before speed-dialing his brother's cell number on his iPhone. "Vin, it's me."

"Where are you?"

"I'm in my van sitting in front of Walgreens. Nancy practically threw me out of the house to get her tampons and Advil. Vin, I need your advice."

"Get the extra-strength."

"I'm serious. Things have changed between us. When we first moved in together, everything was great. And now my life has changed in oh so many ways."

"Douche bag, it's called the end of the honeymoon phase. You think you were just going to get endless *schtuppie* without the emotional baggage?"

"I just want her to stop yelling at me. 'Do this. Do that.' Why can't *she* put the toilet seat down?"

"You want my advice? Apologize."

"You misunderstood. She's the one yelling at me. Why would I apologize?"

"You're apologizing because God gave you a penis. In the bible it's referred to as 'original sin.' Adam bit the apple, stuck his *schmeckle* in Eve, and man has been apologizing to women ever since, even though Eve made Adam eat the damn apple. And by the way, if you think it's bad now, just wait until you get married and Nancy pops out a few kids. You'll be buying stock in Advil."

"I don't know. It doesn't feel right to me."

"Jacob, do you want to be right, or do you want to get laid twice a week?"

"Yesterday we got into a fight over which way the toilet paper hangs."

"I've been married to Helen for fifteen years, and I still can't get her to replace the roll so the paper hangs over the top. Sure, it used to bother me. That was my ego talking. Then I realized that, by losing, I was actually winning."

"I don't understand."

"Women's brains are wired to rule the nest; it's the natural order of the jungle. Take the lion, the king of beasts. Who hunts for food? The lioness.

Who takes care of the cubs? The lioness. You know what the male lion does all day? He lies around and licks his balls. Who really wins? The male, that's who. All you need to worry about are those five days a month when the devil possesses her brain."

"Lana warned me about those days. She told me to buy Nancy a white foofie dog. She said it would stabilize our home."

"Actually, a dog could work. Women need someone to hug and blab all their problems to. Gay men and dogs are great for that. There's a pet store on Hillsboro Boulevard not far from you. Get her the dog, and by tonight she'll be licking *your* balls."

Jacob found Wags and Purr located in a strip mall next to a kosher Chinese restaurant. A litter of kittens occupied the front window pen, enticing passing shoppers to *ooh* and *ahh*. Inside, lined up in rows, were baby cribs, each padded cell holding a different breed of puppy.

Jacob entered the store, his presence attracting the attention of a flamboyant gay man in his early forties dressed in a sky-blue lab coat and white crocs. "Welcome to Wags and Purr. My name is Cyril, and I'll be your adoption counselor. And you are?"

"Jacob."

"Well, Mister Jacob, have I got fabulous news for you. We've got kitties for sale, only twenty dollars each. That comes with a litter box and two jingle toys."

"Actually, Cyril, I'm shopping for a puppy."

"Oh, come on, kittens are fun too. Take home two, and I'll toss in a bag of catnip. Slip some in your pants pocket, and your new feline friends will work you like a pro." Cyril meowed, pawing his own groin.

Jacob took a step back. "That's … really tempting. But I'm looking for a Bichon, for my *girlfriend*."

"Stupid cats. I can't even give the damn things away. Okay, Mister Jacob, wash your hands with some antibacterial gel and follow me."

Cyril waited for him to cleanse before leading him past two cribs of puppies to the last padded container in the row. Inside the crib, standing on its hind legs, was an eight-inch-long whimpering white fur-ball of joy.

The salesman scooped up the adorable nine-week-old Bichon in both hands and cradled it to his face, allowing the puppy to lick his open mouth. "He's so cute, isn't hims?"

Jacob glanced at the price tag. "Sixteen hundred bucks? For a dog?"

"That's right, daddy. Plus you'll need a bowl and

a puppy leash, and don't forget the food. Now he's had his vaccination—"

"He?"

"Yes, handsome. See, some puppies have pee-pees and some don't. This one does, so we call it a he."

"What about protection?"

"I usually wear a rubber."

"I meant the dog. Can it be trained to protect my girlfriend?"

"Why? Is she in danger?"

"You know what I mean."

"Daddy, this is a Bichon, not a Rottweiler. It barks at every noise and pees on the carpet, but it'll come when you call it—Jesus, it sounds just like my boyfriend, Felipe. Trust me, your girlfriend will love him. Women love the breed. This little brute is the last one we have left from a litter of six, and they just came in on Tuesday. Let me guess, this is going to be a surprise."

"I'll say. She's expecting Advil."

"Okay, I have no idea what that means. Tell you what, why don't you pick out a pretty, butch collar and a doggy bowl. Then we'll fill out the paperwork, and you can take your precious bundle of love home in a special Wags and Purr puppy box."

14

Sam

IT WAS NEARLY FIVE in the afternoon by the time Jacob returned home. Shutting off the engine, he calmed his new best friend, grabbed the cardboard box off the passenger seat, and exited the van.

Nancy was lying on the sofa. Doubled up with cramps, she had been calling her boyfriend for the last five hours, but his cell phone had been going straight to voice mail.

Hearing Jacob key in, she muted the television, ready to wage war. "You left five hours ago. Where the hell—" She sniffed the air, catching a disturbing scent coming from the front of Jacob's pants. "Oh my God, you went to a nudie bar!"

"Nudie bar? I didn't go to a—"

Her anger seething, she stood, poking her index finger against his chest. "Do you actually believe a naked woman grinding her stink all over your lap isn't cheating?"

"Oh, that stink—that's not from a lap dance. I was being licked."

"Get out!"

"Nancy, it wasn't another woman. It's a special gift. Something Lana suggested I buy to make us a family." From behind his back he revealed the pet store box.

Nancy's demeanor changed. Cheeks flushed, tears in her eyes, she carefully opened the container, removing a dog bowl. "Oh my God, Jacob, oh my God … did you buy us a puppy?"

"Yes I did. He's in the van, waiting to meet his new mommy!"

Nancy's heart raced. Suddenly her cramps were gone, and her rage evaporated. Barefoot, still in her pajamas, she pushed past Jacob and raced out the front door. "Where is he? Where is my precious little puppy?"

She yanked open the van's side door and was instantly bowled over by a black, tan, and burnt-orange tornado of muscle, fur and slobber that knocked her backward onto the ground before assaulting her with its tongue and stench.

The 110-pound male German shepherd circled Nancy, barking and wagging its tail.

Jacob attempted to step between them. "Isn't he

amazing? His name is Sam. He's five years old. I got him at the pound. Can you believe they were going to kill him?"

Breaking off its licking frenzy, the dog sniffed an invisible trail to the nearest flower bed, lifted its hind leg, and peed.

Nancy sat up, bewildered. "This isn't a Bichon. A Bichon is a small, white, foofie dog. This … this is a horse."

"Silly, it's not a horse; it's a German shepherd. They're loyal and smart and very protective. The cops use them to sniff out drugs."

"And I suppose you left your stash buried in my flower bed?"

Nancy pointed over Jacob's shoulder where the dog was using its front paws to dig out a scarlet bromeliad.

"Sam, no! Sorry. I'll replant that."

"Jacob, I don't want a big dog. How could you make a decision like this without asking me?"

"It was supposed to be a surprise."

"Mission accomplished. Now please take it back."

"I can't do that. Sam's owner abandoned him. If I bring him back to the pound, they'll gas him."

"That's not my problem."

"It sort of is. The pound closed twenty minutes ago."

Exasperated, Nancy stood, her cramps returning. Doubled over, she hurried back inside the house, slamming the front door.

Sam circled Jacob, wanting to play.

"Now what am I going to—*owff!*" Jacob dropped to his knees in pulsating agony, the dog having shoved its long wet nose into his groin, flicking Jacob's balls up to his belly like a pinball lever.

I am the keeper of my own fate, emancipating myself from the self-imposed bonds of my gender.

Four Advil and forty minutes later, Nancy emerged from the master bedroom, her psyche recomposed, her temper cooled. To his credit, Jacob had dinner delivered and laid out on the kitchen table, the aroma of the eggplant parmesan momentarily replacing the overpowering scent of a kennel.

Jacob was already seated, his facial expression and body language showing submission. The dog was lying on its side on the linoleum floor by its metal water bowl, panting hot, humid, tongue-laced breaths across the room.

Nancy stepped over the smelly animal to take her usual seat, but Sam's bulk was preventing her from pulling out the chair. "Can you do something about this?"

"Here, Sam! Here, boy! Sam, come here!"

The dog refused to move.

Jacob shrugged. "Maybe he only understands German?"

Refusing to switch places, Nancy wedged herself into her chair. Still unable to move the dog, she pushed the table into Jacob's stomach, forcing him to surrender territory. "What time does the pound reopen?"

"I don't know. Tomorrow's Monday. I'm guessing nine."

"You'll take him back in the morning."

"Which means he'll be gassed by noon. I'm Jewish, Nancy. Gassing innocent beings doesn't sit well with my people."

"Then drop the dog off at the nearest synagogue. I don't care. This smelly animal is not staying in my house."

"What if I bathe him?"

"No."

"If I bathe him, he'll smell just like a Bichon."

"When he's as small as a Bichon, then he can stay. Tonight he sleeps in the garage."

"It's gotta be a hundred degrees out there."

"Then let him sleep outside or in your van. I don't care, as long as he's out of my house."

"Our house."

"Excuse me?"

"You said it was your house. Technically it's our

house. My name's on the lease too. I pay half the rent—that makes it our house."

"Fine! Keep the damn dog!" More angry than hungry, Nancy attempted to push her chair back in order to stand, but the dog refused to budge. Maneuvering sideways, she managed to squeeze her way onto her feet only to kick the water bowl, spilling half its contents onto her bare feet.

"Ugh!" She stormed out of the kitchen and back inside the master bedroom, bolting the door behind her.

Jacob went after her. He tried the door. It was locked. "Nance? Can we talk about this please?"

She opened the door a minute later, shoving his clothes and toothbrush against his chest. "This is my bedroom, roommate. You can take the guest room. You can also do your own laundry. And cleaning. And cooking!"

She slammed the door, the noise covering up the *schlerping* sound of eggplant parmesan being licked off Nancy's plate as Sam, standing on his hind legs, devoured the Italian take-out.

15

Dead Man Walking

THE GRAYNESS OF DAWN peeled away the South Florida night in its humid vapor. A surge of traffic converged on Interstate 95, forcing motorists to adhere to the speed limit. Trash trucks crawled through a maze of neighborhoods, their rear orifices squealing as garbage men in overalls fed the vehicles piles of refuse.

Monday morning rush hour. Children heading off to school, adults shaking off the remains of the weekend.

Inside the house with the uprooted scarlet bromeliads, the sound and scent of dueling sphincters soured the air.

Stretched out on the La-Z-Boy recliner was Jacob Cope, his pale, hairy right leg curled over the leather arm of the chair. Stretched out on the sofa was Sam, the dog's hairy right hind leg mirroring that of its sleeping master. Man and dog on their backs, their rectums blowing out farts to welcome the day.

At precisely 7:49, the door to the master bedroom was unlocked and opened. Nancy emerged dressed in her business attire. A meeting between the radio psychologist, the station owner, and the new programming director had been scheduled for 9:00 a.m. sharp, and she would arrive on Vincent Lombardi time, if not sooner. All she needed as a cup of coffee, a nonfat yogurt and her Tory Burch flats. She had the right shoe; the left one was still missing.

Must be in the den.

She entered the kitchen to start the coffee only to be greeted by a trail of feathers. Still a bit sleepy, she followed the goose down into the den, her blood pressure soaring as her eyes shifted from her mangled throw pillow to the four-legged mongrel stretched out on her new sofa. "Get the hell off of my sofa, you mangy mutt!"

Startled awake, Sam slunk off the couch, his tail tucked between his hind quarters.

Nancy turned to the two-legged mongrel snoring in the La-Z-Boy recliner. "Jacob, wake up."

The shaggy man belched in his sleep and rolled over on his side.

"Jacob!" Grabbing the remains of the pillow, she beat him over the head, feathers flying across the room like volcanic ash.

Jacob sat up, groggy. "Wha?"

"Your dog chewed up my good pillow!"

He rubbed his eyes, looking around dumbfounded. "You sure it was Sam?"

"Gee, I don't know. Maybe an alligator snuck in last night and—" Nancy paused, sniffing the air. "What's that smell?" Leaving the den, she entered the hallway and gagged. "Jacob!"

Jacob rolled out of the La-Z-Boy recliner to join Nancy, who was pinching her nose at the stench from the white ceramic-tile floor, which has been cluster-bombed with smoldering brown blobs of doggy diarrhea.

Jacob covered his mouth. "He must have gotten into the eggplant. I'll get a mop. It'll be okay."

"It's not okay. Do you know why it's not okay, Mr. Y?"

"Who's Mr. Y?"

"Mr. Y is the tiny voice in every man's head that says, 'Don't worry about how your actions might affect other people. Just do it.' Do you know where that tiny voice is coming from, Jacob?"

"From my dick?"

"It's coming from your male ego."

Nancy pushed past him, returning to the den. She would grab her coffee and yogurt and escape this Monday morning speed bump of aggravation. She would seek refuge in her car and listen to her *Best of Enya* CD. She would meet with her boss and the new programming director, excitedly accept their ideas for marketing her show, and then devour a spinach salad for lunch before performing an amazing radio broadcast. In essence, the unflappable Nancy Beach, Ph.D., would use her willpower and emotional self-control to change what could have been a disastrous morning into a glorious day. But first, she must find her other shoe.

Retracing her steps, she returned to the master bedroom and located the missing Tory Burch flat— in the dog's mouth.

Tail wagging, Sam stood in her doorway, the canine's teeth biting down on her prized leather shoe.

"Drop it now, fleabag," Nancy growled, "or I swear I'll give you away to a hungry Korean family."

The German shepherd dropped down on its front paws, ready to play.

"Not a chance in hell," Nancy muttered, lowering her center of gravity.

The dog bolted past her, underestimating the tenacity of the seething Ivy League grad and former varsity field hockey goalie, who lunged sideways and tackled the kennel-reeking, four-legged, 110-pound missile of muscle and fur around its hips, her right hand reaching up to its mouth to secure the shoe.

But Sam wouldn't let go, tug-of-war being far more fun than tag. Rolling out from under Nancy, the dog regained its footing and backed away in seismic two-foot jerks, dragging its unintended playmate with it.

Nancy refused to let go, years of Pilates having prepared her core muscles for this very moment. Balancing on her free hand and knees, she battled the hound like a mother fighting off a carjacker attempting to drive off with her infant.

Rising to the challenge, the dog shook its head back and forth, saliva flying across Nancy's undone blouse as Jacob watched from the kitchen. He was a dead man walking, unsure of what to do first—call the tile cleaners, the dog pound, or hurry to the bathroom and relieve his aching bladder.

With a guttural scream, Nancy called the end of the fight. She had fought valiantly, but the dog had better leverage, its jaws far stronger than her grip. Releasing the shoe, she regained her feet and limped into the bedroom, slamming the door behind her.

Still wagging its tail, Sam approached Jacob and dropped the shoe by his feet.

Jacob inspected the mangled, tooth-marked entanglement of spit-soaked leather. "Hey, uh, Nance ... I got your shoe back."

16

The Cabots

IT WAS 9:03 a.m.—eighteen minutes past Lombardi time—when Nancy frantically keyed in at the Lifestyle Revolution lobby. Ignoring the chocolate-faced receptionist's wild hand gestures, she made a beeline straight for her producer, Trish Kieras, who was waiting anxiously at the end of the hall.

"Olivia Cabot's already in the conference room with her father and Pistol Pete. Go!"

Nancy took a deep breath and entered the conference room. Seated at the end of an oval walnut table was Olivia Cabot. The fifty-three-year-old CEO's face resembled a tan Kabuki mask, the smooth inanimate look courtesy of an early morning session of Botox. On Olivia's left was Peter Soderblom, the station's new programming director. Fair-haired and in his late thirties, "Pistol Pete" had been an associate producer at KYW News Talk Radio in Philadelphia when Olivia had hired him away to run her radio station.

Three seats over was Olivia's eighty-two-year-old father, Truman Cabot. The retired millionaire and founder of Cabot Enterprises was preoccupied with watching *Jeopardy!* on an iPad while slurping spoonfuls of green pea soup from a Styrofoam take-out bowl.

"Olivia, I am so sorry—"

"Sit down. Peter has something to discuss."

The programming director avoided direct eye contact with the perky blonde radio host. "I'll keep this short and sweet: In order to attract bigger sponsors, we're dropping 60 percent of our Lifestyle radio hosts in favor of syndicated talent. Starting Monday, you'll be replaced with Dr. Laura."

Nancy winced, the blow registering in her gut. "But why?"

"Do you mean Y as in my male chromosome, or why as in why were your winter Arbitron ratings a 0.06?"

"I've only been on the air six months. I have some new strategies devised for the third quarter that should bring in at least a 3.5."

Peter handed her a printout sheet. "These are results from a radio survey mailed to homes within the station's signal strength. According to listeners, you're not connecting."

Nancy scanned the paper. "Thirteen listeners? You're basing your decision on thirteen listeners? What about my Internet listeners?"

"The decision's been made." Olivia tapped her father on the top of his head. "Daddy, eat before your soup gets cold."

Peter Soderblom's cell phone rang, cutting off Nancy's Hail Mary offer to do her Internet feed topless. "Pistol Pete, never retreat." The programming director's expression dropped. "When did you figure that out? Yeah, well, thanks for fisting me, ass wipe." He hung up. "Olivia, may I speak with you in private?"

"Let's talk in the lobby. I need a cigarette." Olivia turned to Nancy. "Stay here with my father, and do not give him any sugar."

Nancy waited until they had left before turning her attention to the old man. Truman Cabot had a reputation for supporting the underdog, provided they showed some moxie.

Moxie was Nancy Beach's middle name.

"Mr. Cabot, we haven't met yet, but I'm a big admirer of yours. My name is Nancy Beach, *Doctor* Nancy Beach." She extended her hand, retracting it as Mr. Cabot picked inside his ear then smelled his finger.

"I want something sweet."

The old man returned his attention to the iPad as Alex Trebek read the next question. "Politics for one hundred dollars: He was elected America's first black president."

"Who was George Jefferson?"

"Mr. Cabot, I'm the host of an up-and-coming radio show on your network called *Love's a Beach*. Given a chance, I just know our ratings will climb. Is there any way you might talk to your daughter and ask her to give our show another ratings book?

"Got any chocolate?"

"Sir, your daughter said no sugar."

"She's my step-daughter, and she's a cunt. You want your show, give me something sweet."

Give it to him. They already fired me. What else can they do? She searched through her purse, locating a miniature York Peppermint Patty. "How's this?"

Before she could lay out her terms for the exchange, the old man snatched the candy from her hand, peeled off the wrapper and popped the quarter-size chocolate snack into his mouth.

"So you'll talk to your daughter about my show, right? Right, Mr. Cabot?"

The old man's face turned red.

"Sir, are you all right? Mr. Cabot?" Nancy's heart beat wildly in her chest. "Oh, geez—please tell me you're not a diabetic."

He gasped in silence, his face turning purple.

"Oh my God, you're choking!" She patted him on the back then gave him a vicious slap between his shoulder blades.

The unchewed, partially melted dark chocolate peppermint patty flew out of Mr. Cabot's mouth— followed by the old man's hearing aid and dentures, everything splattering in the plastic bowl of green pea soup.

"Oh, God … I am so sorry. Can you breathe? Mr. Cabot?"

The old man was breathing and fiddling with the iPad, cranking up the volume.

Using his plastic spoon, Nancy attempted to fish his teeth and hearing aid out of the soup when she heard Olivia and Peter approaching from down the hall. On the verge of a nervous breakdown, she stuck her hand in the bowl and retrieved the two objects, hiding them behind her back just as the female CEO led her boy toy back inside the conference room.

Olivia took one of her father's paper napkins and wiped lipstick from Peter's neck. "It would seem Lady Luck is on your side, Dr. Beach. We can't syndicate Dr. Laura until April 15th, and Peter feels it would be easier to keep you in your time slot than to reshuffle the deck again in three months."

"Oh, God, thank you. Thank you, thank you, thank you. I promise my next Arbitron numbers will kick ass."

"Then getting a new job in April should be that much easier for you." Olivia turned to Peter. "Darling, I'm late for my pedicure. Do me a favor and handle things with that wacko psychic and the vegan yoga instructor. Then see to it that my father is dropped off at his new retirement home."

"Of course."

Olivia Cabot slung her purse over her shoulder and left.

Nancy quickly followed her out.

Peter Soderblom used the conference table intercom. "Lynnie, you can send the gypsy in." He turned to Mr. Cabot. "This shouldn't take long—oh, geez."

Old Man Cabot's dentures were hanging upside-down in his mouth, his left ear oozing gobs of green pea soup and chocolate mint.

17

Patel

IT WAS AFTER ELEVEN by the time Jacob arrived at work, having spent the morning cleaning up doggy diarrhea.

His supervisor, Sanjay Patel, intercepted him on his way to his desk. "My uncle wishes to see you in his office right away."

Great. Can this day get any worse? Leaving his thirty-two-ounce soda and chocolate doughnut on his desk, Jacob followed a short corridor past the supply room to a closed door bearing a brass name plate: "Patel."

Amir Patel was the senior manager of I-Guru USA. Jacob had met the man only once, when he interviewed for the job. He had never been invited into his supervisor's office.

He knocked and then entered.

The rectangular chamber was more Buddhist monastery than office, its walls covered by purple velvet drapes, its white marble floor clustered with enormous colorful pillows. The only office furnishings were a curved glass desk and wicker chair which occupied the near-right corner of the room. The desk was barren, save for a laptop and an emerald-shaded brass banker's lamp.

"Remove your shoes, please." Amir Patel was seated with his back to Jacob on an Indian rug, facing the front wall curtain. Incense burned from a glass holder by his feet.

Jacob shrugged. Kicking off his sandals, he approached the short, balding, brown-skinned Hindu, his moist bare feet squeaking on the marble floor.

The middle-aged Indian was dressed in a black tennis warm-up suit. "Sit and pray with me, Jacob."

"What are we praying for?"

"Enlightenment."

Jacob flopped into a seated position. "Sorry I was late. Domestic problem. See, I brought home this dog and—"

"Apologize with your silence." Patel pressed a small remote control by his left foot, causing the front velvet curtains to part, revealing an altar and the five-foot-high statue of a Buddha-bellied, four-armed human possessing the head of an elephant.

Jacob took one look at the Hindu deity and

expelled a bloodcurdling scream.

"What is it? What is wrong?"

"Shut the curtain!"

Patel hit the switch.

Jacob rolled onto his back, hyperventilating.

"Are you in need of medical attention?"

"I … don't … like … elephants."

"Ganesha is not an elephant. He is one of the five prime Hindu deities."

"Dude, I'm not praying to Babar the Elephant or any other pachyderm."

"Who do you pray to?"

"Geez, I don't know. God, I suppose. I'm not very religious."

"One can be spiritual without being religious. Spirituality is the act of connecting with the Creator. We do this through prayer. Prayer itself is the perfect belief in a higher power."

"I'm not into praying."

"Perhaps this is why you are so consumed with fear."

"That's a little harsh," Jacob said, sitting up. "So I'm a little uneasy around elephants—big deal. Amputees rattle me—can't help that. The hydrophobia comes from nearly drowning in a sprinkler when I was eleven."

"Is that everything?"

"Yes. Actually, no. I was beat up in seventh grade by Gertrude Mulder, which explains the Dutch-phobia. But, again, that one could have led to a fear of women, which, thank God, I don't have. Batman was afraid of bats, so we have that in common. And I happen to think my fear of constipation helps me to maintain a balanced diet, so that's a good thing."

"Your logic is baffling. Your diet would kill half of Jakarta."

"I used to suffer from lachanophobia, which stemmed from my mother threatening to home school me if I didn't finish my veggies. That passed when I was sixteen."

"Are you on drugs?"

"I was on Thorazine after the whole deal at Lehman Brothers, but I stopped using it after it led to a fear of leprosy."

"Enough!" Patel grabbed Jacob by his wrist. "None of these fears are real; they are symptoms. This morning I prayed to Ganesha, asking him if I should replace you. Ganesha helped me to recognize the true cause of your fears."

"Who's Ganesha?"

Patel motioned to the curtain.

"You asked a statue of Babar the Elephant if you should fire me?"

"Ganesha is the lord of success and destroyer of

evils and obstacles, things you are clearly lacking in your life."

"What'd the elephant say?"

"Please stop calling Ganesha an elephant!" Patel drew a soothing breath. "Anger is the cause of your fear. Anger causes heat. Heat rises to the head. Tell me about your upbringing. What were your parents like?"

"My father died when I was young."

"And your mother?"

"She lived."

Patel stood, standing before him. "Jacob, do you know why so many American companies outsource their IT departments to India?"

"Because it's cheaper?"

"Yes, but it is also because Indian culture promotes tranquility, while American culture thrives on being reactive. In order to succeed, a computer tech must know how to deal with irate, irrational customers. When it comes to analyzing and fixing computers, there is no one better than yourself. When it comes to dealing with people, you are a hothead. Therefore, you will either learn to control your anger or you will find another job. Am I clear?"

"Yes sir."

Jacob's cell phone rang the moment he left his boss's

office. "Nancy?"

"Did you have the floor cleaned?"

"It's clean."

"What does that mean?"

"It means I cleaned it."

"What about the dog?"

"I left him in the garage with the door cracked open."

"So you've decided to keep it?"

"I'm putting an ad in the paper to give him away."

"Have it your way."

"What does that mean? Hello? Nancy?" Jacob hung up.

18

Bitch Session

MONDAY'S BROADCAST crawled into its third and final hour. Nancy remained at the microphone —a captain sinking her own ship. She had spent her first hour discussing the recent assault in Deerfield Beach, but with few details and no practical experience of her own, the topic had dead-ended rather quickly. In hour two, she opened the phone lines to discuss any topic on the listeners' minds, but there were only three callers—one being Lynnie, who was pushing for a blind date show with her gardener as the top prize.

Heading into the last hour, she decided to come clean with her audience.

"So that's the story, guys. Dr. Beach is officially beached unless I can get my ratings up. I'm willing to talk about anything, so call me at 561-222-WOWF, or you can text star-WOWF on your mobile phone.

Trish, do we have any callers on the line?"

Trish was in the control room, reading the Help Wanted ads. She shook her head then returned to the newspaper.

Nancy groaned. "Hour number three and still no callers. Is there anybody out there with a pulse? I realize it's Monday. … Want to know how my Monday started? It started when my live-in boyfriend's two-thousand-pound German shepherd tore apart my brand-new throw pillow, chewed the heel off of my new Tory Burch flats, and diarrhea'd all over my hallway. Want to join the bitch hour, give us a call at 561-222-WOWF, or you can text star-WOWF on your mobile phone. Woof, woof, woof."

Trish knocked at the glass partition.

"Will wonders never cease? We actually have a caller. This is Dr. Beach, what's your bitch?"

"Hi, Dr. Beach. I'm a first-time caller. Actually, I've never listened to your show before. I happened to be flipping through the dial when I heard you say something about a German shepherd. We breed shepherds. They're wonderful dogs."

"Yes, well, I don't plan to keep ours very long. In fact, when I get home tonight, I'm telling my boyfriend he needs to choose which bitch he wants to live with."

Trish held up another sign.

"Line two from Boca. Speak."

"Hi, Dr. Beach. It sounds to me like the problem's your boyfriend, not the dog."

"Very astute, Boca. Actually, it's not my dog; it's his dog, and they have a lot in common. Neither one of them listens, they're both slobs and they both smell like wet carpet. Line three from Wellington, you're on the air with Dr. Bitch, er, Beach."

"You're not a dog lover, are you?"

"Not true. I like small foofie dogs. Big dogs poop big turds and chew up the furniture. Then again, so does my boyfriend."

"Well, you have to train them."

"The dog or my boyfriend?"

"Both."

The human brain processes four hundred billion bits of information a second, and yet we only allow an infinitesimal percentage of that data to breach our stream of consciousness. How do we select what to focus on? Which random thoughts should be flushed and which harvested? Where do the seeds of inspiration that yield the oak trees of success come from?

The answer: They often come when you least expect it.

"Well, you have to train them."

"The dog or my boyfriend?"

"Both."

Nancy's heart pounded in her chest as the epiphany seeded a thought in her mind's eye that quickly sprouted roots. "My esteemed caller from Wellington is right! It's not the dog's fault it crapped all over my house. Sam needs to be trained. Sam, by the way, is my German shepherd, not my boyfriend. If you're a dog trainer, or you know of an experienced dog trainer, call me right away at 561-222-WOWF or text me at star-WOWF on your mobile phone. The first caller recommending a qualified dog trainer will receive—Trish, do we have anything to give away?"

Trish shook her head no.

"Nothing? Hold on. How about a free massage at the Lifestyle Revolution Spa? No? What if I pay for it? Yes? How much does an hour massage run?"

The producer wrote down a number on a flash card.

"A hundred and fifty dollars? Are you for real? Does that come with an anal bleaching? It does! Okay, listeners, the first caller providing me with the name and phone number of a qualified dog trainer receives an hour massage and the optional anal— and it looks like we have a winner! Who's this?"

"Lynnie Ruffington, I got your dog trainer right

here."

"Lynnie, the contest is for my listeners."

"I'm a listener. Heck, sometimes I'm all you got."

"You're an employee of Lifestyle Revolution. You can't participate in any on-air contests."

"Damn it, Doc, I want that anal bleaching."

"Sorry, Lynnie, guess you'll have to sit bare-ass in a bucket of Clorox. Line four, we have Judy from Coral Springs. Speak to me Judy."

"Dr. Beach, last month we had a dog trainer come out to the house and work with our cocker spaniel, Damian."

"And did the trainer exorcize the devil from Damian?"

"Sorry, I don't know what you mean."

"Does your cocker spaniel still crap in the house? Is he housebroken?"

"Oh, absolutely. Plus he sits and gives you his paw."

"Sounds perfect. Give us the trainer's first name, Judy. Trish will get the rest of the contact information from you off the air."

"The trainer's name is Anita, and she was fantastic."

19

Lord and Masturbator

JACOB PARKED THE VAN in the driveway and exited the rusting steel beast before its engine choked itself off. In his hand was a pet store bag—inside: a simple tool that he hoped would allow him to domesticate his dog and hopefully appease Nancy.

Sam heard him approach. The dog clawed at the inside of the garage door, thrusting its sizeable bulk at the aluminum barrier.

"Easy, boy. I'm coming. Just need to set this up for you, big guy."

Jacob walked around the side of the house to the backyard. From the bag he removed a three-foot-long spiral metal spike attached to a twenty-foot-long dog chain.

Wile E. Coyote ... genius.

For ten minutes he labored to twist the spike into the hard, dry ground. When he finished, he tugged on the chain, testing the strength of the device. Satisfied, he walked back around to the front door of the house and keyed in.

The German shepherd bellowed a ferocious bark that put a smile on Jacob's face. *Foofie dog, my ass. No burglar or rapist in his right mind would break into this house with my dog guarding it.*

He headed for the interior garage door, opened it, and was immediately bowled over by Sam. The dog jumped and spun and ran through the house into the master bedroom. It leaped on top of the bed, stripping the linen as it leaped off again and bolted past Jacob into the living room and onto the sofa, wagging its tail, wanting to play.

"No!"

The dog barked at him.

"Hey, don't bark back at me. I am your lord and master. God gave me opposable thumbs, not you."

The dog laid on the floor, contorting its head and neck between its hind legs to nibble on an itch along its groin.

"Okay, admittedly, a longer neck also has its advantages."

Sam jumped up, clawing at the back door.

"I get it—you need to pee. Got you all set up." Jacob unlocked the sliding glass door and closed it before Sam could escape. Retrieving the end of the chain, he opened the door and clipped it onto the dog's collar.

The dog dashed outside, the chain nearly wrapping around Jacob's ankles. Sam sniffed an unseen trail along the lawn before lifting a leg to pee. Its bladder relieved, the German shepherd took a leisurely jaunt across the open yard—the chain cutting it off, preventing it from leaving.

"Technology—it's a beautiful thing." Jacob closed the glass door and headed back through the house to the garage, seeking to relocate Sam's water bowl out back.

"Ahh! Ahh!" The blood rushed from his face as he spotted the severed arm of a child lying on the garage floor!

In full panic, Jacob turned and ran, his forehead smacking into the side of the interior door. Spinning back around, he eyeballed the detached limb. His woozy brain determined either a small child or a midget must have seen the partially open garage door and crawled inside to rob him, only to have his arm torn off by his dog.

"Where are you, midget?" *Do they prefer to be called "midget" or "vertically challenged"?* "Answer me, or my dog will amputate your other limbs!"

That you, Vice?

"Mr. President?" Jacob retrieved the rest of the

Bush dummy from behind a spare tire. One arm was gone, its head spun around, its right ear partially chewed.

Was it Al-Qaeda?

"No sir. It was my dog."

Damn fleabag gave me a tea bag. As the decider, I've decided that Nancy was right, and the mongrel must go. See to it, Jakester. Then reattach my arm and swab my wood with alcohol.

"Sorry sir, but the dog stays."

That so? You might be singing a different tune once you see what that four-legged monster did to your little Asian dish.

"Yoko?" Jacob stared at the cardboard box, its flaps chewed, the container lying open on its side. Having dragged the sex doll out onto the floor, Sam had gnawed its pliable flesh as if it were a rawhide bone. Yoko's face was mangled, her left eye stretched and deformed.

"Oh … Yoko."

You love me long time, Jacob?

"Sorry Yo-Yo, but I'm not into freaky zombie sex."

Ten minutes later the garage door opened. Jacob exited wheeling a trash can to the curb. Yoko's head and upper torso protruded from the open receptacle, the sex doll's remains wrapped in a plastic garbage bag so the neighbors wouldn't see.

Don't do this, Jacob.

Jacob hummed, blocking out the shrill woman's voice in his head.

Just so you know, I faked every orgasm.

Leaving the trash can by the curb, he returned to the house, closing the garage door behind him.

He never saw the two ten-year-old boys ride past the house on their bicycles.

Sam did.

Tail wagging, the dog attempted to chase after them, easily ripping the stake from the ground. The German shepherd sprinted around the side of the house to the front sidewalk, the trailing length of chain bouncing wildly and looping around Yoko's neck.

Chasing after the kids, Sam dragged the naked life-size sex doll down the street, the plastic trash bag quickly shredding as it was hauled along the tarmac.

Nancy turned off Hillsboro Boulevard, texting her producer as she drove through the residential neighborhood. The excitement she felt back at the studio had waned as her idea had fallen under her own self-scrutiny. *How do you know this will even work? How can I market it to my listeners? Is it fair to Jacob? Sure, it might help his phobias, but what if he catches on?*

Her mind occupied, she never saw the dog running in the street, heading for her car.

Jacob had been filling Sam's water bowl at the kitchen sink when he heard the dog barking like crazy. He glanced out the window just in time to see the German shepherd race out of the back yard, trailing chain.

Jacob hurried out the front door as Sam sprinted down the middle of the street, dragging a familiar object. A car turned the corner, approaching fast.

"Sam!"

Nancy looked up and screamed, slamming on the brakes.

The naked pedestrian struck her windshield a split second later. The impact simultaneously shattered the glass and inflated her air bag, which bashed the startled psychologist in the face, knocking her woozy.

Asshole, you just killed someone. The cops'll know you were texting. Your life is over.

Jacob ran down the street as fast as an out-of-shape man in sandals could run. His heart nearly pushed out of his chest as he saw the naked Yoko doll spread-eagled across the car's shattered windshield.

Holy shit, your dog just killed someone. The cops'll know you were fucking the doll. Your life is over.

Jacob grabbed Sam by his trailing chain, dragging the dog around to the driver's side of the car to check on the driver, whose face was pinned behind the inflated air bag. "Hold on, buddy!" Using the spike still attached to the dog chain, he punctured the safety device, powder exploding all over what now appeared to be a female figure.

Then he recognized the woman.

"Oh my God—Nancy! Oh geez, I didn't realize it was you." He attempted to brush her off.

"Jacob? Oh God, Jacob, I killed somebody!"

"No you didn't, baby. It was just my sex—my sexy new ventriloquist dummy, Yoko. Sam broke loose from the back yard, and the chain must have wrapped around the dummy's neck."

"I didn't kill anyone?"

Jacob smiled nervously. "No, babe."

The smile evaporated as he saw the neighbors close ranks from all directions. "Nance, pop the trunk so I can hide the body, I mean, the doll—the dummy!"

"Why?"

"Just do it!"

She spit out a mouthful of powder, her eyes focusing on the naked vaginal anatomy of the object adorning her windshield. "Oh my God."

"I'll get rid of the dog. Just please pop the trunk."

Feeling along the bottom of the dashboard, she released the hatch as Jacob dragged the disfigured sex doll off the car's hood and tossed it into the trunk in front of a dozen startled neighbors.

"You see that? He just threw the dead woman into the trunk."

"She was naked. Probably his mistress."

"Somebody call the cops."

"I already did. They're on the way."

Jacob released the dog to the wild and climbed in the passenger seat, accepting the role of fugitive. "Nancy, drive!"

The neighbors quickly stepped in front of the car, preventing the driver from leaving the crime scene. Before he could react, his door opened, and two black men dragged Jacob out of the vehicle, pinning him to the ground. The stupid dog was wagging its tail instead of coming to his aid.

A Hispanic woman wearing a purple surgical top

checked on Nancy. "You may have a concussion."

"Are you a doctor?"

"Dental assistant. I don't like the look of those gums. How often do you floss?"

Two squad cars arrived, adding to the chaos. Two policemen exited to eyewitness testimony.

"Blondie killed the woman. The chubby bearded guy shoved the body in the trunk!"

Jacob rolled over, gazing up into the barrel of a gun. "Don't shoot! No one died. There's no body!"

"Got a body, partner—naked as a jaybird, no pulse."

Neighbors armed with iPhones snapped photos of the naked woman.

Face to the asphalt, Jacob struggled to speak as his arms were twisted painfully around his back, the handcuffs biting into his flesh. "Jesus, it's a dummy!"

The Hispanic woman kicked him in the ribs. "That's my lord and savior you're talkin' about, you animal."

The cops argued over who should start mouth-to-mouth.

Nancy yelled at a third cop who was reading Jacob his rights. "Let him go, you idiot. It's a sex—"

Her words were buried under another wailing siren as an ambulance arrived. Two emergency medical technicians hopped out, one checking on the victim, the other opening the van's back doors to retrieve a gurney.

"Officers, we'll take it from here. Wow, she's hot—oh, God, look at her face. Artie, bring a blanket. The hooker's naked."

Jacob was dragged to his feet in time to witness his sex doll, now partially covered beneath a blanket and strapped onto a gurney, being loaded into the back of the ambulance.

Twelve minutes and two attempts with a defibrillator later, the Yoko Ono sex doll was officially pronounced dead.

After two hours and a coroner's examination, Jacob was escorted from the Broward County Sheriff's Office holding cell. He was led to the front desk where Nancy was waiting, his red-faced girlfriend sandwiched between two of the arresting officers.

"Sorry, Mr. Cope," one smiling cop muttered. "Just a bad misunderstanding."

"No hard feelings, Mr. Cope," snickered his partner.

"I don't see what you assholes are laughing at. You were the ones giving mouth-to-mouth to her blowhole."

"Are you some kind of sexual deviant?"

"No." Jacob started the Volkswagen van's engine, his forehead pressed against the fur-covered wheel. "I was lonely. I just needed someone to talk to. Even if it was a doll."

She stared at him. Reaching out, she took his hand. "From now on, talk to me."

He smiled through the tears. "I love you. I'll get rid of the dog."

"No."

"No? I don't understand."

"I'm giving him three months to straighten out. Then we'll see."

Jacob bear-hugged Nancy, her blouse still harboring remnants of powder from the air bag. "Three months is great. By then you'll love him so much you'll never want to let him go."

20

Ruby Kleinhenz

FOR DR. VINCENT COPE, the morning had not gone well. Fifteen Medicare patients in two hours sandwiched around two cases of genital warts and a call from his wife reminding him that their son, Dylan, had early hockey practice tonight.

He checked the chart outside Exam Room 3. Ruby Kleinhenz was one of his favorite patients—a fifty-two-year-old divorcée with the body of a thirty-year-old. Since her divorce settlement, Ruby had had new breasts implants, her teeth bleached and a Lifestyle Lift, a less invasive facelift that had removed her sagging jowls and the last fifteen years of aging.

Wanda joined the gynecologist as he knocked and entered.

Ruby was lying on the exam table in a dressing gown, her jet-black wavy hair highlighted with a ruby-red streak.

"Morning, Mrs. Kleinhenz. My apologies for canceling our last appointment."

"It's okay, Doctor. Were you able to save her?"

"Save who?" Vincent glanced at Wanda, who shot him a nasty look. "Oh, the emergency labiaplasty, yes. Looking at her now, you'd never suspect she pumped three kids out of that vag."

"Sign me up. I'm serious. I wasted thirty good years with that no-good prick, Emilio, but boy did he have to pay out the ass in the settlement. Let him keep the beach house. I told my attorney I want cash. A million for every bimbo I caught him with."

Wanda's eyes widened. "Exactly how many bimbos did ya'll catch him with?"

"Enough to buy a share of an arena-league football team. The Cougars—that's me. I'm a cougar, and I'm on the prowl."

"Good for you," Vince said, scanning her chart. "Just take precautions."

"That's why I'm here."

"Mrs. Kleinhenz—"

"Ruby."

"Ruby, you don't need an IUD. While you may look thirty-five, your ovaries are still fifty-two; they stopped producing eggs years ago."

"Yes, but my thirty-six-year-old boy toy doesn't know that, and I want to keep it that way. So fit me for the IUD, and then schedule me for that twat lip surgery, or whatever you call it. The sooner the better."

"You're the boss." He worked a pair of rubber gloves over his hands then helped Ruby secure her feet into the table stirrups. "Wanda, hand me the speculum."

Wanda was about to pass him the instrument when they heard a commotion coming from the outside corridor.

"Mr. Cope, you can't go back there! Your brother is with a patient."

"It'll only take a minute. Vince?" The door swung open, and Jacob barged in.

"Jacob, get out of here! Can't you see I'm with a patient?"

"Oh, I don't mind," Mrs. Kleinhenz said, straining in the stirrups to look at the bearded young man. "Hi there. I'm Ruby."

"Jacob, Vince's brother."

"Are you a doctor too?"

"Ventriloquist. Vin, can I talk to you a minute?"

"No!"

"Dr. Cope, he's your brother. Whatever you have to say, Jacob, you can say it in front of me."

"Thanks. Vin, I need to borrow some money—twenty-five hundred. I'll pay you back as soon as I can."

"It's not for an abortion, is it?"

"What? No! It's for Sam."

"Who's Sam?"

"My German shepherd."

"You named the German shepherd Sam? Jake, seriously, you need help. What's the money for?"

"I need to fence in our back yard. Maybe get Sam a doghouse."

"Get one with a spare bedroom so you have a place to stay when Nancy throws you out."

"This was Nancy's idea, part of a three-month reprieve for Sam. You'd be saving the dog's life."

"Speaking of saving a life, I saw an interesting video on YouTube this morning of two cops scrambling to give CPR to a naked Asian chick. Turns out it was just a sex doll."

Wanda turned to Jacob. "Asian? I hear you like Asian women."

Jacob's neck flushed. "I happen to enjoy the company of all women, thank you very much. Vin, can you spot me the money or not?"

"Not. This is a medical practice, not a bank. And the next time you interrupt me while I'm with a patient—"

Ruby slapped Vincent on his wrist. "What's wrong with you? Your brother needs your help to save an innocent animal's life." She turned to Jacob.

"Are you really a ventriloquist?"

"Yes ma'am."

"I'm hosting a black-tie affair next Friday evening at the Ritz-Carlton. We're still looking to add local entertainment. Is your ventriloquist act entertaining?"

"The cops thought so," Wanda muttered.

Jacob smiled nervously. "I do a lot of policemen's balls. I mean, I perform comedy for the cops. They laugh a lot. ... It's funny. Uh, how much does the gig pay?"

"Enough to take care of your dog. The show's on the 14th at 6 p.m. You'll sit at my table for dinner. Then you'll perform during dessert."

"Sounds amazing ... wow. Thank you."

"Very generous, Ruby," said Vincent. "Jacob, if you'd leave now so I can treat my patient."

Ruby reached out and grabbed Jacob's hand. "Stay. These things can be tricky. You seem like the well-adjusted, supportive type."

"Yes, I've been told that."

Vincent rolled his eyes at Wanda, who was holding her mouth to keep from busting out laughing. "Alrighty then. Slight cramping here, Ruby, while I take the Pap smear."

21

Anita

NANCY CHECKED THE TIME on the white foofie dog clock. *Nine-oh-eight—she's late. Not a good way to start her first day with a new client.*

Sam was out back, whining to come inside.

"Forget it, flea bag. Your days of sleeping on my sofa are over."

The doorbell rang, sending the dog into a jumping frenzy.

Nancy left the kitchen, heading down the hall. She paused to check her face in the hallway mirror then opened the door.

Standing on the front stoop was a gum-chewing white woman in her mid-thirties, her short, mouse-brown hair spiked, her slender neck tattooed with three Japanese letters. She was wearing a black strapless tube top, silver capri pants and high wedge heels. Slung over her shoulder was a leather backpack.

"Anita Goodman."

"Don't we all. Sorry, I'm Nancy Beach."

"Nice ta make your acquaintance." The accent was a nasal Bronx, the handshake firm. Anita entered, looking around. "So where's the puppy?"

"The puppy? The *puppy's* out back." Nancy led her to the kitchen where Sam was pawing and scratching at the sliding door, muddying the glass as he attempted to gain entry and greet the stranger.

Anita's expression dropped. "That's not a puppy. That's a dog."

"No shit."

"Okay, here's the thing: Dogs are like people —the younger you get them, the easier they are to train. This dog's gotta be, what, four or five? In doggy years, that's like thirty. Ever try to teach a thirty-year-old a new trick?"

"As a matter of fact, yes, but I'd still like to try."

"Not try—do. In order to do, I charge thirty-five dollars an hour, plus any necessary supplies."

"Agreed. Uh, how many lessons do you think he'll need?"

"We'll know when we know, won't we? First, let's see how trainable he is. You said on the phone your husband picked him up at the pound?"

"My boyfriend, yes."

"Based on my vast years of experience, I wouldn't

set the bar too high. A lot of pound refugees were beaten by their previous owners. What's the expression? Life is like a box of chocolates; you never know when you're going to bite into a nut. Let him in, but keep him restrained. These are new pants."

"That's the problem. I can't restrain him. He's too big."

Anita winked. "Girlfriend, trust me. It's not about the size; it's about knowing where to grab hold." Rummaging through her bag, she removed a large chain. "This is a choke collar. When I slip it around the dog's neck and pull thusly," she demonstrated on her hand, "the noose tightens, restraining the bitch or butch as I like to call them. Okay, what's the animal's name?"

"Jacob—I mean *Sam*."

"Let Sam in."

Nancy slid open the door. Sam entered like an excited locomotive, licking and jumping, spinning around in circles.

"Sit, Sam! Sit. Sit!" Anita managed to grab the dog by its neck and slip the choker collar over its head. "We pull thusly—" she yanked the chain hard "—and the animal is restrained."

Sam sat.

"Oh, I like that."

Fishing again through her backpack, Anita

removed a small bag of dog treats. She took one out, the scent exciting the dog.

"I'm a firm believer in the reward system—rewarding your animal when it does something good. Who's a good boy? Sam's a good boy. Give me your paw, Sam. *Paaaaww.*" She held out her hand.

The dog raised its front right paw.

Anita shook it then gave Sam the treat.

"There's a good boy. Always reward the desired behavior immediately and then repeat it right away. The animal learns through repetition. Let's try it again. Sam, paw."

Sam placed his paw in Anita's hand.

"Wow, he did it by himself."

"German shepherds catch on fast. They're a smart breed, but virtually any animal can be trained. It's all about conditioning."

22

Dog Training the American Male
Lesson One: Conditioning

AT PRECISELY 5:57 p.m. Jacob Cope entered his home. "Nance, I'm home."

He placed the newspaper on the shelf by the hall mirror and kicked off his sandals as per Nancy's wishes, leaving them by the front door (a logical dispersal point, steeped in ancient Japanese tradition).

His bladder full, he headed straight for the hall bathroom. He unzipped, lifted the closed lid and seat and urinated. He flushed the toilet, rinsed his hands and removed the neatly folded hand towel from the rack to dry off, leaving the towel on the sink (as a common courtesy to the next user).

He entered the kitchen to the dog leaping and barking at the glass sliding door. "Hey, boy! I missed you." Jacob opened the door, unleashing the spinning, nipping, licking, 110-pound, fur-shedding motion of muscle. In between dog hugs, Jacob gazed outside. The backyard had been transformed into a sixty-by-forty-foot grass-covered rectangle, bordered on all sides by a six-foot-tall wooden privacy fence. In the right-rear corner of the yard was a dog house with a five-foot-tall A-framed roof adorned in olive-green tar paper.

"They did a nice job on the yard, eh, boy?"

Ignoring the muddy paw prints on the linoleum floor, Jacob opened the refrigerator and grabbed a bottle of beer. He searched through three kitchen drawers before he located the bottle opener.

Prying off the cap, he left the drawers open and the opener on the kitchen counter (as a common courtesy to the next user), and searched the pantry shelves. Locating the box of doggy treats, he tossed a bone to his tail-wagging companion and headed for the den.

Exhausted from work, Jacob flopped down on the leather sofa with the beer. Feeling between the cushions, he located the remote control and flicked through the TV stations. Sam seated beside him on the couch. The dog's churning jowls turned the biscuit into a trail of crumbs.

Suddenly alert, Sam bolted for the front door, the dog's howling chorus of barks greeting Nancy, who keyed in with one hand, her other holding a steaming-hot take-out bag.

Suddenly alert, Jacob bolted for the front door, his olfactory senses stimulated. "Hey, babe." He kissed Nancy quickly on the lips. "Is that a Philly cheesesteak I smell?"

"From D'best Sub Shop. Took me a half an hour to fight through traffic."

"Honey, you are d'best." Jacob reached for the treat only to have Nancy snatch it away. "Unh unh." She pointed to his sandals. "Shoes in the bedroom closet."

"Shoes? Oh, sure." He grabbed the sandals then hurried into the master bedroom, blindly tossing them into the open closet, returning in time to find Nancy in the hall bathroom. "Wipe the rim."

"The what?"

"The toilet rim has pee on it. Wipe it clean. Now put the seat down … good boy. (It's always important to offer verbal encouragement. Animals can sense if their owners are pleased.) And what do we have here, a wet hand towel that I just washed and folded?"

Jacob attempted to fold and rerack the towel but succeeded only in mangling it through the loop (some skills are gender biased), and it was off to the kitchen.

"Jacob, look at this kitchen. Look at the floor!"

"I'll wash it, no problem."

"Do you think you could close a drawer after you open it?"

"Sorry." He slammed the three drawers shut.

"The can opener?"

Opening a drawer, he tossed the can opener inside.

"It goes in the middle drawer with the steak knives."

He opened the drawer on the left, removed the can opener and deposited it in the middle drawer.

"Jacob?"

He slammed the two open drawers shut.

"Well done." Nancy pointed to one of the kitchen chairs. "Sit."

Jacob sat, his mouth watering.

Smiling to herself, Nancy tossed him the cheesesteak.

23

Old Habits

AT PRECISELY 5:57 p.m. the next day, Jacob Cope entered his home. "Nance, I'm home."

He placed the newspaper on the book shelf by the hall mirror and kicked off his sandals, leaving them by the front door, the urge to pee overwhelming his five senses. Rushing into the hall bathroom, he lifted the lid and seat and urinated, his eyes fluttering in relief. *Geez, that was close. My back teeth were floating.*

Shaking it twice, he tucked his penis inside his boxers, zippered his fly, flushed and rinsed the urine sprinkles from his hands. Removing the neatly folded hand towel from the rack, he dried off, leaving the towel on the sink.

He entered the kitchen to find the dog leaping and barking at the glass sliding door. "There's my killer watch dog." Jacob let the dog in, knelt to allow the German shepherd to lick his face, and then grabbed a bottle of beer from the fridge. Opening the middle drawer (conditioning through repetition) he located the bottle opener and opened the beer. Tossing the opener back in the drawer, he left the drawer open (in case he wanted a second beer), removed a dog biscuit from the pantry and headed for the den, Sam jumping on the sofa ahead of him.

Flopping down next to the dog, he gave Sam the bone then located the remote control as the dog bolted for the front door, wailing its greeting at Nancy, who keyed in with one hand, holding a steaming-hot take-out bag in the other.

Right behind the dog was Jacob. "Mmm, I smell Chinese food."

"From Uncle Tai's. Took me forty minutes to fight through traffic—and what the fuck are your sandals doing on the floor?"

"Oops." Jacob grabbed the odor-laced leather shoes, hurried into the master bedroom and blindly tossed them into the open closet, returning in time to find Nancy inspecting the hall bathroom. "Seat up, pee on the rim and the floor—can't you aim that thing?"

"Sorry."

"And what a surprise—my neatly folded towel tossed in a pile … unbelievable."

"Sorry. Hey, want me to set the table?" He reached for the bag of Chinese food only to be whacked on the head with the rolled-up newspaper. "Sorry Jacob. You don't get rewarded for negative behavior. Guess I'll have to share this delicious dinner of jumbo shrimp, egg rolls and General Tso's chicken with Helen—at least she'll appreciate it."

Satisfied that her negative reinforcement would make an impact on her salivating mongrel, Nancy left the house, slamming the door behind her.

Confused, Jacob looked down at the dog, bright eyed, its tail wagging. "Hey boy, wanna go for a ride to McDonalds?"

🐾 🐾 🐾

Vincent Cope had just entered his gated community when his cell phone rang. "What do you need now, Jacob? A loan for a new sex toy?"

"Advice, Vin. I just got into a fight with Nancy, only I have no idea what just happened."

"I'm not a marriage counselor, Jacob."

"I'm not married."

"You're living with your girlfriend—same thing."

"Did Helen ever swat you on the head with a newspaper?"

"Helen's a yeller, not a hitter. Wait, did you just say a newspaper?"

"Right on the head."

"What'd you do? Shit on the carpet?"

"No. I got a little pee on the rim of the toilet. No big deal. Certainly no reason to swat me or take away my dinner. She's on the way to your house with my Uncle Tai's."

"Good. I love Uncle Tai's." Vincent turned into his driveway, pressing the garage door opener. "Gotta run, Jake. I've got twenty-eight minutes to eat, change my clothes, drop off Dylan at the hockey rink, and get Wade to baseball practice."

"Vin, what should I do about Nancy?"

"Apologize."

"Apologize for what? And don't tell me because God gave me a penis. God gave me a set of balls too, you know."

"Enjoy playing with them by yourself, dickweed. Nancy went out of the way to bring home your favorite dinner, and all you give a shit about is yourself."

"Listen, Vin—"

"No, you listen. Between your neuroses and that dog, living with you is probably akin to being stuck on the *It's a Small World* ride at Disney World. As your brother and a skilled surgeon, my advice is to apologize to Nancy or else hide the kitchen utensils before she gives you a second circumcision."

Vincent disconnected the call and climbed out of the car, registering the soreness in his lower back and knees. He had been on his feet working since eight o'clock that morning, and there was no rest for the weary.

God had blessed Vincent Cope with three sons—and all three were heavily involved in sports. Thirty years before when Vincent had been entering his teens, kids' athletics consisted of pick-up games in the backyard—sandlot football and softball, street hockey on skates and half-court basketball in the driveway. If you were good enough you tried out for the high school team. If you had talent, you extended your playing career in college. Otherwise it was intramural and adult leagues. Whatever the level, you played because you loved to compete and you loved the camaraderie.

Today, kids' sports had evolved into community-generated leagues organized by adults who dreamt of their offspring receiving college scholarships and a shot at the pros. Competition began at ages five and six—two mandatory practices a week, plus games. And if your kid was good enough to make the travel team, like ice hockey defenseman Dylan Cope, then it was additional practices plus weekend jaunts to Orlando and Jacksonville. And God help the "lucky" parent whose kid's team advanced in the tournament. In the last year, Dylan had played in more hockey games than the average professional in the NHL, Vin escorting him to weekend tournaments in Minneapolis, Tampa, Las Vegas and Toronto.

The exhausted gynecologist entered his home through the garage. Helen was in the kitchen stirring some kind of red sauce-based concoction onto a plate.

"How was work?"

"Horrible. My last patient was as feisty as an alligator and had more wrinkles on her twat than a bag of prunes. I need to eat fast. What is that slop?"

"What's the difference? You either eat it or go hungry."

"Pour a little rat poison in mine, just for flavor. Where's Wade? Baseball practice starts in twenty minutes."

"He's in his room, playing on the Wii. What happened with your brother? Nancy called. She's on her way over. Did Jacob ever get rid of that dog?"

"It's complicated. He named the dog Sam."

Helen shook her head. "He's psychotic."

"Who's psychotic?" Nancy followed Dylan in from the hall.

Vin spotted the take-out bag, his stomach rumbling. "The Uncle Tai's for a free Gynnie Gusher."

"Make it two, just like the one Jeanne had." She

tossed him the bag. "So who's psychotic?"

"Your live-in boyfriend," said Helen, snatching the bag from Vin. "He named the dog after his father."

"I thought his father's name was Friedrich?"

"That's what our psychotic mother told him when he was a kid." Vin circled his wife, who was scooping the Chinese food out of the cartons onto three plates. "Technically, that's mine."

"We're married. I get half."

"Vin, were you and Jacob close to your father?"

"Jake was five when Dad left for Desert Storm. The father I grew up playing ball with was different from the soldier who returned from Iraq after losing both legs. When Jacob saw Dad in the VA hospital, he freaked out."

Amputees … "Vin, Jacob said your father committed suicide."

"Dad was depressed. He suffered from posttraumatic stress before the army docs had even classified it. He was home less than three months before he killed himself. We hid it from Jacob as long as we could."

Helen rolled her eyes. "So instead, your wacko mother told him your father suffocated under a pile of elephant shit? Exactly how does that soothe the blow?"

162

"The VA sent my father home, not realizing he was a ticking time bomb. Jake and I were staying at our grandparents' the morning my father put a gun in his mouth. My mother was sleeping in the same room when he did it."

Nancy covered her mouth. "The poor woman."

"Ma skipped the funeral. She was pretty traumatized. The elephant story was her way of protecting Jacob while venting her anger at my father."

"That's an excuse, Vincent," Helen said, venom in her voice. "Your mother is nasty to everyone. I'm not speaking to that woman, not after what she said to me on Thanksgiving."

Vincent sighed. "Okay, what did she say?"

"She told me the reason you became a gynecologist and not a brain surgeon was because you weren't getting enough sex at home."

"Helen, the woman's seventy-two years old. Being raised Catholic, you may not know this, but after the age of seventy some Jewish women experience a debilitating neurological condition that causes their mouths to disengage from their brains. We call these episodes bubbameisters. It's like going through a second menopause, sort of a rite of passage. Trust me. It's best just to ignore them. Nancy, can you pass me the duck sauce?"

She handed him the condiment. "You know,

Vin, I think your mother and I have a lot in common. I'm still dealing with my own anger issues over my father's death, plus the stuff with my two fiancés. It's hard to trust again once you've been hurt."

"You sound like one of my patients," Vince said, stuffing his mouth with shrimp. "She was married thirty years when she found out her husband was cheating on her. Now she sleeps with men half her age and is livin' life large."

Helen grabbed his fork mid-bite. "Would this patient happen to be Ruby Kleinhenz?"

"Yeah, so?"

"According to Wanda, Ruby was coming on pretty strong the other day."

"To Jacob, not to me." *Oh shit.*

"Kleinhenz?" Nancy turned on him like a hawk circling a pink-eyed bunny. "Isn't that the woman who hired Jacob to do the Ritz-Carlton gig?"

"Did she? I can't remember."

"And this woman wants to sleep with Jacob?"

"Wade, Dylan—get in the car!"

"Vin, answer her."

"Nancy, Ruby Kleinhenz is fifty-two years old."

Helen interjected. "She has the tits of a porn star and hasn't looked a day over thirty-five since her facelift. Wanda told me you have the cougar scheduled for labia surgery."

Vin picked up a piece of General Tso's chicken with his fingers and shoved it into his mouth. "Yes, Helen. Ruby Kleinhenz is scheduled to get her lower lips tightened. I'm a vagina doctor. Restoring outstretched labia is one of the surgical procedures I offer to women who have birthed children."

Helen's face flushed red. "Are you insinuating that my lips need tightening?"

Torpedo in the water! Launch countermeasures! "Of course not. If anything, your lips are too tight. And why the hell is my RN talking to you about my patients? That's a strict violation of the doctor-patient code. You're lucky I don't report the two of you."

"And you're lucky I offered you half of my dinner!" Helen snatched Vin's plate of Chinese food. "Go change your clothes, *vagina doctor*. You're going to be late."

Vin started to say something then thought better of it and left. He made it halfway up the stairs before he stopped. *Apologize. It's a strategic surrender. It won't get you laid, but at least you'll be able to watch* Sports-Center *tonight in peace.*

Vincent reentered the kitchen. "Helen, honey … I'm sorry."

"Shut up and get the boys to practice. And stop encouraging cougars like Ruby Kleinhenz to redo their goolie lips!"

Forget the white flag. She's at DEFCON 1. He trudged back up the steps, passing Dylan on the way down. "Hey, kid—twenty bucks if you snag your old man an egg roll."

24

Old School

SIXTY-SIX-YEAR-OLD Sandra Beach stretched out on a towel-covered lounge chair on the lido deck of the cruise ship beneath a cloudless cobalt-blue sky. It had taken three days and several mango mojitos for the widow to finally loosen up enough to enjoy the seniors' cruise. That morning the ship had arrived at their first port of call along the Mexican Riviera, but Sandy had no interest in leaving the sun deck now that her Chinese suitor had finally made his move.

A steward had introduced her to Dr. Jun Dong two nights before at a cocktail party. The wealthy acupuncturist from Beijing was a slight but virile man a few years younger than Sandy, his shaved head polished and tan, a twinkle in his hazel eyes. Dong, as he preferred to be called, was traveling in one of the more expensive suites on the ship and claimed he had been keeping tabs on the widow Beach since Sandy had boarded in Los Angeles. They had eaten dinner together the previous night, and she had been his "arm candy" at the casino, where he had played blackjack, losing over three thousand dollars as if it were pocket change. A late-night dance had led to their first kiss—the first real kiss she had shared with a man not named Brian Beach in almost forty years.

Her friends (two of whom were also widows) had pushed her to take the cruise and be open-minded to "new experiences." Spending time with a divorced Asian man certainly qualified. They met again for breakfast early this morning, played three games of badminton (she had to stop when her calf muscle had cramped), and now they were in bathing suits by the pool, Dong working up a sweat as he lovingly massaged her sore calf and feet.

Brian had been a hairy man—hairy back, hairy shoulders, hairy groin. As far as Sandy could tell, Dong was hairless. She wondered what would happen if they ended up in bed together. Would his hairless dong cause her to laugh or turn her on? Recalling her late husband's hairy ass, she decided that a change might indeed be a good thing.

Her cat nap was interrupted by her ringing cell phone. She checked the caller ID. "Nancy?"

"Hi Mom. How's the cruise?"

"Wonderful. Tell your sister there are lots of eligible men on board. Men with penises." She winked at Dong, who had produced a small packet of wooden acupuncture needles from his robe pocket.

He nodded reassuringly, whispering, "To help your leg pain."

Sandra ignored him. "So what's new darling?" She asked Nancy, twirling her badminton racket, "How's Lawrence?"

"Jacob, Mom. I want to know how you did it. How did you manage to stay with the same man for thirty-seven years?"

"Forty years. We lived together for three years before Lana was born. Men are like clay, darling; they need to be shaped in order to be good companions. It requires a lot of patience—son of a bitch!" She whacked Dong across his sweaty bald skull with her badminton racket. "That fucking hurt! Enough with the goddam needles!"

"So sorry." Dong bowed, quickly removing the needle protruding from the arch of her foot.

"Unbelievable. Where was I? Oh yes, patience. It really is the key to molding the man. Nancy, be honest. Do you love Louis?"

"It's Jacob, Mother. And, yes, I love him."

"As I remember, you said the same thing about

Dan and Sebi. My point, sweetheart, is that some-times love isn't enough. That's where behavior modification comes in. Of course, some women take it too far. Why just last night I read a news report that said there were over ten thousand battered husbands living in America. Ten thousand! And do you know why?"

"No, Mother. Why?"

"Because, darling, they don't fucking listen. Hold the line." She pulled her foot away from Dong. "That's enough with the massage. Why don't you be a good boy and get us something to drink?"

He offered her a thumbs-up, blew her a kiss, then jaunted over to the bar, catching himself as he tripped over an empty lounge chair.

Well, it was fun while it lasted. "Nancy, are you still there?"

"Behavior modification—I'm trying that."

"It takes time. Try to be patient with this one, darling. You're not getting any younger, and I'd really like some grandbabies before I'm too old to enjoy them. Gotta run. Kisses to Louis."

Sandra disconnected the call then stood and limped off to join a water aerobics class, lugging her bag with her in the hopes of losing her would-be Chinese suitor. *It would have never worked out. Going through my adult life as Sandy Beach was bad enough. I don't think I could handle Sandy Dong.*

25

Dog Training the American Male
Lesson Two: Ball Playing

SEATED OUT BACK on a partially chewed patio chair, Anita Goodman kept a watchful eye on Nancy Beach as she used a treat to bribe the exuberant male German shepherd into a sit position.

"Well done. I think you and Sam have mastered the sit and paw. Let's move on, shall we? Dogs that eat shoes or seat cushions are either lonely or bored. My English springer spaniel, Daisy, used to drive me crazy chewing on my leather sofa. God, I could have strangled her. Then I started tossing the Frisbee with her twice a day and—voila—no more chewing. Sam is a big, frisky dog, and big frisky dogs love to play fetch."

Anita removed a tennis ball from her backpack and showed it to Sam. "You like the ball, baby? Go get it!" She tossed the ball off the back of the fence.

171

Sam chased after it and then brought it back, chewing on it.

"Wow, he did it."

Sam nuzzled Anita with his mouth but refused to let go of the ball.

"See how Sam wants me to engage him, forcing me to physically remove the ball from his mouth? Only I don't want to engage in the game of tug-of-war, (a) because Sam may accidentally bite me, and (b) because I just had these nails put on."

"They do look great."

"You don't think the fuchsia is too much for my toes?"

"I think you need it with the white pants."

"I agree. Sam, drop the ball. *Draaaahp.*" She bribed the dog with a treat.

Sam dropped the ball.

"Always remember to repeat the desired behavior. Rinse and repeat, just like shampoo. Now you try."

Nancy took the ball and tossed it high into the air. "Get it, boy!"

Sam ran under it and leaped, snagging it in mid-air.

"Did you see that? Good catch, Sam. Now bring it here."

Sam brought the ball to Nancy.

"Sam, drop!"

The dog dropped the ball, earning his treat.

"Excellent mastery of the ball toss."

"Now if we could only train him to put down the toilet seat."

"Without an opposable thumb? Not likely."

"I meant my boyfriend. He's not as quick a learner as Sam."

"Ah, gotcha. Girlfriend, do you know the *real* difference between a man and a dog?"

"No opposable thumb?"

"No. The difference between a man and dog is that a dog can lick its own balls." Anita nodded coyly at Nancy.

🐾 🐾 🐾

At precisely 5:57 p.m., Jacob Cope entered his home. "Nance, I'm home."

He placed the newspaper on the shelf by the hall mirror then thought better of it and tossed it in the powder-room trash can, forgetting to remove his sandals, which left a trail of dirt. Hearing the dog leaping and barking at the glass sliding door, he entered the kitchen to find Nancy standing by the refrigerator wearing a bathrobe and spiked heel shoes.

"Hey, Nance. Nice shoes. Are you going out somewhere?"

"No. I'm staying right here so I can fuck your brains out." She opened her robe, flashing him a quick view of her physique, her nipples and shaved groin just barely concealed beneath a red G-string bikini.

"Holy shit." No longer exhausted, Jacob approached Nancy like a dog in heat.

"No!" She closed her robe again. "Come with me."

Jacob practically skipped behind her to the front door.

"Jacob, do you know what gets me wet?"

"No. I mean, of course I know, sure. But I'd rather hear you tell me."

"What really gets me horny is when I walk into my house and I don't have to trip over these smelly sandals, which you're still wearing and have left dirt all over my clean floor."

"I can fix that!" Removing his sandals, he opened the door and tossed them outside then, on his hands and knees, swept the dirt into a neat pile. Using a wad of wet toilet tissue (the anti-dingleberry brand worked best) he swept up the mess, tossed the dirty swab in the toilet with a resounding splash, and proceeded to strip.

"Jacob, what are you doing?"

"Getting ready to get you wet and wild, baby."

"Get dressed."

"Get dressed? Why?"

"Because tonight I'm going to get you all wet and wild, er, hard and wild. But first I need to use the powder room. Is there anything in the powder room that might turn me off? Anything at all?"

"No."

"Are you sure?"

"I haven't even used it."

"Be sure, because I'm really horny, and I thought I just heard a splash."

Jacob climbed back into his Bermuda shorts and entered the hall bathroom, the toilet seat covered in water. Using another wad of toilet paper, he wiped down the seat, tossed the wet tissue inside the bowl and then closed the lid.

He found Nancy waiting for him in the den. She was posed seductively, her open robe dangling halfway down her back. "Very good boy. Come."

Jacob approached.

She kissed him forcefully, probing the inside of his mouth with her tongue as she ran her hand between his legs.

He reached for her, but she smacked him across the head with a rolled up *Time* magazine.

"Ow!"

"That was just a treat until after dinner." She pushed past him, swishing her hips as she returned to the kitchen.

Jacob followed.

"I'm going to make us some dinner. Then, after we clean the dishes, I'm going to screw your brains out like the most expensive whore in Las Vegas."

"Damn. … But could you make it the cheapest whore? The kind of stuff I'm imagining I can't really afford."

"Tonight you can afford it all because I'm going to give you an opportunity to earn it."

"Yes! Wait, did you say earn it? How?"

She sniffed the air. "Do you smell something?"

He sniffed then smiled. "Sorry. I'll go and shower. Oh, is there anything you want me to shave while I'm in there?"

"It's not you I smell, well, besides your feet. I meant the dog."

Sam sat outside the glass door, wagging his tail.

"While I make dinner, why don't you shampoo Sam like you promised you'd do last week? Do it out back with the hose."

"Yes ma'am." Jacob hurried off to the laundry room to fetch the dog shampoo and towels.

An hour, a bathed dog and two barbequed steaks later, Nancy stood from the kitchen table and walked behind Jacob, nuzzling his neck as she rubbed his inner thighs.

Jacob turned to kiss her and belched, earning a smack on his forehead.

"Ow."

"You don't burp in a woman's face."

"I thought tonight you were an expensive whore?"

"The whoring starts as soon as I digest my food. That should give you plenty of time to wash the dishes and clean up dinner."

"But I made dinner."

"And it was delicious, but we're going to start taking turns cleaning up the dishes. Would you rather I clean up or ride you like a Vegas whore?"

"Can I use the dishwasher?"

"Of course you can. Just make sure the dishes are clean before you put them in, and be sure to take out the trash before the dog tears into it. When you're all finished, you can come in the bedroom and help me with a special treat, a new sex toy I ordered from eBay. Better bring a few double-A batteries with you."

Nancy walked out, leaving both Jacob and the dog panting. *Mom was right. It's all about behavior modification. Now I just need to incorporate that wisdom into my radio show.*

26

W.O.M.B.

ADRENALINE KEPT NANCY'S heart racing the entire drive in to work.

It had been exactly two weeks before that the psychologist had launched her new radio show: *Dog Training the American Male*, and so far, the new format seemed to be working. Comparing men to dogs was nothing new, but Nancy was offering practical advice on getting the Y chromosome to comply with her female audience's needs. And because her directions were based on her own experiences, her delivery had become warm and enticing. Her information was also often sexually explicit, which kept the phone lines lit. While it was too early to measure the ratings results, she did notice that the station's managers were no longer treating her like the slow camper trying to outrun the hungry bear. Yesterday, Peter Soderblom had even managed a smile—a first for the new programming director.

Along with the change in format, Nancy laid the groundwork for a new weekly morning support group—Women Overcoming Male Bondage, or W.O.M.B. Replacing the failed Sunshine Hour, each W.O.M.B. "delivery" would be a hard-hitting, take-control-of-your-life, slap-on-the-ass therapy session designed to empower women to reverse their own male-dominated mentality, a mentality Nancy held responsible for her own failed relationships.

The question now was whether anybody would show up.

Heart pounding, she turned into the parking garage twenty-five minutes before the first W.O.M.B. meeting was scheduled to begin.

God, please, give me at least twenty women in attendance. Twenty pays for the use of the room and keeps me off Olivia Cabot's shit list for another week.

Exiting the car, she hustled to catch the garage elevator as the doors began closing. Her ears burned as she eavesdropped on two middle-aged women in business suits.

"Last year for our anniversary, Anthony gave me a card and perfume which he bought at Walgreens while he was picking up cigarettes. Two days before this year's anniversary, I handcuffed him to the bed and teased him for an hour before riding him into submission. Well, guess what. Last night he surprised me with these diamond earrings!"

"They're gorgeous. Last night, John insisted I teach him how to do the laundry."

"Amazing."

Nancy heard the woman whisper, "I told him I'd lick his balls if he did the ironing."

She bit her lip to keep from smiling.

The elevator doors opened, revealing the Lifestyle lobby packed with women.

Lynnie Ruffington was out of her kiosk, the rotund receptionist red faced and sweating profusely as she handed out and simultaneously collected completed registration forms. Seeing Nancy, she pushed her way through the crowd.

"Doc … ," she wheezed, "what'd you promise these broads … free drugs and booze? Cause if you did … you better save some … for me."

Nancy could barely contain herself. "Lynnie, how many women are here?"

"I don't know … shit, maybe a million. I put you in the Liza room. Bet it's already standing room only."

"I'd better get in there. You have been collecting the twenty-dollar seminar fee, right?"

"Seminar fee? A few … I think. Can I get back to you on that? I need to check my cleavage."

"Lynnie, we talked about this. Each guest must sign and complete a registration form. When they hand it in you're supposed to staple the cash or check to the form, otherwise make sure they filled out the credit card information."

"Right. Got it. Only I ran low on staples. Didn't consider that, did you, Dr. Hotshot? Thank God I decided to wear the old double-D slingshot, huh?"

Heads turned.

You're a celebrity now. Don't be seen arguing with the help. "Thank you, Lynnie. Good morning, ladies. I'll see you inside.

🐾 🐾 🐾

Dr. Nancy Beach stood before the podium, humbled by the applause coming from her 217 guests. A banner draped across the blackboard behind her read, "W.O.M.B.: Women Overcoming Male Bondage."

"Good morning, ladies. If you'll open up your information packets, you'll find a laminated card with our pledge. Let's stand in unity, and we'll say it together: 'Knowledge is power. With power I enlighten my soul. With knowledge I begin my rebirth, emancipating myself from my male bondage.'

"Very good. From now on, after you say the pledge, try doing this." Nancy demonstrated the salute. "Okay, now you try."

Palms over their faces, the women slowly pushed their noses and foreheads through their separating hands like a baby's head emerging from its mother's vagina.

"And we are reborn, excellent. I know it seems silly, but that simple composing gesture will allow you to quiet your mind when every fiber in your body wants to whack your growling, belching, reactive, dumb animals on their snouts with a rolled-up newspaper."

Nancy smiled, acknowledging the applause.

"Ladies, the X chromosome is found among both males and females, but only the male possesses the Y. Why? Before I discovered the secrets of establishing a healthy home, a healthy sex life, a balanced relationship, I used to ask *why*: Why must they make us cry? Why must they piss us off? Why must they lie around and scratch their balls and drink beer and watch football every Sunday and Monday and now Thursday nights while we clean and cook and put up and put out?"

Applause reverberated through the small auditorium.

"Well, ladies, I figured out the secret to the Y. The Y chromosome stands for *you*. You must teach your Y the responsibilities of being a good husband

and provider, father and friend. And yes, while it may seem at first that the secret to controlling our Y is simply to be his sex slave, his personal ball-licker, as some callers have suggested, in fact, we are creating an obsession. And the object of that obsession is us—not football, not porn, not beer—us! Our sex, given to us by God, can be used to modify our Y's behavior in a more positive, productive way. Creating, fueling and controlling that sexual obsession can keep your Y from turning to drugs or alcohol when he gets laid off or prevent him from straying into the arms of another Double X. The illusion of that obsession in the work place can turn the tide in business and politics so that we can finally cut the ties of male bondage and create a better, safer world for our children!"

The standing ovation rocked the WOWF offices, causing Lynnie Ruffington to drop the wad of moist twenty dollar bills she has just fished out of her brassiere.

27

Managing the Game

BODIES SWELTERED IN THE Sunday afternoon heat. Parents squirmed on the hot aluminum bleachers. Coaches sweated profusely in their baseball uniforms. Park employees broiled behind the flaming grills of their hot dog and burger concession stands. And God help the umpires, clad in their long black pants and shirts beneath stifling layers of protection.

Least affected by the heat of the South Florida midday sun were the players themselves, fourteen-year-old Little Leaguers—teen boys whose adolescent thoughts drifted from the game to the teen girls milling about the stands.

Baseball in West Boca Raton—four baseball diamonds, their backstops forming a quadrant to the brick structures that housed the bathrooms and food concessions. Eight teams competed every two and a half hours. The weekend games began running non-stop at seven in the morning, ending at ten at night.

Today, Coach Vincent Cope's team was scheduled to play a doubleheader in the noonday broil-a-thon.

The manager sat in his designated dugout, a concrete and aluminum bunker devoid of any breeze. It was still game one, top of the third inning of a scoreless contest, and his team was in the field. Wade was pitching. Vinnie's eldest son struggled to keep his offerings in the strike zone.

"Ball four; take your base," yelled the home-plate umpire to a chorus of groans. Runners on first and second with one out, and Wade Cope was feeling the heat.

His father and manager stepped out of the dugout, clapping his support. "Shake it off, kiddo. Just play catch."

Wade nodded, acknowledging his father's advice: "*Ignore the batter; focus only on the catcher's mitt.*"

"Strike one."

"That-a-boy." Vin allowed his ego a moment's flight—*Would'a made a great minor league pitching coach*—as he took his seat on the bench next to his younger brother. With the team's regular first-base coach away on business, Jacob was sitting in as Vin's assistant.

185

What surprised Vincent was that his brother, who grew up hating sports, had actually *volunteered*. And the schmuck had been smiling all day.

"Ball. One and one."

Vin removed his baseball cap, wiping sweat from his eyes. "Goddam doubleheaders. Feels like my nuts are being slowly roasted in a crock pot. So, little bro, what's going on with you?"

"What do you mean?"

"Come on, Jacob. You've been walking around all day with a stupid grin on your face. Things really that good at home?"

"Can I ask you a personal question? How often do you and Helen … you know?"

"Ball two!"

"What? Have sex? Lately maybe twice a month."

The three bench players at the opposite end of the dugout glanced their coaches' way.

"Eyes on the field, ladies. Heads in the game."

"Two times a month? That's all?"

"I'm married. Sex comes in waves, like the tide. Right now Helen's tide is out. You try raising three boys. See what it does for your libido. Soon as the last little monster goes off to college, Helen gets a facelift, boob job and her varicose veins lasered off. Then I'll ride the high tide into my retirement."

"Ball three."

"So it's true—marriage really does change your sex life."

"It has nothing to do with marriage. It's about the kids. Helen and I used to do it two or three times a week before Wade was born. Diapers, preschool, kindergarten. Then sports kick in, plus we're both working. One kid is a shared obsession; three in six years is a merry-go-round. Now she's in bed early, and I stay up late."

"Watching ESPN?"

"Strike two. Full count."

"ESPN? No, dawg. I watch porn. Every night a different fantasy. I masturbate more now than I did when I hit puberty. Use it or lose it—that's my philosophy. Unless you want to end up like one of those pathetic old men popping Viagra."

"That's more than I needed to know."

"What? Don't tell me you, the Plastic Ono Band Casanova, suddenly has a problem with milking the one-eyed lizard?"

"No. I just didn't think married men would have to do that kind of thing anymore."

"Yeah? Well you've got it all wrong. Among its many other benefits, masturbation maintains the health of the prostate, improves the immune system and can decrease the desire for a man to participate in an extramarital affair. Look at me. Do you have any idea how many hot women come into my office, strip naked and spread their legs for me just so I can probe their privates? Masturbation saves lives, my friend. Think about this: If Clinton had jerked off instead of allowing that chunky Jewish broad to suck on his cigar, Gore would have won the election back in 2000, and we'd have never invaded Iraq. That blow job cost our country thousands of soldiers' lives and three trillion dollars. And I'll bet your left nut she didn't even swallow."

"Ball four. Take your base."

Boos from the home stands rent the humid afternoon air as Wade Cope walked the bases loaded.

"Time!" Vin stood, pulled his sweaty underwear from the crack of his ass, and left the dugout, trotting out to the pitcher's mound where his son was waiting. "Getting hot out here. How's the arm holding up, kiddo?"

"Dad, please don't take me out. Marie McGuire's watching, and it's embarrassing."

"Cheerleader Marie? No shit?" Vin searched the stands.

"Dad, don't look."

"Okay, but be honest. Are you focused on the catcher's mitt or the girl?"

"The mitt, I swear. I can't help it. My fastball's wild today."

"That's because you're rushing your pitches. Listen to me carefully. Are you listening? Before you throw each pitch, I want you to take a slow, deep breath, count to five and imagine the ball pounding the catcher's glove. Can you do that for me?"

"Yes sir."

"Good man." Vincent Cope patted his son on the rump and then walked back to the dugout, only to be greeted by a catcall from Ernie Whitman's father, Bruce, a Palm Beach County trial lawyer.

"Hey, Doc, we all know he's your kid, but he's killing us. How about replacing Junior before this game gets out of hand."

"You gave your wife genital herpes, Whitman, but she hasn't replaced you. Now sit your ass down and support the team." *Jackass.*

Whitman's already sunburned face turned red. A few parents smiled. A few voiced their outrage.

Vincent Cope could give a shit. He'd been coaching Little League games since t-ball, and all he ever asked in return was for the boys' parents to alternate bringing drinks and snacks to every game and to keep things positive.

Whitman's got some set of balls attacking my kid. Maybe I'll use syrup of ipecac instead of peppermint in his wife's next Gynnie Gusher. See how much he likes going down on her then.

Vin entered the dugout bench, greeted by his brother's fist bump. "Well played. Your coaching style reminds me of Ghandi."

"Let the jerk-off sue me. And you can bet the house Wade strikes out the next batter. So what's up with you and Nancy?"

"Honestly, Vin, I'm seeing a side of her I never saw before … and I like it."

"Like what? Wait, you mean sex?"

The bench players turned.

"Eyes, gentlemen."

"Strike one!"

"Atta boy, Wade." Vin lowered his voice. "Talk to me, pal, and don't hold back any sordid details."

"All of a sudden she's really into sex. We've done something kinky almost every night for the past two weeks."

"Kinky? Like what? Bondage? Whips and chains?"

"Yes, chains. Last night after I finished the laundry, we took Sam for a walk, and she hooked me up to a leash. It was kind of weird at first, but it really made me horny."

"Strike two!"

"Nice, kiddo." Vin turned back to Jacob. "Go back. Did you just say you walked the dog *after* you did the laundry? Why the hell are you doing the laundry?"

"It's no big deal. I help out and—"

"—and she gives you sex. That little vixen. … She's out to break your spirit as a free-thinking man."

"You're crazy."

"Strike three!"

"Good job, Wade. One more, baby. Do it again." Vin grabbed his brother by the arm. "Crazy? She's playing you like a violin. Haven't you ever read Sun Tzu? *The Art of War*?"

"Was he a sex therapist?"

"Sun Tzu was a warrior. Twenty-five hundred years ago he wrote the ultimate guide to ensure victory on the battlefield. All warfare is based on deception. Hold out bait to entice the enemy. Feign disorder and crush him. Wake up, pal. Nancy has your balls in the palm of her hand, and she's squeezing the man-juice right out of you."

"I don't believe it."

"That's because you don't *want* to believe it. Like it or not, you're being conditioned. All this sex—it'll start tapering off, only you'll still be doing the laundry every week. You're like the lazy frog relaxing in a pot of cool water simmering on a stove. Everything seems wonderful to you now, only the water will gradually get warmer and warmer until it's boiling your skin off while you're happily cooking with a stupid grin on your face. What else does she have you doing? Wait, let me guess. … Taking out the trash? Doing the dishes?"

"Yeah, tonight I'm supposed to help her faux-paint the powder room."

"That heartless bitch. We've got to do something now, Jacob, or by next week you'll be watching *Martha Stewart* and subscribing to the Home Shopping Network."

28

Faux-Painting

NANCY, DRESSED IN A see-through negligee, slipped on a pair of oven mitts and removed a brisket from the oven. Using a serving fork, she placed the steaming-hot roast beef on a cutting board on the counter to cool. The dog hovered close, watching her every move.

Her cell phone rang. She tossed aside the oven mitts and answered. "Dr. Beach, can I help you?"

"Nancy, Pete Soderblom. That was some crowd you attracted this morning."

"It's only the beginning. By next week we'll need a bigger room."

"Let's hope so. I'm actually calling to tell you your show picked up two new sponsors—Super Smiles, an A-rated dentist in North Lauderdale and Beauty Factory, a salon in Pompano. Keep this up, and come July first we may actually renew your contract."

Nancy's eyes teared up. "That would be wonderful. Thank you."

She disconnected the call, pumping her fists. *You did it! You showed those bastards. You, Nancy Beach, are the keeper of your own fate; you've emancipated yourself from the bonds of your past.*

The dog suddenly became alert, wagging its tail.

Jacob entered his home, greeted by Sam. "Hey, boy. Nance, I'm home." Casually strolling by the open powder room, he opened the sink cabinet and tossed the newspaper inside.

He found Nancy in the den, lying on the sofa in a sexy negligee, a pint of paint dangling from her fingers.

"Welcome home, Picasso. This paint's water based. After we finish the bathroom, I thought we'd paint each other."

"That sounds pretty wild, only I can't do it tonight. Mrs. Kleinhenz called. She's got two tickets to tonight's Heat playoff game and wanted to know if I wanted them. *Duh!*"

"Oh. Well, sure … I'd love to see the game."

"Sorry, babe. I kind of already asked Vince." He checked his dive watch. "Did you want to have a quickie?"

"No, I wanted to faux-paint the bathroom."

"Maybe tomorrow. Oh, wait—tomorrow night

is Ruby's event. Tell you what. Why don't you just paint the bathroom without me? I gotta change." Cutting through the kitchen, he entered the master bedroom, Nancy right behind him.

"Jacob, I'm not mad, but I am a little perturbed by this."

Jacob pulled off his tee-shirt then took a whiff beneath each armpit. "Gonna need some deodorant. Sorry, what's perturbing you?"

"You mean besides what you just did? Blowing me off, for one thing. And since when did Mrs. Kleinhenz become Ruby?"

"I don't know. What's the difference? It's just a name."

"Is she coming on to you?"

"Come on, I'm like half her age." Jacob rubbed a deodorant stick along each armpit. "Are you asking me this because you wanted to have sex? I'll be home by midnight. We can do it then."

"You think I'm having sex with you after you cancelled the paint job?"

"Paint job?" He squeezed a glob of toothpaste from the tube directly into his mouth and then brushed. "Are ru raying ra roni reron roo—"

"Just finish brushing—God." Placing her hands before her face, she pressed her nose and head through her separating fingers.

Jacob rinsed out his mouth, spitting white residue across the basin. "I said, 'Are you saying the only reason you've been initiating these wild sexual fantasies is so I'd be your Stepford boyfriend?'"

"Of course not."

The dog barked, and a car horn honked in the driveway.

"That's Vin. Gotta go." He kissed her quickly and exited the bathroom, leaving the cap off the toothpaste.

Nancy growled at her reflection in the mirror. *Stay calm. Remember, behavior modification takes time.* She put on her bathrobe and returned to the kitchen to eat dinner alone only to find the slab of roasted meat gone.

"Sam, you son of a bitch, where the hell are you?" She found the dog eating the remains of the brisket on the leather sofa. "Bad dog! Get out of my house!"

Nancy opened the sliding glass door, chasing the dog outside.

29

Black-Tie Elephants

LOCATED ON SEVEN ACRES of exclusive beachfront property in Lantana, Florida, the Ritz-Carlton Palm Beach was a five-star luxury hotel with the kind of amenities that catered to the upper class.

Jacob cruised north on A1A, the Atlantic Ocean on his right as he followed the scenic two-lane roadway to the hotel entrance. He had hoped Nancy would have joined him on this, his first officially paid gig, but after last night's fiasco, she had banished him to the silent treatment.

She did look sexy in that negligee. Maybe you shouldn't have listened to Vin?

Stop! You need to focus on the gig. Your future clients are in tonight's audience. Do a great job. Pass out your business cards. And who knows what can come from this?

It was nearly 8 p.m. by the time he arrived at the entrance to the resort. The last golden rays of sunset bled into the crimson hue of evening, the trunks of the hotel's palm trees illuminated with landscape lighting as the Volkswagen van wheezed its way around a circular entrance to the valet parking.

The valet, a Hispanic man in his forties, knocked frantically on Jacob's window. "Deliveries are on zee north-side entrance."

"I'm not a delivery. I'm the entertainment."

"Jess, well we don't got any clown parking spots, so jews need to move this hunk of jit, okay?"

"Not okay. I'm a guest of Mrs. Kleinhenz. She told me to valet, so I'm valeting. And be careful with jit. Jit's a classic." Jacob turned off the engine, but the engine continued to run until it choked itself into a burst of carbon monoxide and died. He handed the valet his lucky rabbit's foot keychain, grabbed the suitcase holding the Bush dummy and strode toward the hotel lobby in his rented tuxedo and matching black canvas Converse sneakers.

The concierge directed him to Salon A.

Chandeliers and dimmed lights, white tablecloths and waitresses circulating with tantalizing trays of hors d'oeuvres—several hundred guests mingled in packs, the women in designer dresses, the men in their penguin suits.

Jacob accepted an offering from a waitress and filled a paper napkin with half a dozen pigs in a blanket. *"Everywhere there's lots of piggies, living piggy lives. You can see them out for dinner with their piggy wives, clutching forks and knives to eat their bacon."* Never thought I'd be back mixing it with the hoi polloi. Bet more than a few of these blue bloods had Lehman Brothers accounts. Wonder if any of them own comedy clubs?

"Jacob! Over here!" Ruby Kleinhenz, sandwiched between an older couple, was waving. The fund-raiser hostess was hanging out of a black satin dress, the neckline plunging clear down to her exposed navel, the fabric defying the laws of gravity in order to keep from revealing more than 30 percent of her tan cantaloupe-sized breasts.

John Lennon was right. Women should be obscene and not heard.

"Jacob Cope, these are my friends, Richard and Lois Babcock—"

The blood rushed from his face.

"—The Babcocks own Babcock Industries. They're one of our biggest donors."

Badcock? Richard … as in Dick Babcock? Holy shit. Don't speak.

The silver-haired gentleman with the dark pencil-thin mustache offered his hand. "Nice to meet you … Jacob, was it?"

Jacob shoved the pig in a blanket in his mouth and shook Mr. Babcock's hand. "Res. Rice roo reat

199

roo too."

"And what line of work are you in?"

Jacob swallowed the glob of food in his mouth. "Entertainment. Comedy, actually."

Ruby looped her arm around his elbow. "Jacob's my after-dinner entertainment."

Smiling nervously, Jacob held up the suitcase. "Ventriloquist. So, Richard, what does Badcock—" he cleared his throat, feeling Lois's eyes on him "—Babcock Industries make?"

"We're into hi-tech instruments."

"Like synthesizers?"

Mr. Babcock chuckled. "More like the kind of instrument you'd find on an Apache helicopter."

"Ah, so you're in the business of killing people."

Mr. Babcock's mustache twitched. "Only the bad guys who threaten the American way of life. We're patriots, Jacob. I'm guessing you've never served your country in the armed forces."

"Imagine there were no countries, Mr. Babcock. It isn't hard to do. Nothing to kill or die for, and no religion too."

Lois smiled. "Are you a poet, Mr. Cope?"

"No ma'am. I am he as you are he as you are me, and we are all together."

Lois frowned then whispered, "Ruby, I think your friend is on drugs."

Ruby winked. "Jacob is such a jokester. Oh look, Lois, I think they're getting ready to serve dinner." She kissed the Babcocks on each cheek and then led Jacob to the head table, her elbow hooked around his arm. "What was that all about?"

"The guy builds weapons of mass destruction, and he's rewarded. The world's insane."

"Jacob, who's to judge what's sane or insane," she said, escorting him to his seat at the end of the table before taking the chair to his right. "My ex-husband was an attorney. He defended a lot of filthy-rich guilty people and donated a ton of money to charities that helped the poor. Did that render him a sinner or a saint? Who knows? All I know is that while I was raising his children and taking care of our home, he was banging his legal assistant. Do you know how I found out he was cheating on me? The legal assistant told me after she found out he was cheating on her. Insane, huh? And you know what I learned?"

"No ma'am."

"I learned that right and wrong is all about your perspective. Love thy neighbor. Live and let live. I also learned that I don't have to agree with a person's politics to like them, only to suck their dick." Reaching under the table, she groped his crotch, causing him to jump.

"Mrs. Kleinhenz, are you trying to seduce me?"

"Seduction is a game, Jacob. I don't have time for games."

"Okay then." He squeezed her hand, guiding it back atop the table. "Why don't you tell me a little about the charity you're raising money for."

She smiled and then whispered into his ear, "This isn't a charity, lover. It's a thirty-thousand-dollar-a-plate fund-raising dinner to benefit the Florida Republican Committee."

Sweet Jesus, I've entered the lion's den.

"Our next entertainer this evening is a well-known member of the Grand Ole Party. Ladies and gentlemen, let's give a warm, South Florida welcome to President George W. Bush and his bodyguard, Jacob."

Jacob approached the microphone and stool to a standing ovation that quickly melted into laughter as the audience recognized the face of the dummy tucked over his left arm.

"Good evening. My name is Jacob Cope. For those of you in the cheap seats, I'd like you to clap your hands. The rest of you can just rattle your jewelry."

The John Lennon quote bombed.

"Um, before we begin, I feel it's important that

I let you know that I am not a Republican. I am instead a registered Libertarian."

The puppet animated. "Hey, Jakester, what's with the Libertarian bullshit? If I had known you were such a pussy, I would have never let you stick your hand up my ass."

Laughs, sprinkled around a few gasps from the blue-haired biddies.

"Be a real man, Jacob. Join the Republican Party, and we'll give you a free assault weapon just for registering."

Solid applause. *God, they do love their meat red.*

"Hear that applause, Jacob? These people love me. Think they care that Al-Qaeda attacked us on my watch or that I led America into a three-trillion-dollar war in Iraq or that I deregulated Wall Street so the banks could lead us into the greatest depression since whatever that last depression was called? No, Jacob. They love me because I'm a real man. I got me a real man's squint. Not one of those wacky Asian squints where it looks like I'm polishing my wood; I'm talking about a Texas-league, Clint Eastwood kinda squint. And I got me a real man's walk—a bow-legged walk, like there's something swinging between my legs that requires hourly swipes of baby powder just to keep from chafing. That walk got me Laura. Can we hear it for my wife, Laura?"

The audience applauded, unsure of where this was going.

"God, I love that woman. Though she's not the friskiest of critters. Just last night I walked out of the bathroom, naked as a jaybird. Laura took one look at my Woody the Woodpecker and started her usual whining, 'George, not tonight. I have a terrible headache.' 'That works out perfect,' I said. 'I was just in the bathroom powdering my dick with aspirin. You can take it orally or as a suppository. It's up to you. Heh heh heh.'"

A few laughs, drowned out by gasps from the members of the religious right.

Jesus, toss 'em more red meat—fast!

"Mr. President, I understand you ran into Chelsea Clinton the other day?"

Boos.

The Bush dummy retorted, "Hey, come on now, she's a married Christian woman. Being a devout Christian man, I asked her, 'Hey, Chelsea, be honest. Did you and your new husband ever have sex before you two were married?' She winked at me and said, 'Not according to Dad. Heh heh heh."

Big laughs, followed by applause.

"Mr. President, have you spent time with many political celebrities since you retired?"

"Been keeping it on the down low, Jacob. Last

week, me and Fat-Ass Limbaugh were out at my ranch clearing brush when we saw my dog, Barney, lying on the trail, licking his balls. Limbaugh says, 'Gosh, Dubuya, I wish I could do that.' I said, 'Big guy, you'd better wait and see if he'll let you pet him first.'"

More laughs, suddenly silenced by the presence of a cigar-smoking man standing by table three. "Who hired this liberal lackey? Debbie Wasserman-Schultz?"

Jacob's eyes widened. *Sweet Jesus, it's Limbaugh!*

"Honestly, folks, I've seen better acts at an abortion clinic."

Gasps from several tables in back.

"Easy. I meant at an anti-abortion rally."

Jacob worked the puppet, his heart pounding. "Hey Rush, how 'bout I tell 'em the joke you shared with us in the men's room before dinner?"

"Joke? What joke?"

"Why can't Helen Keller drive?"

"Obviously because she was blind."

"Nope. Because she's a woman."

Limbaugh slapped the table, hooting a red-faced laugh. "See? Now that's funny. Stick with the women jokes, kid. Just watch out for the Femi-Nazis."

The young woman in her thirties seated beside the conservative broadcaster abruptly stood and left.

"Aww come on, honey. It was a joke. Bush got to tell his Helen Keller joke!"

"Thank you, folks. My name is Jacob Cope, and I hope I passed the audition."

30

Bad Dog

NANCY KEYED IN THE front door ahead of Lana and Jeanne, the disturbance setting Sam to paw at the sliding glass door and bark to get inside the house. "Can you hear the hairy monster scratching on my glass door?"

"I thought you were training him?" Lana asked.

"I have been. Watch." She unlocked the back door, letting the excited dog in. "Sam, sit! Sit, Sam!"

The dog ignored her, more interested in licking and jumping on the two strangers.

"Sam, get down! Wait, let me get a doggie treat."

"Aw, he just wants to play. Don't you, boy?" Using her open palms, Jeanne boxed with Sam, jabbing at his open jowls.

"Jeanne, don't roughhouse with him. He gets riled up very easily."

Sam nipped and bit, yapping a high-pitched bark

as he circled Jeanne before suddenly sprinting around the house, knocking over a floor lamp on the second lap.

When the dog diverted into the spare bedroom, Jeanne pulled the door shut, trapping him inside. "Sorry, Nance. My bad."

Lana shook her head. "What kind of dog trainer did you hire?"

"I thought she was good. Sam can sit and play fetch."

"Those are basic tricks, not training," Jeanne said. "This dog lacks any sense of discipline."

"She's right," Lana chimed in. "And from what you told us at lunch, Jacob needs that same kind of discipline. Jeanne, isn't there a guy in your beach combat training group that works with the Broward K-9 division?"

"James Adams. Nance, I'll call him and find out who trains their German shepherds and text you their phone number."

"I don't know. Things have been going really well down at the radio station. I'd hate to upset the applecart by introducing something—what's that noise?"

"It's the dog. Sounds like he's chewing on something." Jeanne opened the bedroom door.

Sam bounded out, an object in his mouth.

"That'd better not be my shoe!"

"Oh my God," Lana laughed, "it's a penis."

"Oh, shit." Nancy chased after the dog and her vibrator. She managed to tackle Sam on the sofa, where a tug of war ensued, the device's rubber testicles flapping in the German shepherd's face. The canine refused to let go, until Nancy managed to switch the vibrator on, frightening the dog.

The radio psychologist slumped to the floor, holding up the mangled sex toy. "Looks like my ex, Dan, after you Tasered him."

The dog came over to lick her.

"Go away. I hate you."

Jeanne helped Nancy to her feet. "I'll get the instructor's number and call you."

Nancy escorted Lana and Jeanne to the front door.

Sam was waiting, wagging his tail.

"Now what?"

"He probably wants you to take him for a walk," Jeanne said.

"Forget it."

The dog barked, insistent.

"He's smart."

"He's a pain in my ass," Nancy growled, searching for the dog's leash.

Dusk—a late afternoon rain shower had cooled the South Florida air.

The dog led Nancy on its leash, dragging her twenty feet before stopping to lift its leg to urinate, only to continue another twenty feet before it stopped again to pee.

"Stupid dog. Can't you just do it all at once? Or are you just doing this to annoy me?"

Reaching the end of the block, they followed the curbed sidewalk around a five-foot shrub that bordered a corner property when Sam suddenly became alert. The dog growled viciously, showing his teeth.

Before Nancy could react, a man in a dark blue running suit appeared. Startled by the big dog's unexpected presence, the jogger tripped over the curb, falling on his hands in the street.

"Oh my God, I am so sorry. Sam, stop!"

The German shepherd refused to let up, growling at the Caucasian man with the buzz-cut red hair.

The freaked-out jogger regained his feet and hurried across the street. "That dog is a menace! You need to do something about that animal, or I'm calling the cops!"

Sam remained tense, growling softly as the frightened man continued jogging down the street.

"Bad dog! What's wrong with you? Is that why you were left in the pound?"

Sam looked up at Nancy, wagging his tail.

Nancy walked into the house in time to hear her cell phone ringing in the kitchen. She answered it, the dog slopping water everywhere as it drank from the bowl.

"Hello?"

"Nancy, it's Mother."

"Mom? Where are you?"

"Acapulco."

Three time zones away, Sandra Beach stretched out in her private tub of mud, fresh lemon slices covering her eyes. "I'm staying at the Las Brisas resort as a guest of my new friend, Fahd Al-Khatani."

"You're dating an Arab?"

"He's a Saud, and he's charming. We met on the cruise ship. He saw me whack my Chinese man-friend with a badminton racket and said he had to have me."

"Mother!"

"Relax. He's not kidnapping me." She peeked out from behind a lemon peel. "Are you kidnapping me, Fahd?"

The naked mocha-skinned man in the next mud tub over laughed. "Not yet, Sandra."

"Fahd says not yet. So darling, are you pregnant?"

"God, no. Why would I be pregnant, Mother? I'm not even married."

"Who cares? It's been twenty-five years since I held an infant in my arms. Now be a good daughter and make me some grandchildren. I'd ask Lana, but your sister's ovaries are as useless as tits on a bull. Tits on a bull—that pretty much describes Jan."

"Jeanne. And I'm not ready for kids."

"Well when do you think you might be ready? You're not getting any younger. Your biological clock's ticking faster than a Muslim's vest. ... No offense, Fahd."

"None taken, my sweet."

The dog barked, wagging his tail as he charged out of the kitchen to greet Jacob.

"Mom, I gotta run. Call me in a few days just so I know you're not being held captive." She hung up as Jacob flopped down in one of the kitchen chairs, exhausted.

"You look tired. How was work?"

"Lousy. I hate Saturday shifts."

"How did it go last night?"

"The gig? Not well. My material wasn't quite suited for my audience."

"You didn't get home until three in the morning."

"I got into an argument at the bar with Rush Limbaugh."

"Rush Limbaugh was there?"

"Yeah. I'm thinking of using him as my next dummy. You can pretty much say any stupid shit and get away with it if you're Rush Limbaugh."

"What happened with Ruby Kleinhenz?"

Jacob averted his eyes. "Nothing. She hosted the event. I barely saw her. Anyway, the fence is paid for. So that's that."

"Good thing too. Your dog attacked a neighbor tonight."

"What?"

"I took Sam out for a walk, and he growled at a jogger. He would have bitten him had I not had him on a choker chain."

"Maybe the guy startled him? Maybe Sam was protecting you?"

"The man was jogging, Jacob. Your dog went after him. Just remember what I told you: Sam's on probation. If he goes after anyone else, you'll have to get rid of him."

31

Speed Bumps

NANCY STOOD AT THE DAIS, gazing around the lecture hall. From a high of several hundred attendees, her weekly W.O.M.B. "rebirth sessions" had dwindled to less than fifty. And the lukewarm energy exuded in today's session did not bode well for next week.

Desperate for answers, she decided to skip the last workshop and find out why things were going south.

"Ladies, tell me what's happening. Why is our attendance dropping? Is it mornings? Would it be easier if we held an evening session, say around eight o'clock?"

A few murmurs, and then a white woman in her fifties stood, egged on by her two companions. "For me, mornings are better. The problem I think a lot of us are having is with your advice. It works for a few days, maybe a week, and then things start to revert. My husband's great right before we go at it, but a few hours later he's back on the couch while I'm cleaning out the pantry. I can't be licking his balls twenty-four/seven."

A few ladies applauded in agreement.

Another woman stood. "I'm tired of always pleasing my Y. Why can't he please me?"

"By *please*, I assume you mean sexually?"

"Hell yeah. Why should I be the one always trying to get him off? I'd trade a good orgasm and a back rub for him screwing up my laundry any day."

The other women nodded and applauded.

Nancy held up her hands, desperate to stave off the anarchy. "You can have that. You can have it all: a man who wants to please you, a partner who speaks to you with respect. Next week we begin the real training, ladies, the serious stuff that will turn your Ys into Stepford husbands and boyfriends and fiancés. Best of all, if you bring a friend, there's no charge for you or your guests. In fact, next week's session is absolutely free to everyone, because you're going to be so excited about what I'll be revealing and how it will change your lives that you'll gladly pay double in two weeks. A preview of what's to come will be delivered on my radio show this week, so keep listening. Sound good? Yes?"

Mild applause. A few encouraging nods.

Nancy ended the session then hustled to the exit to say her goodbyes.

Pete Soderblom was the last one in line. He smiled, wiggling his index finger in the direction of her breasts. "Beep, beep, beep."

"What's that supposed to be?"

"It's my bullshit detector. Your ship's sinking fast, Dr. Nancy, and you haven't a clue how to fix it."

"You're wrong. This was nothing more than a speed bump. You watch. After next week it'll be standing room only again."

"Hope you're right, because I spoke to Dr. Laura's agent this morning. He sounded real anxious to sign a syndication deal."

"Don't—" Her cell phone reverberated with a new text: "NANCY—dog trainer's name is Spencer. Call him at 551-236-6879. Tell him I referred you. KISSES.—JEANNE."

"Ha! Speak of the devil. That was my relationship expert assuring me we'll be getting together this week to organize our new training, I mean, strategy. You watch. By the time I'm done, Dr. Laura will be blurbing my book … on your station, of course."

32

Spencer

THE WHITE VAN LABELED "K-9 Kinder-garten" wove through the neighborhood, parking curbside at the designated address. Climbing out of the vehicle was a lanky Englishman in his mid-sixties with a salt-and-pepper mustache and short-cropped hair and dressed from his cap to his army boots in desert camouflage. Striding up the driveway to the front door, he paused, tilting his head like an engaged canine to hear the dog barking out back.

Good hearing, though certainly not great. Lacks training. Too deep to be a poodle or bearded collie. My guess … German shepherd. And a lazy one at that.

Proceeding to the front door, he knocked then stood at ease with hands behind the small of his back.

Nancy opened the door.

"Ms. Beach? Sergeant-Major Spencer Botchin,

retired. Formerly of the British Canine patrol, reporting as requested. German shepherd?"

"Thanks, but I already have one."

"Indeed. By its bark, I'm guessing a male, forty-nine to fifty kilos, about 110 pounds."

"I'm impressed. Would you like to come in, or can you train him psychically?"

"I'm sorry?"

"Never mind. Please come in. He's had a little training already. He can sit and give you his paw."

Spencer was incredulous. "Sit and give his paw? What's next? Balancing on a high-wire while carrying an umbrella?"

"No. I just meant—"

"Never mind all that. Show me the dog."

Nancy led him through the house to the kitchen where Sam was leaping at the sliding glass door.

"Ah, yes, I see he's mastered the scratching at the back door trick."

"That's why I called you. Should I get his box of treats?"

"Treats? My dear Ms. Beach, this is a German shepherd, an animal of extreme intelligence, bred to serve man. I don't know who the devil trained it, but if it were up to me, they'd be drawn and quartered! Come."

"Excuse me?"

"Come. With me. Quickly." Spencer led her back out the front door and down the driveway to his van. He opened the rear doors, revealing a cage holding a fearsome German shepherd. Twenty pounds lighter than Sam and not nearly as bulky, the dog barked viciously, its snout curled back, exposing every fanged tooth.

Spencer unlocked the cage, sending Nancy backing away in fear.

"No worries. She's trained to respond that way. Tilda, come!"

Tilda jumped down from her cage and sat on all four paws by Spencer's right heel, the dog's weight on its feet, not its belly, the snarling personality completely doused.

"We call this the ready position. From here, we'll proceed with a small demonstration." Spencer walked down the sidewalk alone. Fifty feet away, he yelled, "Tilda, heel!"

Tilda sprang to her feet and hustled to Spencer's right flank.

The trainer walked toward Nancy, the dog keeping pace. When Spencer turned, the dog turned with him. When he stopped, the dog stopped—all without looking.

"Tilda, stay."

Tilda returned to her ready position on all fours.

Spencer left the dog and walked over to Nancy. "Tilda, come!"

Tilda raced over then assumed the four-paw ready position at Spencer's feet.

"Tilda, house!"

Tilda sprinted back to the van and jumped inside her cage.

"Wow. I mean … wow! I never imagined a dog could be trained like that."

"That, madam, is what discipline and proper training can achieve. No babying the animal. No bribing it with cookies or any of that childish rubbish—just hard work and praise. Ready to begin?"

"Teach me, Obi Wan."

33

Dog Training the American Male
Lesson Three: Utilizing the Leash

SAM DRAGGED NANCY out of the house by his leash, the dog honing in on his would-be bitch like a bee to honey.

Tilda remained in her cage, gazing at the big male with feigned interest.

Spencer took the leash from Nancy. Gripping the chain close to Sam's collar, he yanked hard, placing the dog in a seated position.

The German shepherd whined but didn't move.

"Now pay attention, Ms. Beach."

"Nancy."

"Very well … Nancy. All dogs descended from *Canis lupus*, the common wolf. As such, all dogs maintain an inherent pack mentality, with each dog vying to find its place within the pack. In Sam's case, your family is his pack, and he obviously believes he's the alpha dog. That must change. Our first step, therefore, will be to put him in his proper place using the walk. I see you have Sam on a choker chain."

"I was told it's the best."

"Yes, and I was told Saint Nick climbs down the chimney every Christmas to deliver toys to all the good little tots in the world—only my family lived in a fourth-floor flat with bars on the windows, rendering the entire story a load of rubbish. Prong collars are better, but this will do for starters, the proper position for a choker collar being high up on the dog's neck, like so. Now watch what I do and say. Sam, heel!"

Positioning Sam on his right, Spencer walked to the next mailbox and turned around, occasionally yanking on the chain to keep the dog close. "Good boy. There's a good boy. Heel, Sam. Good boy."

The dog trainer walked the route three times, ending the exercise by putting Sam into a sit position.

"All right, Nancy, take command. Remember, dogs can sense weakness. You are the alpha."

"I am the alpha."

"You are the alpha."

"Please stop saying that." Nancy gripped the

leash. "Sam, heel!" She walked, praising the dog while keeping him close. She ended the drill as Spencer did, placing the canine in a sit position.

"Very good. Now that we've associated a voice command with the desired behavior, we'll test the animal, using discipline to correct any independent thoughts, or, as I call it, separating the peas from the corn."

From his utility belt, Spencer removed a thirty-foot nylon leash, swapping it out for Sam's short chain leash. "*Take a break* is the command we'll use to allow Sam to wander off. When we want him back we use the *heel* or *come* command."

"What's the long leash for?"

"Retrieving the dog. You don't expect him to learn without any corrections? Sam, heel!"

Spencer walked, Sam keeping pace on his right. When they reached the next mailbox, Spencer said, "Sam, take a break," and stopped walking.

The dog looked back and continued walking, its pace increasing.

Spencer allowed Sam to wander away a good twenty feet before yelling, "Sam, heel."

The spell broken, Sam continued to sniff the neighbor's lawn.

"Sam, come!" Spencer yanked hard on the long leash as he reeled the dog in, forcing Sam to double-time it back to his side. "Good boy. Sam, heel."

They returned then repeated the drill several times until Sam came back to Spencer on his own.

"All right, Nancy, now it's your turn. Always remember, you are the alpha dog."

34

Dog Training the American Male
Lesson Four: The Stay Command

THE TWO-TONE VOLKSWAGEN VAN idled roughly through the neighborhood, the sound muted from its driver by the 8-track cassette blaring the Beatles' *The Ballad of John and Yoko*.

Jacob lowered the volume to answer his cell phone. "Hello?"

"You're a bad boy, Jacob."

"Ma?"

"It's Ruby. Why did you run out on me Friday night?"

"Run out? I didn't run out, did I?"

"Yes, you did. You were in my suite raiding my snack bar while I was in the bedroom, changing my clothes. When I came out you were gone."

"Mrs. Kleinhenz—"

"Ruby."

"Ruby, you're a stunning woman, but I have a girlfriend."

"Which I totally respect."

"You do?"

"Absolutely. My interest in you is strictly business. I want to manage your career."

"Then why were you changing into a see-through leopard teddy?"

"I think best when my tits are exposed. My investment banker and I meet every first Wednesday of the month at the topless beach in Miami. It's a dog-eat-dog world out there, Jacob. Using my God-given attributes is how I maintain an edge."

"I thought they were implants?"

"That's not important. What is important is that we meet tonight to discuss your next booking. Be at the Improv Comedy Club at City Place at 7:30. I have a meeting set up with the manager."

"You do? That's great. Should I bring the George Bush dummy?"

"That won't be necessary. The owner's a personal friend of mine."

"Ruby, I don't know what to say."

"Do you own leather pants?"

"What?"

"Never mind. I just thought your ass would look good in leather. See you in a few hours."

He rode in silence for a moment, then turned up the volume on the 8-track in time to hear, *"The way things are going, they're gonna crucify me."*

"If Nancy finds out I'm meeting with Ruby tonight, *she'll* crucify me."

At precisely 6:14 p.m. Jacob Cope entered his home. "Nance, I'm home."

He placed the newspaper on the shelf by the hall mirror and kicked off his sandals, retrieving the shoes and the newspaper as Nancy approached. The dog was walking calmly by her side.

"Sam, heel. Good boy. Sam, take a break."

The dog darted to Jacob, wagging its tail.

"Sam, heel!"

The dog hurried back to Nancy, circling her until it sat, statuesque, on her right side.

"Wow. How did you do that?"

"Lots of practice."

"That was amazing." Jacob kissed Nancy passionately on the lips. "Gotta change. I promised my mother I'd come by and see her tonight. You don't mind, do you?"

Nancy's reaction was unexpected. She got in his face, backing him up against the door. "Actually, I do mind. We've been together three months, and the woman still refers to me as the *shiksa* whore who stole her son. I also mind that you come home every night and still leave your smelly shoes on my floor."

She ripped the sandals from his hand and tossed them down the hallway.

"Finally, I mind that the only time you're interested in me is when you're horny." She grabbed his Johnson, squeezing it. "You want to visit your mother tonight? Fine, but this time you'll bring me with you."

Sweat dripped from every pore on Jacob's body. "You really want to meet Ma?"

"Absolutely. Now put those toe-jam-festering shoes away and wash up for dinner."

"Yes ma'am." Jacob fetched his sandals and hustled into the master bedroom.

Nancy looked down at Sam, the dog still seated by her right leg. "Let that be a lesson. Nobody messes with the alpha dog."

35

The Alpha Dog

CARMELLA COPE WAS IN THE rec room watching television from a wheelchair, not because the seventy-two-year-old's sciatic nerve was bothering her (it wasn't), or because she wanted to give the kibitzers another opportunity to spread her C.C. Rider nickname to the new arrivals (okay, partially true), but because her most faithful son had just called her out of the blue to announce that he was on his way, and Carmella believed an infusion of Jewish guilt was a B-12 shot for the soul.

Nancy followed Jacob through the lobby of the senior citizen complex into the rec room, immediately registering a musty "old people" scent.

"There she is, in the wheelchair. Ma, what's wrong? Did you fall?"

"It's my sciatic nerve, Jacob. It's been bothering me all—who the hell is this?"

"Ma, this is my girlfriend, Nancy Beach. Nancy, this is—"

"You brought the hooker?"

"Stop it. Treat her with respect, or I'll leave."

Carmella grumbled, her mind flipping through a mental Rolodex of responses. *Start with tears, the pain and suffering from the sciatica unbearable.*

Nancy pulled over a chair, refusing to be intimidated. "It's so nice to finally meet you, Mrs. Cope. I must say, this is a beautiful facility."

"What do you know? The food's horrible, and you should see how small the portions are. So Fancy Nancy, what do you think of my Jacob? Hung like his father, no doubt. Little Sammy Cope, I used to call him. I've ridden saddles that went deeper."

"That's it, Ma. Come on, Nancy. We're leaving."

"It's okay, Jacob. Your mother's just upset because she has to share you. We have to help her learn to finally cut the umbilical cord. Mrs. Cope, there's two things you should know about me. First, it's not about the size of the saddle; it's about the fit, and your son fits me just fine."

Jacob smiled, his grin quickly chased away by his mother's glare.

"Second, I'd never do anything to come between you and your son. I happen to believe that—" Nancy paused, her eyes locking onto an old man watching them from across the room, his face familiar. "Would you excuse me a moment?"

Jacob watched as his girlfriend made her way across the room.

Carmella blew her nose in a Kleenex. "I take it back. She's not a whore; she's a conniving, manipulative witch."

"She's not a witch, Ma. Why do you have to be so rude?"

"It's my nature, Jacob. Your mother's old. Every day I feel death's cold fingers creeping up my—" Carmella shifted uncomfortably in her wheelchair. "Oh my."

"What is it? Is something wrong?"

"Suddenly my hootie feels as cold as ice. Jacob, be a good son and tell these cheap bastards to turn up the heat."

"Ma, it's ninety degrees in here."

Selma Krawitz joined them. The silver-haired senior and queen of the women's gin rummy league pointed beneath Carmella's wheelchair. "Good grief, C.C., you dropped trou again. Your giggle flower's buck naked to the vinyl."

Jacob looked beneath the chair. "Jesus, Ma. How'd you manage to lose this?" His face contorted involuntarily as he retrieved the adult diaper.

"Don't be a drama queen. I didn't soil it. I wear

231

them to keep my bare ass warm."

The men turned like tumbling dominoes to stare at Carmella.

"Look at 'em, dirty old men. Hey, Selma, watch this!" Carmella lifted both legs in the air, offering the men an unobstructed three-second beaver shot. "First one's free, boys. The rest'll cost you next month's social security check."

"Jesus, Ma—stop!"

"Relax, I'm performing a civic duty. The old farts' hearts can use the exercise."

Across the room, Truman Cabot was seated at his private table. The retired millionaire and founder of Cabot Enterprises was dressed in a bathing suit, bathrobe, bathing cap and swim goggles, having just completed his evening walk in the pool. Saliva oozed from the old man's open mouth as he stared at the flashing vixen in the wheelchair.

"Mr. Cabot?"

"Look at that hellcat. Goddam, she makes my blood boil."

Nancy glanced over her shoulder at Carmella Cope, who was spinning around in her wheelchair, her spread legs held high to catcalls.

Oh dear God. "Sir, would you like to meet her?"

Mr. Cabot looked up as if seeing her for the first time. "You know the goddess?"

"She's my boyfriend's mother. I'm Nancy—Dr. Beach."

"You're my doctor?"

"No sir. I work at your daughter's radio station. My show used to be called *Love's a Beach*. I recently switched it to *Dog Training the American Male*. I'm the host, Nancy Beach."

"You host the doggy show?"

"Actually, sir, it's a relationship show. I use dog training techniques to empower women … and men. I could teach you how to begin a relationship with the goddess."

"One million dollars."

"Excuse me?"

"Hook me up with the goddess, and I'll pay you a million dollars."

Nancy's pulse raced. "Stay right here!" She crossed the room, her mind on fire. *Be nice. Flatter her. Show her respect. Build trust. And if that doesn't work, drug the bitch.*

"Go on, Ma. Apologize to Nancy."

Carmella averted her gaze. "Sorry."

"I'm the one who should be sorry, Mrs. Cope. The mother-son bond is forever. I only hope you'll allow me to get to know you better so I can be a part of your life."

Carmella looked up, suspicious. "Who's the old

fart you were talking to?"

"His name is Truman Cabot. His daughter owns the radio station where I work. It would mean the world to me if you'd allow me to introduce him to you."

"Not interested."

"Ma—"

"I'm already seeing two men."

"Nancy's not asking you to date him, just to say hello."

"Eh."

"Please, Mrs. Cope."

"Fine, if it'll shut you up."

Nancy waved Mr. Cabot over.

"Jacob, help me sit up. I think I may have pulled something in my gynnie. Might have to see your brother. Bet that would send him running back to brain surgery school."

"Truman Cabot, I'd like you to meet Carmella Cope."

Mr. Cabot offered her a denture-filled smile.

"What are you grinning at, you old fool?"

"You look just like my beloved Rachel, just before she died."

"And you look like an enema. Take off that ridiculous bathing cap. You're embarrassing me."

He peeled the rubber cap from his silver-haired

skull. "Go out with me, and I'll buy you a Mercedes."

"I wouldn't be caught dead in a Kraut car. Besides, I'm already seeing Goldman and Schwartz."

"You're dating a law firm?"

"I'm a free-wheeler, Cabot. Only you're not my type."

"I'm every widow's type—an eighty-two-year-old with a three-hundred-million-dollar bank account, a bad heart and a case of Viagra."

Carmella reached for her pincer cane and used it to part Truman Cabot's robe, revealing a sagging chest and a paunch belly that obscured a red Speedo bathing suit and whatever lay beneath. "Like I said, you're not my type."

Cabot panicked. "I was just in the pool. You have to allow for shrinkage."

"Looks like it's been shrink-wrapped. Now beat it, Richie Rich, before I use my gripper to check your prostate."

Dejected, Mr. Cabot glanced at Nancy and left.

36

Dog Training the American Male
Lesson Five: Dealing With
Separation Anxiety

SPENCER WATCHED APPROVINGLY as Nancy walked Sam up and down the sidewalk using the long leash. "Very good. I think that's enough for today."

"Thank God. How about an iced tea?"

"That would be lovely. First, let's see if Sam remembers his new command."

Nancy detached the leash from the dog's choke collar. "Sam, house!"

The German shepherd sprinted through the open backyard gate and entered his dog house.

Spencer followed Nancy into the enclosed yard, locking the gate behind him.

The moment they were inside the house, Sam

went wild, sprinting around the yard before digging in the garden.

"Look at him, Spencer. He does this every time I leave for work. Damn you, dog! I just planted those bromeliads!"

Spencer watched the German shepherd tear apart the row of colorful red plants. "I'd say Sam has a bad case of separation anxiety."

"You're joking, right?"

"My dear, I never joke when it comes to the welfare of a canine. Separation anxiety is the second-most common reason dogs are abandoned by their owners and eventually euthanized. Remember, dogs are pack animals; being left alone is against their nature. A dog suffering from anxiety will bark excessively, can become destructive, and, if given the opportunity, will defecate in the house. The animal may become so nervous that it will chew parts of its own body down to the bone. I knew of one dog that chewed on its tail so much the appendage had to be amputated."

Great, another roommate suffering from panic attacks. "Okay, Obi Wan, what am I supposed to do?"

"For now, I'd suggest walking Sam before you leave for work every day. Unfortunately, a dog of this size and intelligence will need something more stimulating to fill your void—at least until he accepts you as his pack leader. My wife and I had the same problem with Tilda when we adopted her."

"I bet your wife would have preferred a small, white, foofie dog."

"Actually, Kate liked the bigger breeds. When we first met, she had a 170-pound Newfoundland."

"I'd love to meet her—your wife, not the dog."

"Unfortunately, she passed away a few years ago. Breast cancer."

"I'm so sorry. I lost my father to stomach cancer."

"It's a frightful disease."

"Do you have any children?"

"A daughter—she's about your age. Married an Aussie. Now they live in Melbourne with my three-year-old grandson. I suppose I'm suffering from my own separation anxiety."

"Have you tried dating? My mother was against it at first. Now she's on a senior single's cruise. At least, she was. God knows where she is today."

"No actual dates, though I've attended a few social functions where I live. Sadly, the women tend to be either hounds or terriers."

"Where do you live, The American Kennel Club?"

Spencer smiled. "Sorry, old habit. I tend to segregate women into show categories. Terriers are your yappers—women who drone on endlessly. Hounds are the sniffers—always prying into your affairs, wanting to know everything from the place you were born to the last time you had a solid bowel movement. Essentially they want to know if you're suitable for marriage. Sporting breeds are your Boca bitches—eye candy relegated to young men or the eccentric rich."

"I know I'll regret asking, but what am I?"

"Well, at first I assumed you were a toy, either a Shih Tzu or miniature poodle, but as I've gotten to know you, I see you more as a working bitch—someone who seeks her own independence. I think a Doberman pinscher suits your style."

"Pretty profound. Just out of curiosity, what was your wife?"

"Kathy? Definitely a herder, like your German shepherd—loyal to a fault, excellent with kids. But, as you can see, my herding days are over. Truth be told, it would be nice to find a sporting dog, certainly not an Irish setter—God help me—perhaps a retriever or, better yet, an English springer spaniel, something with a little fight in her."

"I know one! She's single and loves dogs. Her name's Anita. What if I set you up on a blind date?"

"I don't know. How physically impaired is she? Can she see shadows?"

"No, no, she's not blind. The date would be the first time the two of you would meet. We call that a blind date."

"Smashing. You set me up with my doggy date, and I'll bring over the equipment you'll need to help Sam with his separation anxiety."

37

Dog Training the American Male
Lesson Six: Breeding Rituals

NANCY DROVE OUT of the gated community with Helen Cope in the passenger seat. "Cabot really offered you a million dollars if Carmella would date him?"

"Actually, he said 'hook him up.' I wasn't sure if he meant a date or sex."

"Either way, it's like paying someone to give you malaria. Does this guy even have that kind of money?"

"Enough to date a hundred Carmella Copes."

"And the old bat refused?"

"She took one look at the size of his Johnson and sent him on his way. Poor guy just got out of the pool. But you know what they say about first impressions. I asked Jacob to work on her, but he refused to question Mommy Dearest."

"What makes you think she'd listen to me?"

"You're her daughter-in-law, the mother of her three grandsons. All you have to do is help me convince Carmella to give Mr. Cabot a chance, and we'll split the bounty."

"Let me tell you a little something about my relationship with Carmella Cope. The first time we met, she called me a whore. She finally stopped a year later when Vin asked me to marry him and threatened not to invite her to the wedding. A year later I was at my baby shower, eight months pregnant with Wade, when Carmella pulled me aside, drunk as a skunk and said, 'I know what you're up to, Helen of Troy. After it's born, I'm having the baby's blood tested just to prove to Vincent that it's not his kid.'"

"My God, she actually said that?"

"Nancy, I was so pissed I refused to allow her to see Wade until he was ten months old. She's mellowed slightly over these last few years. I think it's because she's getting laid or whatever it is these old people do in these senior cities of theirs."

"I guess that means you're out."

"For half a million bucks? Oh, I'm in. In a worst-case scenario, I can always use the money to hire someone to kill her."

It was dusk when Spencer Botchin assaulted the two flights of concrete stairs to reach Apartment 3-F, the bouquet of roses held firmly in his left hand. He took a moment to wipe perspiration from his brow and then knocked on the door.

After a minute the door opened, revealing Anita Goodman. She was wearing a short black leather dress, her bulging cleavage held together between the plunging neckline with a leather string. The matching leather boots rose clear up to her knees.

Spencer's eyes widened. "Major Botchin Spencer Sergeant—I mean, Spencer Botchin. I'll be your blind date for this evening."

"Anita Goodman."

"I'll do my best. I mean, happy to meet you." Spencer's mustache twitched as he imagined Anita in her bra and thong panties on all fours while he inspected her body like a dog show judge.

"Are those flowers for me?"

"Flowers? Yes."

She took them and tossed them inside. "Okay, let's go."

"Perhaps you might want to put them in water?"

"Nah, I'm not big on flowers. I appreciate the effort. You get one gold star. Next time try candy."

"Plain or with peanuts?"

"Surprise me."

243

Spencer led her down the stairs and across the parking lot to his van. He held open the door then hustled to the driver's side and climbed in.

Anita sniffed the air. "Smells like dog in here."

Spencer started the van. "Not just a dog, madam, but eighty-two pounds of sinew and muscle, possessing bloodlines that trace back to eighteenth-century Europe."

"Very impressive."

"Indeed. So I thought we'd start with dinner at Ruth's Chris Steakhouse and then catch the 9:30 showing of *Sharkman*."

"Let's do Thai. And I wanted to see *Eternal Love*; it's playing at the Regal."

"Thai food and a chick flick? Not in this lifetime."

Anita rubbed her left hand along the inside of Spencer's thigh. "Eighty-two pounds of sinew and muscle, huh? Is that when it's angry?"

Spencer's eye's fluttered. "You know, I haven't had good Asian food in quite some time."

🐾 🐾 🐾

While Spencer was on his blind date, Nancy found herself in Mr. Cabot's three-bedroom suite, helping him with his cummerbund. The millionaire was dressed in a classic white dinner jacket, white shirt, black trousers and a matching bow tie—what the quirky retiree referred to as his "James Bond pick-up attire."

Arm in arm, she led him out of the apartment to the elevators. They rode downstairs to the rec room, which had been converted into a senior citizen's rendition of *Casino Royale*. There were blackjack and poker tables, roulette and a Wheel of Fortune. Several hundred residents dressed in evening wear and dinner jackets were gambling with fake money provided by the staff, with prizes promised to the top twenty earners at the end of the night.

Mr. Cabot signed in at the registration desk and received his envelope of fake money.

Nancy spotted Helen dealing cards at one of the poker tables. "There she is, dealing cards at Carmella's table. The moment you approach, my friend's arranged for one of the players to give up their seat. Are you ready to dazzle C.C. Rider with your card-playing skills?"

"Not yet. Give the Viagra another few minutes to kick in."

"You took Viagra? I thought you were here to play poker?"

"I'm here to poke her all right—*poke her* with my one-eyed trouser snake. Last time Carmella saw it, it was hiding beneath my two rocks. This time, watch out, sister."

Why do men get more disgusting as they age?

"Go on over, Dr. Nancy. I'll be there in a two shakes."

Nancy headed over to the table where Helen was dealing cards from a shoe. Seated around the green felt from left to right were Sol Rabinowitz and his hearing-impaired wife, Esther; Morty Goldman and Carmella; Janie Honeywell, a three-hundred-pound redhead gigglepuss; and Bill Blackmon, a retired cardiologist from Des Moines, Iowa.

"Hi, Helen. How's it going?"

"Good, Nancy. Are you my relief?"

"Looks that way."

Carmella watched the two women suspiciously as they traded places. "What's she doing here?"

"Nancy's a volunteer, just like me. Watch out for my mother-in-law, Nance. I think she's looking at Janey's cards using the reflection from her lapel pin."

The heavyset redhead reached for her shiny silver Weight Watchers pin, causing the lump of jiggling fat beneath her arm to knock over Carmella's stack of chips.

"Easy, Rush Bimbo."

"C.C., have you been looking at my cards?"

"Of course I've been looking at your cards. So has Doc Blackmon."

"Actually," the retired cardiologist grinned, "I've

been looking at her breasts. Professionally, of course."

Helen glanced over Nancy's shoulder to see Mr. Cabot approaching from across the room. She nodded at Blackmon, who pocketed his chips. "Think I'll check out the big wheel. Janey, why don't you bring the twins over to my apartment later, and I'll raise the stakes, heh heh."

"Oh, behave." She slapped him playfully on the back, the powerful blow sending him stumbling into Mr. Cabot's erection.

"Aww!" Cabot dropped like a sack of potatoes.

"Oh no!" Nancy rushed over to him in full panic. "Mr. Cabot, what's wrong? You're turning red. Just stay calm and breathe. Can you tell me what hurts?"

"My … hard … my hard …"

Sol Rabinowitz leaned over and listened. "He said his heart. My God, he's having a heart attack! Quick, somebody get the number for 911!"

Janie Honeywell grabbed Dr. Blackmon by his arm, tearing the fabric of his jacket as she dragged him over. "He's having a heart attack, Doc. Do something!"

"And be sued for malpractice? Forget it. Allow the man to croak in peace."

Helen leaned over Nancy. "Hang in there, Mr. Cabot. An ambulance is on the way."

"Where's … Carmella? Must … show her …"

Nancy rushed over to Jacob's mother's side. "He's asking for you."

"Do I look like a priest?"

"Stop being so selfish!" Nancy led Carmella by the elbows to Mr. Cabot as whirling scarlet lights illuminated the rec hall. Seconds later, two EMTs were making their way through the jittery crowd of seniors, wheeling a crash cart on a gurney.

"Out of the way, folks. Give us room. What seems to be the problem, sir?"

"He says it's his heart," Nancy answered.

The EMT stared at the pretty petite blonde. "Don't I know you?"

"Yeah," Carmella said, "she's your whore."

The other Emergency Tech worked on Mr. Cabot, getting his vitals. "Blood pressure's 145 over 80, pulse 92. Where's it hurt, big guy?"

"My … dick. I took Viagra, and … he hit me in the groin."

All eyes focused on Mr. Cabot's hard-on, wedged painfully beneath his cummerbund.

"What did he say?" squawked Esther Rabinowitz.

"He said it's his *schmeckle*." Sol yelled back.

"His pickle?"

"Exactly. Play your cards."

The EMTs loosened Mr. Cabot's cummerbund

then strapped him down onto the gurney, his erect penis pitching tent beneath his trousers.

Nancy stopped them. "Wait. If it's not his heart, why are you taking him?"

"His blood pressure's elevated. It could be a Viagra overdose. We'll admit him overnight and keep an eye on it."

"I don't understand," Janie said. "They're going to watch his hard-on all night?"

Morty snickered. *"Die Hard 5: Viagra Stakeout."*

Carmella leaned over Cabot as they wheeled him away. "Nice try, Truman, but that's not the kind of saddle I ride. Maybe they can fix you while you're in the hospital."

38

Dog Training the American Male
Lesson Seven: Exercise

"I HAVE A DILEMMA, LISTENERS. A friend of mine—an older gentleman—seeks the company of a controlling, egotistical woman who won't give him the time of day. I'm asking all you dog lovers out there for a solution. Call me at 561-222-WOWF, or you can text a solution to star-WOWF on your mobile phone.

"Looks like we have our first caller: Eric from Lantana. Talk to me Eric."

"Dr. Beach, life is like a penis—simple, relaxed and hanging freely. It's women who make it hard."

"Well said, Eric. And if it wasn't for women, men would spend their entire day flaccid on the couch, drinking beer. Next caller: Felicity from Weston. Felicity, do you have a solution for my hard-up older gentleman?"

"I was just wonderin' if this older guy knows how to mow a lawn. 'Cause if he does, I'll let him do me doggy style."

"He doesn't mow lawns, *Felicity*."

"What about Eric? He sounds like a guy who could trim a mean hedge."

"Good-bye, Lynnie. Stacey from Wellington, one of our regulars. Help me out here, Stacey."

"Nancy, it sounds to me like you've got two alpha dogs in the mix. My advice is to have the male take on the role of the submissive partner."

"How does he do that when the female refuses to engage him?"

"Does she engage in other male-female relation-ships?"

"In fact, she's allowing two other males to hump her leg, if you catch my drift."

"So you have a bitch in heat, but she's particular. All your friend has to do is figure out what these other two males have that he doesn't have and get it."

🐾 🐾 🐾

The white K-9 van was already parked by the curb when Nancy arrived home from work. Spencer Botchin greeted her with a limp and a Band-Aid covering the bridge of his nose.

"My God, what happened to you?"

"Your friend, the English springer spaniel. She doesn't need a man; she needs a muzzle."

"Spencer, I am so sorry."

"Ah, no worries. I'll be in full assault gear when we reconvene later tonight. Meanwhile, I've brought along a few accessories to help rid your dog of his separation anxiety. Exercise is the key to keeping your pet mentally and physically fit, Nancy, and Sam could certainly stand to lose a few pounds."

"Isn't walking exercise?"

"Walking is bonding time, and, with your schedule, I suspect you skimp on that too. Face it, Nancy, your dog is lethargic. He sits at home all day lacking stimulation, surrounded by a sensory-blanketing wood fence while he yearns for his pack. What Sam needs is something to jolt him out of his sedentary ways. Exercise can do that, provided we make it both fun and challenging."

Spencer opened the van's rear doors. The cage holding Tilda was gone, the space now occupied from floor to ceiling with a variety of equipment.

At precisely 6:13 p.m., Jacob Cope parked his Volkswagen van in the driveway. He felt tired and depressed, stuck in a job that kept him just over broke, his new career dependent for the moment on a woman more interested in having sex with him than promoting his act. He envisioned himself as a hamster on a wheel—perpetually running but getting nowhere.

The idling van began to heat up, forcing him to engage reality once more. Shutting off the engine, he pushed open the rust-encrusted door and slid off the torn seat cushion. Sleepwalking his way up the driveway, he ignored the newspaper lying on the front stoop and keyed in.

Jacob wiped the bottom of his sandals on the new doormat and entered his home. He bypassed the bathroom and trudged into the kitchen, surprised to find the sliding door's drapes closed.

Seated in the dark was Nancy.

"Nance? What are you doing?"

"Shh. Listen."

The two of them listened to the dog barking out back. "Doesn't he sound happier?"

"I don't know. I guess. Why are the drapes closed?"

"It's a surprise." She opened the curtains, revealing a yard filled with colorful plastic equipment.

"What's all this? Looks like you robbed a McDonald's play area."

"It's a doggy obstacle course. Let me show you."

He followed her outside, wondering what the elaborate setup would tally on next month's expense ledger.

Nancy yelled, "Sam, come!"

The German shepherd hustled over to her right side.

"There's a good boy. Let's show Daddy what we can do."

"Daddy?" Jacob grinned. "I like that."

"We begin with the doggy crawl." Nancy directed Sam through a three-foot-high, six-foot-long porous plastic tube. "Good boy! Then it's a quick run around the zigzag."

Sam raced after Nancy, following a serpentine pattern created using bright orange cones.

"Then it's the Rover jump-over, set at beginner's height."

Sam leaped over the two-foot-high soft plastic hurdle.

"Up and over the teeter-totter."

The dog walked up then down the kid's toy, maintaining its balance.

"And finally we end with our reward—a dip in the wading pool."

Wagging his tail, Sam climbed inside the foot-deep, plastic kiddie pool and rolled in the water, cooling himself off.

Jacob clapped. "That's awesome. We should enter you guys in *America's Got Talent*."

Nancy wiped sweat from her face. "Pretty wild, huh? Spencer says it builds the dog's confidence and self-esteem. Plus Sam will be a lot healthier if he loses ten pounds. And he loves it, don't you boy?"

The dog wagged its tail from inside the pool, waiting for Nancy's next command.

"How much did all this cost?"

"Nothing. Spencer is lending it to us while Sam gets over his separation anxiety. Speaking of which, I have a surprise for you inside."

She led Jacob back inside the house to the spare bedroom.

Nancy's home office was gone, replaced with a treadmill, bench press and assorted dumbbells.

"You set up a gym?"

"I'd rather you joined a gym, but I know you don't like crowds. Jeanne's friend had the equipment in her garage and wasn't using it, so it didn't cost us a thing. And I'll use it too."

"Um, thanks."

"What's wrong?"

"Is this your way of saying I need to lose weight?"

"It's my way of saying you don't seem happy. By working out regularly, you'll feel better about your-self, less anxious. Exercise stimulates your brain to release endorphins, engaging your pleasure centers."

"I tried exercise but it turns out I'm allergic to it. My skin flushed and my heart raced. I got sweaty and short of breath … very dangerous."

"Ha-ha."

"Seriously, I get a good workout just from having sex."

"We'll have sex after you walk a mile and do a few lifting exercises."

"A mile?"

"Okay, half a mile. But do it at a brisk pace."

"You know, Nancy, this sounds really great, but I don't have any running shoes."

"Check the closet. Size 10½ Nikes."

"Thought of everything, did ya?"

Nancy kissed him. "I love you, Jacob, and I want you to be happy. I gave Sam a chance. Try this. For me."

He opened the closet door, slipped off his sandals, and put on the white athletic socks and running shoes.

Unsure, he stepped onto the treadmill.

Nancy started the machine, showing him how to set his speed and incline. "How does it feel?"

"Feels pretty good." *Like a hamster on a wheel.*

"You look great. Remember, half a mile without stopping. I need to freshen up. Helen asked me out to dinner. Back in a second!"

Nancy hurried into the master bedroom, her adrenaline pumping. *This is great! We can work out together, lose weight, stay in shape. He'll be less anxious, easier to deal with. Plus he's gained a good ten pounds since we've been living together, so a little exercise can go a long way. Maybe he'll get his confidence back … get a job again with a major investment firm. This is a win-win.*

Nancy changed into a skirt, heels and a blouse. She brushed her teeth, touched up her make-up, spritzed a shot of perfume across her shoulders and then emerged from the master bedroom to check on Jacob, three minutes and fifty seconds having elapsed.

He was gone.

"Jacob?" She hurried into the kitchen, suddenly fearful. *He's been depressed. Is he suicidal?*

She searched the house then found him lying in the kiddie pool drinking a beer.

39

Dog Training the American Male
Lesson Eight:
Toys and Accessories

HELEN COPE STARED at her reflection in the lighted passenger visor mirror. "Look at my eyes, Nancy. It's like they're permanently bloodshot."

"I didn't want to say anything, but you look exhausted."

"Who wouldn't be with my schedule? Up at six every day to get the boys off to school, followed by four hours at the real estate office. Then it's grocery shopping and running errands before picking the boys up at two, clean the house, yell at them to do their homework while I make dinner before driving them to another baseball game or hockey practice or karate lesson. And weekends are just as bad. If it wasn't for caffeine and Vivance …"

"What about your social life?"

"Social life? You're kidding, right? Vinnie and I used to have a mandatory date night every Saturday. Now we come home from the boys' games and fall asleep on the couch. Don't get me wrong. I love watching my sons compete, but tonight's the first time in four months I ate dinner with someone who wasn't wearing a uniform."

"What about … you know—"

"Sex? Who has the time? I'm usually in bed by 9:30, while Vin stays up all night watching Netflix. Wanna know my biggest fear? In ten years Austin will be off to college, and then it'll be just me and Vin. Except I'll be going through menopause while younger women continue to spread their legs in front of my husband, who by that time should be going through his own midlife crisis."

Helen's lower lip quivered.

"Hey, come on now. A Double X never crawls back into her womb; a Double X attacks the problem. You're a beautiful woman, Helen Cope. What's missing in your life is your Y."

"I'm sorry. I'm not getting the whole X-Y-Z deal."

"The Y is you and your own purpose for being. The Y is the man in your life who has forsaken his marital commitment. Instead of treating you like a princess, Vin's turned you into the castle wench, the chauffeur and chef … the team manager. Tonight, we're going to change all that."

"We are? How?"

"Behavior modification."

"This is more of your dog training stuff, isn't it? That crap may work with your boyfriend, but Vincent and I have been married fifteen years. Even a Twinkie has an expiration date."

"Vin's still a man, Helen, and, like most men, he's a creature of habit."

"You got the *creature* right. This morning I accused him of not having feelings. Do you know what he said? He said, 'Helen, I have feelings. Right now I'm feeling hungry—so how about making me my damn breakfast!'"

"I'm serious. We need to shake things up. We need to get Vin to look at you as his own personal sex goddess—someone who's suddenly come into possession of a forbidden carnal knowledge that will ignite his loins. By the time we're through, he'll be chasing you around the house like a panting dog begging for its master's attention."

"You've got me panting. So how do we do all this?"

"Prong collars."

Twenty minutes later, Nancy turned off the main road into a parking lot, a flashing pink neon sign reading, "SEX EMPORIUM."

Helen followed her inside, slipping on sunglasses to prevent someone from recognizing her. "I can't believe you actually brought us here."

They walked through aisles of triple-X DVDs, past display racks filled with inflatable dolls, vibrators, dildos and contraptions that dated back to the Renaissance.

Helen stared at a glass gizmo that was equipped with a two-pronged, penis-shaped insertion. "Oh my God, do women actually use these devices on themselves?"

"Abso-fucking-lutely." A black saleswoman approached, the masked female dressed in a leather Bat Girl outfit and spiked heels. "Welcome to the world-famous Sex Emporium, home of the Whopper with sleaze. Can I interest you ladies in Dr. Z's latest dual Nipple Pleaser? The convenient Y-converter allows for simultaneous vacuum control and—*Mrs. C.*?"

"Wanda? You work here?"

"I'm one of the minority owners. And no, that ain't a black thing. Well, actually I guess it is, since it got me a small business loan."

"Does Vin know about this?"

"Hell yes. Who do you think he comes to for the latest DVDs?"

"So it's not enough that my husband dabbles in strange women's vaginas all day; now he has to watch porn too?"

"Listen, ya'll don't have to worry about Dr. C. He's what we call a sniffer."

"I'm afraid to ask, but what's a sniffer?"

"Ever see a dog sniff another dog's ass? Looking at strange buck naked old women with leaky vaginas all day can affect a man's libido. Watching porn helps Dr. C achieve what I call "hootie balance." Believe me, it's necessary after sniffing at some of the dogs' asses we see and sniff all day long. It's the quiet ones, like his brother, that you got to watch out for." She turned to Nancy. "Hi, I'm Wanda."

"I'm Nancy. The quiet one's girlfriend."

"For real? Well—*oh shit*." Wanda looked over Nancy's shoulder. "Can I help you, Mrs. K?"

Helen and Nancy turned to find Ruby Kleinhenz standing outside a dressing room. The cougar was wearing a black see-through baby-doll negligee, her bra-covered breasts protruding through the outfit's open cups.

"Wanda, do you have this in red? I need it for—*Helen*?"

"Ruby?" Helen feigned being pleasantly surprised.

"What are you doing here?"

"I'm here every week. The question is what are you doing here?"

"You know … this and that. Have you seen Dr. C's latest dual Nipple Pleaser? The convenient Y-converter allows for simultaneous vacuum control."

"You mean Dr. Z—your husband's Dr. C—and I own two of them."

Wanda stepped between them. "We don't have the teddy in red, but we just got in something hot, a Chemise with nipple clamps and clit and anal loops. And I'm pretty sure it comes in red. Why don't ya'll wait in the dressing room, and I'll bring you one to try on."

"Perfect. Size 36-D." She winked at Nancy then sashayed back to the dressing room.

Nancy's face flushed bright red. "Wanda, we're gonna need a shopping cart."

At 9:36 p.m. Vincent Cope arrived home, having completed his one late-night office shift for the week. Parking his Lexus in the garage, he entered the kitchen carrying his briefcase and an aching lower back.

"Hello?" He hung his keys on their peg by the coffee maker and checked the stack of mail on the counter.

"Helen? Boys?"

No reply.

Any empty house? Is it possible?

Heart pounding, he opened his briefcase and removed the new DVD from its brown paper wrapper. "*Mary Todd-Lincoln: Lesbian Hunter.* Probably more historically accurate than they know."

He dashed upstairs to the master bedroom, opened the door and screamed.

Helen, dressed in a leather S and M outfit, was lying above the four-post bed in a love swing.

"Helen? Have you lost your mind?"

"This is what you want, isn't it, Vincent—to live out your fantasies?"

It's a trap! It's a trap! Don't say a word. Sweet Jesus, look at her tits! Propped up like ripe melons …

"Well? Don't just stand there gawking at me with your mouth hanging open, say something."

"I, uh … nice outfit. Is that new?"

"It came with the love swing. Come closer. I won't bite."

His heart beating wildly, his trousers tightening, Vincent Cope inched closer. "Love swing, huh? Good color. Goes with the lamp shades." *Jesus F-ing Christ, she shaved!*

"Silly, it's not a throw pillow; it's an accessory that allows you to move me while you thrust in and out, in and out of my hot … wet … pussy."

Vinnie broke into a cold sweat, his voice high pitched and stuttering. "Love swing … what a great idea."

"I hope you like it. Wanda tells me it's endorsed by Dr. Ruth."

"Wa—Wanda?"

"You remember Wanda. Your own personal porn dealer!"

He pivoted, attempting to hide the DVD behind his back. "I—I—I don't know what you mean."

"Lying to Momma, huh? Just for that, I'm going to beat your ass raw." Wielding a leather riding crop from behind her hip, Helen snapped it across Vinnie's right hip.

"Ow! Are you crazy?"

"Shut up and take off your clothes."

"Wait, for real? Please say it's for real, because if this is a joke—"

"The boys are sleeping over at my sister's. Now get over here and ride me like a mule, you big, dumb, hairy orangutan."

"Oh hell yes!" Vinnie kicked off his shoes. "Baby, you look unbelievable." He quickly pulled down his pants and underwear without unbuckling his belt. "God, I love you. I love you so much. And I respect you. Totally."

"Tonight you get to disrespect me."

"Oh dear God." He tore off his shirt without unbuttoning it—"Wanda's definitely getting that raise, no pun intended"—and rushed into his goddess's outstretched legs.

"Come on, fat boy, work up a good lather! I want you nice and sweaty when you fuck me silly."

Nancy smacked Jacob's bare ass again with the riding crop as her boyfriend jogged at a brisk pace on the treadmill, naked, save for his jock strap, white socks and Nike sneakers.

40

Stray Dog

THE GUN CLUB WAS LOCATED in West Palm Beach off Okeechobee Boulevard. Jacob parked his van in the half-empty lot and stepped into the blinding noon-day sun. *Now I know why Clint Eastwood was always squinting in those spaghetti westerns.* He checked his dive watch, estimated what time he had to leave in order to get back to work for his afternoon shift, and then entered the building.

An assortment of handguns and knives were displayed in locked glass cases; assault weapons lined the walls. A female clerk, heavyset and graying at forty, was showing a pistol to a well-endowed redhead and her skinny tattooed boyfriend.

"This is a Glock-26 subcompact, nine millimeter. It's very popular, great for a concealed carry. Your boyfriend may prefer the Glock-19, which has a longer grip—" She glanced over at Jacob, offering a cherub smile. "Be right with you, sweet britches. Why don'tcha look around."

"Actually, I'm supposed to be meeting someone … Mrs. Kleinhenz?"

"Ruby's on the range with the women's group. Through that door and turn left. Grab yourself a pair of earmuffs when you go in, honey buns."

"Thanks." Jacob opened the door and entered a small alcove that led to a glass door which sealed off an air-conditioned egress corridor. Inside the shooting area, half a dozen women encircled a gray-haired male firearms instructor.

Ruby Kleinhenz spotted Jacob and waved him over.

"Good afternoon, ladies. My name is Mr. Appleseed, and I'll be your firearms instructor for today. As you know, these are dangerous times. Just this morning I read about a fatal carjacking in Fort Lauderdale. Last week another woman was raped and assaulted in Palm Beach County. Ladies, there are three kinds of people in the world. Most are sheep—frightened creatures dependent on the flock. Then there are your wolves—the animals that prey on society, the assholes who force us to live in fear. Finally, there are sheepdogs—the ones who don't take shit from the wolves."

The instructor held up a nine-millimeter semiautomatic handgun. "This, ladies, is the instrument that turns sheep into sheepdogs."

Jacob growled beneath his breath.

Ruby snickered, nudging him with her elbow.

The instructor recited a few safety regulations then assigned each woman to a stall, the targets: cardboard male silhouettes.

Jacob watched Ruby expertly snap a loaded magazine into place. "You look good, Jacob. Did you lose weight?"

"Five pounds. Been exercising." He glanced one stall over where the instructor was observing a timid brunette. The college sophomore aimed her pistol down range, her slender arms shaking. Looking away, she squeezed off a shot, the recoil nearly hitting her in the face.

Mr. Appleseed shook his head in disgust. "That's no way to discharge a weapon. Look at your target. You've got one shot before he rapes you! Shoot to kill. Now, fleabag!"

Suddenly the timid brunette became Dirty Harry, scattering six holes across the target.

"That's better. Load another clip. Only, this time, try aiming." The instructor moved over one stall to watch Ruby. The divorcée spread her legs in an exaggerated horse stance and fired a perfect cluster, punching holes over her target's groin.

"Impressive cluster, Ruby. Only those aren't kill shots."

"I wasn't trying to kill him. I wanted to make him suffer."

Jacob cringed.

Ruby loaded another magazine and turned to face him. "You're up, lover."

"Whoa, not me. I'm afraid of guns."

"You're afraid of a lot of things. Now get your sweet ass over here before I put a bullet in your crack." She handed him the loaded weapon then stood behind him, positioning his arms. "Strong arms. Aim and squeeze the trigger."

His body quaking, Jacob aimed and fired, flinching at the recoil. The bullet hole was visible over the target's heart.

Ruby kissed him on the cheekbone. "See that? You're a natural."

"Ruby, why am I here?"

"You're here because I got you an amazing gig, a private birthday party on a millionaire's yacht. The job's in two weeks and pays five Gs."

"Five grand? Holy shit."

"There's a catch. The woman arranging everything wants to see your act first. She's a friend, but she's a hardcore feminist. So you need to revise your act accordingly."

"How do I do that?"

"I don't care. Just do it. There'll be a lot of deep pockets at the party, including a few television producers, so take this seriously. No Helen Keller jokes."

"Yes ma'am. When and where is the audition?"

"Friday at noon. I'll text you the address." Turning to face the target, she rapidly discharged eight more rounds until the gun's slide popped out.

Jacob nervously checked his watch. "I better go or I'll be late for work." Mindful of the gun, he offered her an awkward hug.

Ruby groped him through his Bermuda shorts. "Why Jacob, is that a Glock in your pocket, or are you just happy to see me?"

Jacob ducked away from her advances and hurried out of the shooting area, never seeing the muscular woman staring at him from her stall.

Jeanne Pratt watched Jacob disappear out the egress door before she turned and fired two Glocks down range, one gun in each hand.

41

Dog Training the American Male
Lesson Nine: Social Issues

NANCY GRIPPED THE dog's leash tighter, half leading, half dragging Sam down the sidewalk, her sister, Lana, power-walking beside her. "What else did Jeanne say?"

"She said Ruby's advances seemed to make Jacob uncomfortable, but he definitely had a hard-on when he left the shooting range."

"That little shit. Know what he said to me the first night we moved in together? He said he'd cut off his balls if he was even tempted to cheat on me." She quickened the pace, tugging harder on the German shepherd's choker collar.

"Want me to send Jeanne and her PMS crew after Ruby? Send a little message about moving in on another woman's man?"

"The bitch carries a gun, Lana. Besides, Jacob's

the one that needs the warning."

They crossed the street, approaching an older black man walking a golden retriever.

Before she could react, the chain was torn from Nancy's hand as Sam went ballistic, growling and attacking the golden retriever. Screaming, "Heel!" she attempted to separate her enraged animal from the other canine, the retriever's owner yelling and dragging his dog away.

Finally managing to grab Sam's choker collar, Nancy pulled it tight, yelling, "Bad dog! Bad!"

Lana's heart was racing. "God, that was scary."

"That was scary."

"Sam could've killed that dog. Then what? The owner sues you."

"Like I don't have enough problems. This is all Jacob's fault."

"Don't blame me," Lana said. "I specifically told your boyfriend to get you a Bichon."

"Can't trust a man to do anything right."

"I couldn't have been clearer."

"Maybe you should've pulled a Ruby Kleinhenz and grabbed him by the balls."

"I did."

Nancy turned to her sister. "What do you mean you did? You grabbed my boyfriend's balls?"

"Not sexually. You know, just to get his attention.

Sort of like Sam's choker collar."

"Don't touch Jacob's balls! Touch your own boyfriend—touch Jeanne's balls. What is it with other women going after my boyfriends' private parts?"

"Take it easy, Nance—"

"Maybe I should castrate my men before I let them move in with me. Maybe that would keep them from cheating on me."

"Just breathe, little sister. Breathe and count to ten."

"Maybe I'll start with his damn dog? Bet that would keep him from being so aggressive."

"Fix Sam? That would certainly get Jacob's attention."

"Hell yeah." Nancy paused, a kernel of thought taking root in her brain. "Wait a second. Oh my God, that's it! That's why Jacob's mother refuses to give Mr. Cabot the time of day."

"What are you talking about?"

"Carmella's Jewish. She's dating Jewish men—circumcised Jewish men. Cabot's not circumcised. She must have seen his foreskin peeking through his Speedo bathing suit."

"Gross."

"It's not gross, Lana. In fact it makes perfect sense. What's gross is what Cabot will have to do if he really wants to be with Jacob's mother."

42

Distemper Issues

JACOB SAT IN HIS IT CUBICLE, agitated. His blood felt like it was flowing ten degrees too hot. His skin was annoying to be inside of, like it was wrapped too tight. His thoughts were helter-skelter, his problems popping up in his brain like a never-ending game of whack-a-mole.

My share of the rent's due again. I already owe Nancy from last month's expenses. And the van's transmission could go anytime. I need this yacht gig, only Ruby won't let up until I sleep with her. Can't cheat on Nancy, but I need the money.

Jacob could feel the anxiety building, the blood vessels in his left arm tightening.

The iPhone on his desk vibrated again: "RUBY CALLING." He turned the cursed machine off.

Sanjay Patel leaned into Jacob's cubby. "Take line fourteen please."

He snatched the headphones off his desktop,

connecting the line. "Name?"

"Excuse me?"

"Can I have your name, please?"

"James."

"What's your problem, James?"

"My problem is my fucking Internet won't work."

"Have you tried rebooting?"

"Three times."

"Close all of your programs then click on *start*, then *run*, then type in—"

"Whoa, slow down, pal. I have to save a bunch of stuff."

Jacob's heart beat faster and harder. *Do you want a career as a stand-up?*

"Okay. Do what now? Hello?"

Jacob saw the squiggly line in his vision. *Migraine coming. This is bad.*

"Yo, dude, you still—"

"Click on *start* then *run*—"

"Where's *run*? Oh wait, I see it. Now what?"

"Type in capital *C*, colon, then capital *R*, *T*, forward slash—"

"Wait, what comes after the *C*?"

"Colon."

"That's the thing with two dots, right? Hello? Yo, pal, you still there?"

Jacob was gone—the toggle switches in his brain having flipped from up to down, all rational thought drowning beneath a tidal wave of anxiety as he ripped the headphones from his ears and tossed them at the cheerleader calendar hanging crooked on the cubby wall.

He found himself outside, the spots in his vision partially blinding him, causing his heart to race faster. He managed to locate the Volkswagen van. Keying in, he started the engine, not to drive (he still couldn't see), just to power the A/C, which hadn't run cold since the unit began leaking Freon six months ago. He crawled in back, feeling the thick brown shag carpet beneath him as he collapsed face-first on a down pillow. He rolled over onto his back, hot and sweating in the airless metal box, suffering and suffocating—hyperventilating thoughts at the moment still too frightening to consider as the migraine stabbed him in the left eye.

Trapped in purgatory, desperate to keep from falling into his own private hell, he felt for the battery-operated fan he purchased a year ago when he was forced to live in his vehicle, out of work, out of money, out of options.

The breeze momentarily restored his sanity.

The rumble in his gut shattered it.

Sliding open the side door, he leaned out and

puked, the ferocity of the act igniting every blood vessel in his head as his brain sought to restore equilibrium.

He finished, slammed the door closed, and searched the back of the van, desperate to quench the burning sensation in his esophagus. Locating a long-forgotten bottle of water, he swished the hot remains in his mouth before swallowing, then laid back down, his body trembling until finally, mercifully, he passed out.

Several hours later, he stirred in his sauna refuge to Sanjay banging on the side of the van. The migraine had passed, leaving him with a dull hangover.

"Jacob, come inside please. My uncle wishes to speak with you."

"You're fired." Amir Patel delivered the news from behind his immaculate desk.

"Please don't fire me, Mr. Patel. I just had a bad morning."

"A bad morning? My friend, you are in a state of denial. You hate your job. You hate your coworkers. You speak with disrespect to our clients. And from observing the way in which you live, I imagine you are at the top of your own shit list. I like you, Jacob, but what am I supposed to do?"

"I don't know. What does the elephant say?"

"The elephant says you are an asshole." Patel shook his head as if to settle an internal debate. "Answer my questions, and do not lie to me. Are you self-medicating?"

"No."

"Drinking?"

"Occasionally."

"Are you seeing a therapist?"

"Sort of. She's not treating me; we're just renting a house together. She's my girlfriend."

"Apologize."

"For what?"

"It doesn't matter. Apologize, start seeing a therapist, get on an exercise regimen and speak to a medical doctor about prescribing an antidepressant. Then come see me next week dressed in a white collared shirt, black slacks and matching dress shoes. If you've done everything I asked, I'll start you out on service calls using one of our company vans. It's less money, but it's a job. You can thank the elephant if you get that far."

🐾 🐾 🐾

The waiting room at the gynecology center was packed with women, Dr. Cope running an hour behind schedule. Wanda grabbed the next chart from the receptionist and opened the door, calling out, "Cory Verdoliva?"

The forty-eight-year-old mother of two gathered her belongings, wondering how long she'd have to wait in the exam room.

Wanda handed the brunette a plastic cup and clean dressing gown. "Bathroom's on the right. Pee in the cup, leave it in the cupboard, then wait in Room 3 and get into this gown. Dr. Cope will be right with you."

Wanda was about to close the door when she spotted Jacob entering the waiting room. "Damn, boy. You look like two miles of bad road."

"I need to see Vin."

"Go wait in his office. I'll let him know you're here."

Another patient grabbed the door before Wanda could close it. "Nurse, I've been waiting an hour. How much longer will it be?"

"Not long, Ms. Kirsten."

"Not long? How many more hours is 'not long'? I am so tired of doctors overbooking their schedules."

"Yeah, it sucks, don't it."

"Is that your response?"

"Well, I could tell you the insurance companies ain't payin' like they're supposed to, forcing doctors to book more patients just so they can afford their malpractice insurance, but you don't really care about the why. Ya'll just want to bitch and maybe extract a little payback for those of us making you wait."

"It just seems like things are moving extra slow today."

"Well, we ain't givin' pedicures back there. We're knee-deep in smelly, leaky, yeast-infected vaginas. Ya'll want speed? Get your pootie tuned up at Jiffy Lube. Otherwise, sit your cute little ass down and wait 'til I call you."

Jacob entered his brother's office. Vincent Cope's desk was covered with stacks of medical files, his two walls with Samurai swords and martial arts weaponry. A suit of Japanese armor adorned a human skeleton.

Damn. Yoko would love this shit.

Jacob removed a short sword from its perch, recognizing it as a blade used by Samurai to commit *seppuku*, a ritual suicide that involved gutting the stomach. Situating himself on the edge of his brother's desk, pressing the tip of the steel blade against his shirt-covered belly, he imagined himself as a depressed Samurai warrior, about to meet his death.

The door suddenly flew open, and Ruby Kleinhenz rushed in, her naked features flirting with the front of her half-buttoned patient's gown.

Startled, Jacob stabbed himself with the blade, the jolting pain causing him to knock over the skeleton clad in its ancient suit of Japanese armor.

"Jacob, are you okay?"

"Fine … good."

"You're bleeding."

"Huh?" He looked down at the specks of blood spreading across his tee-shirt. "It's okay, just a flesh wound. Why are—what are you doing here?"

"I was waiting to see your brother in the exam room across the hall when I saw you come in."

"I meant, why are you in here, in my brother's private office, naked?"

"It's been three weeks since my surgery. I just wanted your opinion." She lifted the front of her gown, exposing her shaved vagina. "Didn't your brother do a great job on my labia?"

Jacob felt the blood rushing to his face as his fingers pressed the torn tee-shirt against his stab wound. "Uh, great."

Vincent entered in a huff. "Jacob, what the hell are you doing in here—Ruby? Pull your gown down and get back to your room, you lunatic. Ah, hell, look at my Samurai armor—and you dislocated Red

Skeleton's collar bone!" He rushed to aid the fallen icon, noticing his brother's pale complexion. "Jacob, are you bleeding?"

"Yes, please …"

Jacob's eyes rolled up, Vin catching him as he fainted.

43

Love Hurts

JACOB OPENED HIS EYES. He was lying on an exam table, his lower belly in agony. Through his delirium, he could make out his older brother washing his hands at the sink … *scrubbing up for major surgery?*

"Vin? Vinnie …"

"Hey, turd blossom, didn't Dad teach you anything? Suicide comes *after* you get married."

"Sick bastard. Just tell me the truth. How bad is it? Did I slice open the intestine? Will I have to wear a colostomy bag like Dad?"

Vin peeled open a bandage and adhered it to Jacob's wound. "Four stitches. It only needed two, but I'm a Zorro fanatic. See me in a week, and I'll take them out. Or we could let Ruby bite them off for you."

"That'd be funny if I didn't think she'd do it. The woman's insane."

"She's not insane; she's in pain. Her ex hurt her pretty badly. Now she's trying to bury the last thirty years by reinventing herself. Having sex with younger men makes her feel alive again while allowing her to maintain control."

"You sound like Nancy. Maybe it's love? The fact that I'm young and adorable—it's a curse."

"Right. The woman probably has a thing for Panda bears. Don't be surprised if she wants you to wear a stuffed animal costume on your next gig."

"Joke if you must, Vincent, but this is a serious problem. Thanks to you, Nancy knows Ruby wants me sexually. It's affecting our relationship."

"Just tell Ruby you're not interested." Vin saw the look on his brother's face. "Uh-oh, don't tell me you tapped that reconstructed glory hole."

"No."

"But you're tempted. You're thinking about it."

"Ruby's not the only one trying to reinvent herself." Jacob winced as he struggled to sit up. "I had a meltdown this morning at work. I'll probably lose my job; at the very least I'll be demoted. Meanwhile, Ruby has some serious contacts in the entertainment industry, plus a gig coming up in a few weeks that can pay off all my debt."

"And the job's yours, but only if you play ball."

"So it would seem. What do I do, Vin? I don't

want to cheat on Nancy, but I'm behind a month on my share of the bills. If Nancy finds out I can't pay the rent again, she may throw me out. I don't want to hurt her. She's a good woman."

"Far better than you deserve. My advice: don't mention anything to Nancy about Ruby or any details about your stand-up gigs. If you cheat on her and she finds out, she won't just throw you out— she'll castrate you."

44

Dog Training the American Male
Lesson Ten: Neutering Your Pet

"IT WON'T HURT," Nancy said, pouring herself another glass of lemonade. "They'll put you under, snip snip, and you wake up with a small bandage on your penis. No big deal."

"It's far less invasive than breast implants," Helen added. "Plus there's the added benefits. For instance, you'll never have to worry about getting cancer of the penis. Plus, adult circumcision also adds a large degree of protection against AIDS. You can never be too careful."

Truman Cabot glanced at the two younger women seated across from him on his third-floor balcony. "Maybe it's no big deal to you ladies, but it's my penis. After nearly eighty-three years, I've grown attached to it—all of it."

"It's just the foreskin," Nancy said. "Trust us, women prefer men without that annoying skin cape. Your penis will smell a lot better, and it'll look great."

"Oh, God, it'll look amazing," Helen agreed enthusiastically. "We'll practically have to beat my mother-in-law off with a stick just to keep her from, you know, grabbing you."

"You're sure the goddess said she prefers men without a foreskin?"

"Absolutely."

"What else could it be?"

He glanced three stories below to the pool deck where Carmella Cope was part of a foursome playing gin rummy. Using his high-powered binoculars, he managed a quick view of C.C. Rider's suntan-oiled cleavage.

"Call the doctor. Set it up. Soon as possible."

"Just one tiny little thing," Nancy said, scrunching up her face. "It's probably better if we don't mention this to your daughter."

Helen nodded. "Not a good idea, you being eighty-two and all. She'd probably object to any kind of elective surgery at your age. Not that there's any danger in this—there's not."

"Are you kidding?" Cabot said, "Do you know what Olivia bought me last year for my birthday?

Sky diving lessons! My step-daughter's in favor of anything that expedites her inheritance."

Jacob Cope entered his home, having spent the last few hours of daylight at the beach contemplating his life. "Nancy, I'm home."

He placed the newspaper on the shelf by the hall mirror and kicked off his sandals, leaving traces of sand by the front door. His bladder ready to burst, he ducked into the hall bathroom, lifted the lid and seat and urinated, flushed and rinsed his hands. Bypassing the neatly folded hand towel on the rack, he used his shirt to dry his hands, mindful of his bandaged belly.

"Nance?"

"In the kitchen."

He found her at the table working at her laptop. "How was work?" she asked without looking up, her voice inflection a telltale bit too high.

"Fine," he lied. "Where's Sam?" He glanced outside, the German shepherd nowhere to be seen.

"I took him to the vet."

"The vet? Why? What's wrong?"

"He wigged out this morning, attacking another dog. I spoke to a friend, who suggested we have Sam neutered. It seemed like a good idea, so—"

"You had my dog's balls cut off without asking me!"

"You bought the dog without asking *me*."

"That's different."

"I don't see how. Anyway, the vet told me Sam should have been neutered when we first got him. It's better for the dog."

"How? How is it better for my dog to chop off his nuts?"

"For one thing, you'll never have to worry about Sam getting testicular cancer. Plus his penis will smell better and look a lot better. It's embarrassing to have company over with that big rock sack flopping around between his legs."

"He was born that way! Jesus, Nancy, you took away his manhood."

"More like his ego. At least now I won't have to worry about Sam attacking every female dog that wiggles her naked ass at him."

Jacob felt the blood rush from his face. A moment later his knees buckled, and he hit the floor.

45

The Vagina Dialogues

THE MANSION WAS SITUATED on an acre of oceanfront property in Manalapan, a small island town just north of Boynton Beach. Jacob drove up to the iron gate with the giant letter C and pressed the button on the speaker. "Hello?"

"Name?" The male voice seemed bothered by his intrusion.

"Jacob Cope. I'm a guest of Ruby Kleinhenz."

The gate retracted on both sides.

Jacob followed the stone paver driveway up to the two-story, twenty-two-room, five-car-garage dwelling.

He parked, and prayed: "Dear God Almighty: Out of love for Nancy, I jerked-off twice today. Please don't let me get horny around Ruby Kleinhenz. I really need this gig. Thanks, God. Oh, sorry for saying 'jerked-off.' That was kind of rude. I should have said 'masturbated.' Actually, you probably already know what I did since you're God and you see everything. Amen."

Reaching across the console, he grabbed the suitcase lying on the passenger seat and exited the van. Heading up the front path, he approached the mansion's entrance. Before he could ring the bell, the right side of the double door opened, revealing a flamboyant gay man in his early forties dressed in a tight-fitting charcoal-colored tee-shirt and white Ralph Lauren slacks, the high hem exposing his bare ankles and hemp loafers. A light-knit salmon-pink cardigan was draped like a cape over his shoulders. Silver bracelets adorned his left wrist.

"*Namaste.* My name is Cyril, and you must be—oh my God, I know you, don't I? This is so embarrassing, but wait—don't you dare tell me. I know. We met on the dance floor at Twist in Miami. It was White Party week and you were dressed in a French cuff with scarab cuff links which intoxicated me like heroin."

"No—"

"Okay, just give me one clue. Did it involve a pirate costume and a fake parrot named Mr. Tweed?"

"It involved a dog."

"Eww, really?"

"You tried to sell me a Bichon at the pet store where you work."

"Okay, but the dog was white?"

"Yeah, so what?"

"Gaydar! It never lets me down."

"Dude, I'm not gay. What are you doing here anyway? Shouldn't you be selling cats or something?"

"Don't get testy. Olivia invited me over to see your act. She's hosting a big gig on the family yacht for her father's eighty-third birthday—as if she really wants to celebrate the occasion. All I can say is you'd better be good, especially after you waited until I filled out all that paperwork to cancel that puppy sale. See, Mr. Jacob, I do remember. Come this way."

He followed Cyril inside. They passed through a two-story grand salon illuminated by a crystal chandelier then trekked across the polished marble floors past a twenty-seat dining room. An alcove led them to an atrium, the indoor greenhouse's glass doors exiting to the back of the mansion.

"Holy shit."

The tranquil azure waters of a zero-line, twenty-meter pool appeared to run straight into the ocean, its southern border melding into a stone-and-wood deck featuring a fireplace, koi pond, waterfall, bridge and sun deck.

"Hi there."

Jacob turned. Ruby waved from a padded lounge chair. She was wearing a blue metallic micro-thong bikini. The woman in the chair next to her was dressed in identical metallic-purple apparel.

Hail Mary, full of face … I ask the Lord my soul to take.

"Jacob, I want you to meet my dearest, most wonderful friend in the world, Olivia Cabot. Olivia, this is the young man I've been bragging to you about all morning."

Olivia Cabot smiled. "He's cute, but he dresses like my gardener. Cyril, think you can style him up a bit for my father's party?"

"Bitch, please. I could dress him in a Hefty bag, and it'd be an improvement."

Jacob forced his eyes away from the two nearly naked women. "So, uh, where do you want me to perform?"

Olivia cooed, "Why don't you perform for us in my romp room."

"How 'bout the sauna?" Ruby responded. "I like it sweaty."

"The whirlpool," Olivia retorted. "The jets act like vibrators."

"My guest room."

"Better in my bedroom."

"Better in my mouth."

"Better in my ass!"

The women high-fived, laughing hysterically.

"In her ass. ... As if." Cyril rolled his eyes at Jacob, who was sweating profusely. "Well, look at you—nervous as a virgin prince at a prison rodeo. Hey cougars? Your friend here just shit himself a brick."

Ruby turned to Jacob, her voice inflecting a motherly tone. "Sweetie, just grab a chair and set everything up right here."

Locating a straight-backed deck chair, Jacob placed it on the koi pond's bridge facing his audience of three. "Ready?"

"Go for it, sweet cheeks." Olivia winked.

"I, uh ... okay. Good afternoon. My name is Jacob, and this," he opened his case, removing a Lisa Simpson dummy, "this is my friend, Lisa. Lisa, welcome to the show."

"Thank you, Jacob." He strained to reach the practiced higher octave, earning applause from Ruby. "Lisa, you told me earlier you had something important to discuss."

"Yes, Jacob. I wanted to talk to you about Mrs. Henderson."

"And who's Mrs. Henderson?"

"She's ... my vagina."

"Oh God!" Cyril burst out.

"I'm terribly worried about Mrs. Henderson. She's getting older and more wrinkled. Plus she's growing hair, only the hair isn't yellow like mine; it's dark and curly. And it itches. I'm afraid to scratch it in public."

"Because you're afraid people might think you're playing with it?"

"No. Because I'm afraid our Tea Party governor will pass some stupid law making it illegal for me to even own a Mrs. Henderson."

Cyril had tears streaming down his face. "You go, girl."

"To be honest, Lisa, I feel a little uncomfortable speaking to an eight-year-old about her vagina."

"That's exactly what my mother said. Fortunately, I found quite a few references to it on the Internet. I'm scared, Jacob."

"What are you so scared of, Lisa?"

"For one thing, high cholesterol. You should see how much meat Mrs. Henderson consumes in some of these videos. The poor dear is being turned into a sausage factory, which brings up a new term I just learned: *blow job*. Does the woman get paid to inflate the man's penis by blowing air into his pee hole? Does the expression, 'This job really blows,' relate to the pay scale or nature of the work?"

"All good questions, Lisa."

"Here's another. If a vegan is someone who only eats veggies, why isn't a lesbian called a vagan?"

"I don't know."

"Did you know the anagram for penis is snipe, a wading bird with a long, hard, stiff bill? Most snipes fall into the genus Gallinago, the closest relative being the woodcock. Pretty deep, huh, Jacob?"

"Very."

"I only ask because my vagina is made of wood. Simple logic dictates that I acquire the services of a wood cock to please Mrs. Henderson."

"Just don't get splinters in your mouth when you're polishing his wood."

"Oh my, I never even considered that! That job really would blow, no doubt pushing me toward a vagan lifestyle."

"You're a little girl, Lisa. You shouldn't be thinking about these things."

"It's unavoidable, Jacob. It's always on television."

"Really? Lisa, what TV show features such graphic sexual content?"

"*Family Guy.*"

🐾 🐾 🐾

Nancy briefed Spencer as she led the dog trainer through her home to the back yard. "Everything was fine until Sam saw that other dog. It was scary. I could barely restrain him."

"I'm not sure neutering him was the solution."

"I needed to set some boundaries."

"You probably had the collar positioned too low. No worries. I brought Sam a prong collar. You'll use it whenever you train him outside the home. As for Sam's aggressive nature around other dogs, you can fix that with a little training."

"Forget it. I'm paying you; you do the training."

"And what good would that do? Sam's your dog, not mine. His aggressiveness is a reflection of your own conscious nature."

"My nature? This is his previous owner's fault, not mine. I barely knew the dog before I let him move in. I mean—oh never mind."

"Let's put that little theory to the test, shall we?" Spencer opened the sliding glass door and greeted Sam. The German shepherd immediately calmed, its ears drooping, its tail low and tucked between its bandaged groin. The former military man leashed the dog and led him out front to his parked van. Nancy following them out.

"Sam, sit!"

The dog waited in a sit position while Spencer opened the back doors, sending Tilda into a frenzy. He opened the cage. "Tilda, heel!"

The female leaped down from her perch to take her place on Spencer's right. Moving Sam to his left, the trainer attempted to walk both dogs, the male Shepherd fighting to get to the female to sniff her behind.

"Sam, stop it. That's disgusting!" Nancy pushed her dog's snout away from Tilda's hind quarters.

"There's nothing to be distressed about. A dog sniffing another dog's genitalia is perfectly natural. Sam is merely attempting to obtain information from Tilda's scent."

"Maybe it's natural to you, but I don't want my dog sniffing another female's ass."

"As you wish." Spencer tugged on the choker chain, sending Sam scurrying back to his side of the trainer.

A minute later both dogs were walking steadily and happily, flanking Spencer.

"Well?"

"Well, obviously cutting off his nuts took away some of his aggressiveness. Besides, this was a golden retriever, not another shepherd. Not a *female* shepherd."

"Fine. We'll visit a dog park with Sam when he's fully mended. For now, know this: A dog will reflect its owner's state of mind. If you're confident, they'll remain submissive. If you're angry, the animal will register your tense feelings and become aggressive."

"What are you implying?"

"I'm not implying anything, Nancy. I'm stating a fact. The problem's not Sam; it's you."

46

Male Bonding

IT WAS HALF PAST TWO in the afternoon when the Volkswagen van exited the mansion's gated entrance, thoughts of a ménage à trois dancing in the driver's head.

Olivia Cabot had loved Jacob's performance. To celebrate his hiring, she and Ruby had insisted he join them for a swim then stay for lunch. With five hours to kill before he had to "return home from work," Jacob agreed.

He had followed Cyril down a stone path to the guesthouse to locate a bathing suit. Decorated like an erotic honeymoon suite, the single-floor dwelling opened to a large living room with dark shades and a projection-screen television that occupied an entire wall. A bookcase featured the latest movies as well as a shelf dedicated to adult videos. The bar was fully stocked, and the thick carpet littered with giant throw pillows. The master bath was done entirely in Italian marble and housed a bidet, sauna and a two-seat whirlpool. The bedroom was kept simple but titillating with its mirrored ceiling and king-size bed. A saddle-like woman's vibrator, called a Sybian, sat next to an exercise bike.

Cyril directed Jacob to a drawer filled with an assortment of men's bathing suits. "Choose whatever you like, not that it matters."

"What's that supposed to mean?"

"Wake up, my dear. The contest is on, and you're the quarry."

"What contest?"

Cyril smirked. "Hello? Five grand to the first one who sleeps with you. Ruby and Olivia play the game all the time—don't look so shocked; it's what rich bitches do when they're bored. So which one will it be?"

"Neither. I have a girlfriend."

"As long as you're not married, they don't care."

Jacob scoffed. "Dude, they can't force me to have sex. What are they gonna do? Rape me?"

"No, you'll go quite willingly. While we're in here picking out your bathing suit, Olivia's spiking your beer with ecstasy."

"Shit." Jacob peeked out the bedroom's Venetian blinds to see a servant wheel out a cart of sandwiches and drinks.

Cyril moved next to him to sneak a peek. "You'll sun and swim while they tease you. Then it's lunch on the veranda. Twenty minutes later you'll be back in here, humping two gorgeous middle-aged women with a combined age of 104."

"Jesus, Cyril, what do I do?"

"Don't you mean *who* will you do? Don't worry about the loser; she'll get double-or-nothing odds on the yacht."

"What if I leave now without doing either of them?"

"Assuming you still want that big pay day next Friday night, you'll need a good excuse. Wait, you drove, right?"

"So?"

"So while you take a dip in the pool, I'll remain here and stick my finger down my throat. I'll stagger back to the pool all sick and pale. You offer to drive me home. Don't even change. Just grab your clothes and a towel and G-O, go, bro."

"Dude, you'd do that for me?"

"No, but I'd do it for little Lisa Simpson. She stole my heart."

The plan had worked to perfection. Forty minutes

later, the Volkswagen was weaving its way through the streets of an upper-middle-class neighborhood in Boynton Beach, the driver parking curbside in front of a two-story home.

Jacob clenched his fist to bump knuckles with Cyril. "Thanks again, man. I owe you one."

"Then you won't mind coming in … just for a minute while I get the lights on. I know it sounds strange, but I get very nervous entering a dark house."

"Dude, it's only 3:20 in the afternoon."

"Yes, and it's dark inside."

Realizing Cyril was not budging, Jacob shut off the van's engine and exited the vehicle, escorting the gay man to the front door of his home.

Cyril keyed in, entered the two-story house and worked his way inside, flipping on light switches, illuminating a professionally decorated, brightly colored interior, not a speck of dust or a magazine out of place.

"Nice digs. See you next Friday night."

"Jacob, wait. Would you mind walking ahead of me to the den?"

"Why?"

"Because I feel funny about coming into an empty house. I'd feel better knowing an axe murderer wasn't waiting for me in the den."

"Dude, seriously, you should get a dog. And not one of those foofie white dogs either. Something with teeth."

"Mr. Jacob, I'm not going to change the way I look or the way I feel to conform to anything. I've always been a freak. I've been a freak all my life—"

"—and I have to live with that. I'm one of those people."

"You recognize the John Lennon quote?"

"Who wouldn't? The man was a game-changer. And don't feel bad. I suffer from a few minor phobias myself." Jacob led him past an oak staircase to a glass-enclosed family room.

Cyril situated himself on a stool by a wrap-around bar. "What are you drinking?"

"Nothing for me. I have to go."

"No you don't. You told me in the van that your girlfriend thinks you're at work. What time do you normally get home?"

"Around six."

"Then sit." Cyril reached for a plastic container shaped like a Hawaiian god and filled two glasses with its copper-colored liquor.

Jacob sat uncomfortably on the cushion of a wicker love seat. "Look, man, I appreciate you saving my ass today at Olivia's, but—"

"Bourbon?" Cyril shoved one of the glasses in

Jacob's hand then powered on the CD player. Music pumped softly from the wall-mounted speakers—Lady Gaga's *Born This Way*.

"Jacob, may I ask you a question, and please be honest. What do you think of me?"

Jacob's pulse raced. "What do you mean?"

"You've known me several hours now. Surely you must have formed some opinion."

"I dunno. You seem like a nice person."

"Did you know I was a homosexual?"

"I've got to go." Jacob stood.

"Sit down. You're going to finish your drink and answer my question. You owe me that."

"Yes, Cyril, I knew you were gay. All of Boca knows you're gay."

"Am I … attractive?"

"Okay, this conversation is now officially weird. I hate to leave you alone in an empty house, but I'm sure your boyfriend will be home from work any minute and—"

"No. Felipe won't be home until tomorrow morning." Cyril smiled, sauntering toward him.

Jacob retreated around the other back side of the love seat. "Oh no."

"What?"

"Oh my God."

"What is wrong?"

"You didn't really think that I'd do something like that!"

"Like what? Tell me."

"For God's sake, Cyril. Here we are: you've got me in your house; you give me a drink; you put on music; you tell me you're gay, which I already knew—which the entire world already fucking knew—then you tell me your boyfriend won't be home until tomorrow morning."

"So?"

"Dude ... you're trying to seduce me."

Cyril situated himself on a barstool, resting his bare right foot on the adjacent chair as he lit a cigarette, chuckling softly to himself.

"Aren't you?"

"Actually, I hadn't thought of it. You told me you had a girlfriend so I sort of took it for granted that you were heterosexual. Don't get me wrong; I'm certainly flattered."

Jacob felt the blood rushing from his face in embarrassment. "Cyril, I'm sorry for what I just said."

"It's all right."

"It's not all right. I'm just seriously fucked up right now."

"It's forgotten. Finish your drink. You'll feel better."

Jacob drained the bitter liquor. "What the fuck

is wrong with me? Ever since the Lehman Brothers disaster I just haven't been myself."

"It's okay."

"It's my future; I'm just worried about my future. Losing my job, depending upon Ruby to get me gigs, all while she tries to … you know—"

"Seduce you?"

"Yeah."

"Jacob, did Ruby mention I was a painter?"

"A painter? No, I don't think so." He inspected the walls. "Everything looks professionally finished."

"Not the walls, silly. I paint portraits. I'm really quite good. Perhaps I could paint you sometime."

"I've got to go." Jacob placed his empty glass on the coffee table and stood to leave.

"Will you stop with the seducing nonsense! I meant paint you with your girlfriend."

"Really?"

"Consider it an early Christmas present. Now would you like to see my work? "

"Yes. Yes I would."

"Come with me." Cyril led him out of the den back to the staircase.

"It's upstairs?"

"Yes. We hung it in the master bedroom."

"I really have to go."

"Jacob, what is wrong with you? I didn't take

you for such a homophobe."

"I'm not a homophobe. I just don't feel comfortable going into another dude's bedroom."

"Would you *like* me to seduce you?"

"What?"

"Now it all makes sense. I mean, what red-blooded heterosexual male wouldn't have given his right testicle to be in a ménage à trois with two beautiful women like Ruby and Olivia? Unless that redblooded heterosexual male was a closet homosexual."

"Cyril, I'm sorry about the whole seduction thing, but I swear to you I'm not gay."

"Prove it. Take a look at my artistic creation then go home to your girlfriend—assuming she really exists."

"Fine." Jacob followed Cyril up the steep wooden steps to the landing.

"The master bedroom is at the end of the hall. Go and take a look. I need to use the little boy's room."

Jacob waited for Cyril to shut the bathroom door before he walked down the hall to the master bedroom, feeling a bit lightheaded from the bourbon. He pushed the door open, stepping inside.

Gray carpet. Pink throw pillows. A white comforter covered the queen-size bed. A framed painting hung on the wall above the headboard—two naked men kissing.

"Yuck." Looking closer, Jacob realized it was a paint-by-numbers canvas.

The bedroom door slammed shut.

Jacob turned to find Cyril clad in a leather dominatrix slave outfit, his groin concealed behind a black thong, his nipple rings trailing matching straps. "Don't be nervous—"

"Oh … God."

"Jacob?"

"Get away from that door."

Cyril locked it. "I want to say something first."

"Jesus Christ."

"If you don't want to sleep with me now, I want you to know you can call me up any time you want, and we'll make some kind of arrangement."

"Let me out."

"I find you very attractive. I also wanted you to know that, well, I'm part of the wager."

"Wait … what?"

"The wager between Ruby and Olivia? I'm part of it."

"You set me up? For this?"

"Yes. But if you sleep with *me*, I'll split the winnings with you."

A car pulled into the driveway, screeching to a

halt.

"Oh, God, that's him!"

Jacob pushed his way past Cyril, unlocked the bedroom door and sprinted down the stairs as Cyril's boyfriend, Felipe, entered.

"Hey, Cyril, is that the *Scooby-Doo Mystery Machine* out front?"

Jacob squeezed past the leather-clad biker and raced out the door.

47

Dog Training the American Male
Lesson Eleven: Scent Training

SPENCER BOTCHIN SAT at his client's kitchen table, perplexed. "Nancy, if you tell me why you wish to train Sam to discriminate between scents, it would make my job a lot easier."

"If you must know, I want to make sure my boyfriend's not sleeping with his manager."

"I see." Spencer nodded, still a bit apprehensive. "Well then, we'll need an article of clothing or a personal belonging that carries the, uh, scent of the suspected female. You don't happen to have—"

"I do." Nancy reached inside her handbag and removed a plastic Ziploc freezer bag containing a pair of women's thong underwear. "They're fresh. Courtesy of a friend who works in the doctor's office the bitch frequents for her weekly labia tightening and boob enhancements and whatever the hell else she does to keep from looking her age."

Spencer inspected the undies. "The average human sheds thousands of skin cells every day, each cell carrying our own particular scent. What we're doing is training the dog to isolate one scent above another, in this case, the stench of this rival female on your boyfriend. To do that, we must first condition the dog so it realizes that making the right choice will result in a reward."

"Wait, am I conditioning my boyfriend to make the right choices, or the dog?" Nancy's cell phone rang. She checked the caller ID. "Would you excuse me a moment?"

"Of course." Spencer waited until she walked away before opening the Ziploc bag. The English gentleman stuck his nose inside, inhaling deeply. "Ahh, Caswell-Massey Lilac skin cream—my favorite."

Nancy took the call from her radio producer in her bedroom. "Trish, what's up?"

"That big W.O.M.B. party set for next Thursday afternoon? I just found out Olivia Cabot will be there. Soderblom too."

Nancy's heart pounded in her chest. "You think they've made their decision about the show?"

"The word around here is that they're still on the fence. Which means Thursday's meeting could be what decides whether we have a job next month. Lean in, baby!"

"I will. Thanks." She returned to Spencer, who was rubbing Ruby Kleinhenz's thong undies over six magazines. The dog trainer spread them out on the kitchen floor then slid open the back door and called for Sam.

The German shepherd hurried to him, tucking its tail as it recognized the alpha male.

"Alrighty then, Nancy. These six similar objects now carry the suspected home wrecker's pubescent stench. In step one of our scent training, Sam will smell the undergarment then be given the seek command. Every time he goes to a magazine, he'll be praised. In step two we'll repeat the exercise, having exchanged a scented magazine for an unscented one. We'll continue the drill, swapping a scented magazine for an unscented one until only one scented magazine remains. Depending upon Sam's progress, we'll then scent and hide a different object with the whore's stink trail on it, preparing him for the moment when you ultimately put Sam onto your boyfriend's scent trail—the dog determining if there is a match."

At precisely 5:57 p.m., Jacob Cope returned home,

having spent the last few hours guzzling coffee at a local donut shop. Regaining his sobriety, he had changed back into his shorts, tossing the wet bathing suit and towel in the donut shop's dumpster—his mind fantasizing about the afternoon that might have been with Ruby and Olivia Cabot.

"Nancy, I'm home."

He placed the newspaper on the shelf by the hall mirror and carefully removed his wiped-clean sandals, depositing them in the bedroom closet on their designated shoe-tree branch. His bladder ready to burst, he headed for the master bathroom, lifted the lid and seat, urinated, wiped the rim with toilet paper and flushed. He rinsed his hands. Bypassing the neatly folded hand towel on the rack, he used his shirt to dry his hands, thus maintaining the high performance score required for what he called "spontaneous sex."

Nancy was waiting for him in the bedroom when he emerged. "Shoes in their proper place, towel not destroyed … I'm impressed. How was work?"

"Stressful. I need to unwind."

"By unwind, you mean sex."

"Sex? Sure, I suppose sex would relieve my stress, but more importantly it would allow me to express the overabundance of love that I feel for you at this very moment."

"Yeah, yeah. Get naked, cowboy, we'll have a quickie."

"Works for me!" Jacob stripped in four seconds flat.

Nancy carefully removed her skirt and blouse. "Wait, you didn't say hi to your best friend. Sam, come!"

The German shepherd came bounding into the bedroom.

"Hey, boy! How are ya?"

"Sam, seek!"

Sam's demeanor suddenly changed, the dog sniffing at Jacob's legs, feet and testicles.

"Whoa, easy boy. I need those."

Satisfied with Jacob, the German shepherd sniffed the pile of clothes. Finding nothing, the dog left the bedroom to search the rest of the house.

"Seek?"

"Affection. It's important to hug your dog every day."

"And your sexy girlfriend." Jacob attacked Nancy, growling like a bear.

Nancy intercepted him with a passionate kiss, her hands groping his groin as she slowly dropped to her knees, kissing and inhaling his scent.

Jacob's eyes fluttered as she reached his hard-on.

"Chlorine?"

"Huh?"

"You smell like chlorine."

"I do?"

"Were you swimming today?"

"Swimming? I—no, I wasn't swimming. Why would I be swimming? That's crazy."

"Then why do you smell like chlorine? Normally when you come home you smell like onions."

Confess, lie, or deny—which one offers the best chance of still getting laid? "Wait, I know what it is. I went to the gym after work to check out a trial membership. While I was there I used the steam room."

"The steam room?"

"My lower back was killing me; I thought it might loosen things up. I was all sweaty after that so I took a shower. I didn't have any soap, so, yeah, I probably do smell like chlorine."

"That makes sense. Which gym?"

Jacob's hard-on shriveled into something resembling a large chickpea and two Fava beans. "Which gym? The one on the drive home from work."

Nancy eyeballed him, suddenly suspicious. "LA Fitness?"

"No. The other one."

"Gorilla Workout?"

"Maybe."

"How 'bout I call them to see if they registered you as a guest?"

"I wasn't a *guest* guest. I didn't work out or anything. I sort of snuck in."

"To use the steam room?"

"Exactly. Then I took a quick shower. It was spontaneous."

She located her clothes, getting dressed.

"Nance, what are you doing?"

"Suddenly I don't feel so spontaneous."

"Aw, come on—for real?"

"Tell me the truth, or it'll be a dog year before we have sex again."

"Fine. I got laid off."

"Jacob … when?"

"Last week."

"Then, every day you left the house for work you were lying to me?"

"It's just temporary. Hopefully I'll work again on Monday, but Mr. Patel said I'd have to switch to doing customer service calls on the road. I have to dress professionally, which means I need to buy dress shoes, which I don't have the money for."

"But you hate going into strangers' homes."

"I know, but we need the money, which is why I went swimming this afternoon."

"You were at Ruby's, weren't you."

"No. I was at some mansion in Manalapan trying out for a gig that pays five grand. I got the job, only the owner invited me to stay for lunch and a swim. Nothing happened. I didn't even stay for lunch. But I did jump in the pool."

"Naked?"

"No. The owner lent me a bathing suit."

"When's the gig?"

"Next Friday night."

"Does it pay well?"

"Yes."

Nancy stripped off her bra and panties.

"What are you doing?"

"Rewarding you for telling the truth. Now lie down and take a break while I see if I can resuscitate the little guy."

48

Blue Monday

THE MAN STANDING before Amir Patel was dressed in a button-down, white collared shirt, black pants, shoes and a matching tie. "Now at least you look like a professional. Sit down, Jacob."

"If it's all right with you, Mr. Patel, I'd rather stand. My butt is a little sore from, uh, working out."

"Then I'll make this brief. I'm giving you a second chance, but you're on probation. Your first repair call is with one of our most important clients. Zev Bourla owns the biggest advertising firm in Miami. They were hit by a computer virus early this morning. I told Zev I would send him our best man."

"You're sending Sanjay?"

"I'm sending you. Here's the address," Patel handed him a business card. "Remember, you are representing my company, so—"

"I know. Always be polite."

The drive south on I-95 was harrowing, the rush-hour traffic weaving from one congested lane to the next at seventy miles an hour, the construction lanes narrowed by concrete shoulders.

An hour after leaving Boca, Jacob arrived at the address in Miami, his nerves frayed, his fingernails chewed down to the nub.

The high-rise building was on scenic route A1A. The advertising firm occupied the entire sixth floor. Jacob was escorted to the president's office, a large corner suite divided into a desk and work area and a small conference table, its white Formica top cluttered with four-color glossy posters. The east wall offered a floor-to-ceiling view of the Atlantic Ocean, the turquoise and blue tapestry partially concealed behind Venetian blinds.

Zev Bourla greeted Jacob with a warm smile and handshake. The advertising executive was trim and in his late forties, with a youthful face and jet-black hair. The Brooklyn accent seemed perpetually upbeat. "So you're Amir's new superstar?"

"No, sir. The truth is, this is my first service call, and I'm a little nervous. Actually I'm very nervous. I don't do well in new environments with strangers

I've just met. That's not to say I can't fix your computer—I can. I just work better alone."

"Do you want me to have the building evacuated?"

"No sir."

"Good. So the computer's over there on my desk, and I'm just going to work over here at the conference table … if that's okay."

"Yes sir." Jacob entered the horseshoe-shaped work area. He carefully moved the leather swivel chair out of the way and knelt by the computer keypad. After typing several commands, he connected his own laptop to Zev's hard drive and began running a diagnostics program.

Several minutes of quiet caused Zev to look up from his work, the shy technician nowhere to be seen. "Jacob?"

"Down here, sir. I'm just waiting for the diagnostic program to finish running."

"You don't have to sit on the floor. You can use my chair."

"It's okay. I don't mind."

"How much longer will the diagnostics program take?"

"Another twenty-nine minutes."

"Twenty-nine minutes." Zev smiled, looking up at the ceiling. "Sent me another one, huh?"

"Excuse me?"

"Jacob, come on out from there and have a seat on the sofa."

Jacob crawled out from beneath the desk, walking over to the sofa as if he had a tail tucked between his legs.

"You seem nervous. Relax, I don't bite. I like you, Jacob. I wonder if you could keep an open mind, say, for the next twenty-nine minutes."

Stranger danger! Jacob felt his skin crawl. "I have a girlfriend, sir."

"I'm sure she's a very nice person."

"I meant I'm not gay."

"Mazel tov to your girlfriend. I simply wanted to share something with you—advice that has helped me over the years. Are you okay with that, or would you rather sit under the desk?"

"No, advice is cool."

"Good, because I love hearing myself talk. Jacob, everything in life is consciousness; the way in which we view things affects us both conceptually and on a physical level."

"If you say so."

"Let me give you an example. You told me that you don't do well in new environments with strangers. When your boss sent you to see me, the way in which you accepted the assignment created an energy field, either positive or negative. Do you follow?"

"No sir."

"I'm talking about being afraid. Fear is a weapon of mass destruction, Jacob. It creates all kinds of negative energy that can manifest in our physical lives."

"Being around strangers—it's not my only fear."

"All of us have fears: fear of dying, fear of catching a disease, fear of losing our jobs, fear of poverty—"

"Amputees."

"Amputees?"

"They freak me out. The water scares me, too—and heights. Maybe you could shut the blinds?"

"Of course."

"And elephants."

"Elephants? Do you come across a lot of elephants in your line of work?"

"Thank God, no."

"God … now there's an interesting subject. Do you believe in God, Jacob? A higher power?"

"I guess so."

"You guess so?"

"I'm not really into religion."

"Neither am I. I'm strictly talking God. Because

if you really believe in a creator, then what's to fear? Why don't you just pray, 'Hey, God, please no amputees riding elephants today. Hey God, I could use more money. Help me to lose weight, to live until I'm two hundred.' If you really believe in God, what are you afraid of?"

"Maybe I should check the computer."

"What you're afraid of, Jacob, is your own inability to connect with the higher power that you say you believe in. Feeling powerless, your life becomes overwhelmed with chaos. Chaos leads to fear. Fear turns you into a victim. Trust me. I've been in your shoes—a member in good standing at Victim.com. What I've learned is that our fears actually create what we're afraid of. It's always the guy who's afraid of amputees that runs into a VA hospital. The people who are afraid of flying—those are the ones who always find themselves on the planes experiencing turbulence. The reason is that fear manifests a negative energy field that brings the actual situation to life. When you're afraid or angry or anxiety-ridden, you've essentially shut yourself off from God. That's the negative energy at work. Instead of drowning in fear, focus your mind on swimming to the solution. It's these positive thoughts that will connect you to the power of the creator— the place where real miracles come from.

"Now, I know what you're thinking. You're thinking, 'Get me out of here. This guy Zev is some kind of nut.' But the information I'm sharing with you is not some hokey conceptual thought or theory. It comes from teachings that are four thousand years old.

"True story: When I was about your age, I was living a textbook life. Beautiful woman, successful business, big house, driving around in a sports car. … You name it, I had it. Then my son was born with an immune deficiency that was undiagnosable. I spent six months sleeping on a cot in Jackson Memorial Hospital while my infant was hooked up to machines to keep him alive. This went on for years. I felt my life spiraling out of control. I felt anger toward the doctors who had no answers. I found myself hating the creator: 'What did I do to deserve this, God? I'm not a bad person. I'm not a drug addict or an alcoholic. I'm not a criminal. Why won't you answer my prayers?'"

Jacob sat up, finding himself relating to the man's angst.

"When my son turned six, we attempted to enroll him in public school. Because he had spent the first years of his life in a hospital, he had never learned to crawl. When a baby doesn't crawl, it doesn't develop the strength or coordination to use its thumbs. As a result, my son couldn't dress himself. Because he wasn't around other children growing up, he couldn't speak properly. No school would take him, the administrators insisting he had to go to a special school for the mentally handicapped.

"Again, I was devastated: 'Why, God? Why is this happening?' I was lost, full of fear. A friend recommended I speak to a man who was teaching a course on spirituality. The teacher told me I wasn't a victim; in fact I was in total control, only I was looking at things all wrong. He explained to me the reason my son was placed in my life and exactly what I had to do to change the situation. He also told me that I had to shed my anger toward the doctors and school administrators and especially toward God, that there was no one to blame, that it was my anger that was causing me to block the creator's energy, what he called God's light. Well, normally my ego would have dismissed this teacher and his ridiculous advice, but at that point I was so desperate that I would have listened to anyone. And so I listened, and I began working on changing my consciousness. And slowly but surely, things began to get better, not just with my son but in my relationships, with my health, and with my career. Today my son is seventeen and in an excellent private school for normal kids where he's a straight-A student. We bike ride together, play sports together and he's become so physically coordinated that he plays the drums in a local band. Instead of being institutionalized, my son is enjoying a full, normal life, all because I changed my consciousness and, with it, my perception of the challenges given to me. Challenges are opportunities, Jacob. In the process of changing myself, I became someone who shared versus someone who received for the self alone."

"This ancient wisdom, is there a book I can read about it?"

"There are books. There are courses being offered at local centers and online. As a way of giving back, I offer a free introduction called Twenty-Nine Amazing Minutes."

Jacob smiled. "Twenty-nine minutes. That's why you wanted to talk to me."

"And why Patel sent you to service my computer, no doubt." Zev searched one of his desk drawers, retrieving a flyer with a Boca address.

"Kabbalah?"

"It's not what you think. Come by. Meet a few of the teachers. See if you like what you hear. Meanwhile, think of your life as a bank account— the more positive things you put in, the more you'll eventually get out. Just bear in mind that you may not reap the rewards you sow right away. If that were true, if we were rewarded immediately after we did something positive, then there'd be no such thing as free will, man's existence reduced to a dog performing tricks in order to receive a cookie from his master."

49

Dog Training the American Male
Lesson Twelve: The Shock Collar

NANCY ARRIVED HOME to find Spencer's van parked by the curb, the dog trainer seated on her front porch. As she approached, he shot her a look of consternation.

"Sorry I'm late. Traffic was a bitch."

"Bitch, as in female dog? I happened to listen to your show on Friday. Am I right in assuming you're advising your listeners to use dog training techniques to domesticate their men?"

Nancy blushed. "Well … sort of."

"Madam, I've spent my entire adult life working with both dogs and men, and, based on my experiences, the canine is the nobler creature. Unlike humans, they are loyal to a fault, their love is unconditional, their motives free of personal gain. A dog's reward for obedience is simply to have pleased its master."

"A man's reward for domestic obedience is to be pleased by his woman."

"Stop it. You're confusing the issue."

"I thought the issue was conditioning."

"You miss the point. Unlike men, dogs are receptive to training. What you're doing is using deception to overcome inherent laziness. The average American male would rather sit on the couch all day, scratch his balls and sleep."

"Sounds like Sam before I had him neutered."

"My point is free will. Man's first priority is to fulfill his own selfish needs. A dog's loyalty is instinctively to its pack."

"Would you consider a frat house a pack? Or a bar room filled with drinking buddies watching football? And correct me if I'm wrong, but isn't a sergeant-major the alpha dog of his platoon?"

"Yes, but—"

"Have you ever performed for a treat, Spencer? Ever peed on a tree or dry humped a woman's leg? Stuck you nose in her groin? Chased pussy? Do you enjoy having your butt scratched?"

"Well, who doesn't?"

"Be honest. Have you ever inspected your own bowel movement before you flushed?"

"What?"

"Ever pick a fight with another man just to prove who's tougher? Dug a hole at the beach? Howled at the moon?"

"Good God … I'm a dog."

"You and the rest of the heterosexual Y population. And, by the way, you should know that since I've been employing dog training techniques on my boyfriend, he's been more content, less anxious and he's lost weight. Even better, he's been more attentive to my needs."

"Does he really inspect his own poo?"

"He gives them names. Torpedoes fire cleanly out the hole. Floaters float. Chunkys have nuts. Corn fritters have—"

"Stop. I just ate Taco Bell for lunch."

"Ah, the Mexican toilet grenade."

"Good lord. Is this boyfriend of yours housebroken?"

"No, but he's getting there. So what's on today's agenda? This is a big week for me, and I could really use something new."

"I've got just the thing." From his jacket pocket Spencer produced a black dog collar with a small built-in, two-pronged metal device, along with a thumb-size, battery-powered control box.

"This is an electrical training collar. Far superior

to a choker or prong collar, the remote trainer gener-
ates a small charge that will shock the dog's central
nervous system, deterring any undesirable behavior
for up to half a mile away."

Nancy inspected the device. "It really shocks the
dog? That seems kind of cruel."

Now it was Spencer's face that reddened. "Cruel?
Nancy, cruel is deporting an illegal immigrant without
his wife and kids. Cruel is sending a National Guards-
man suffering from depression on a fourth tour of
Afghanistan. Cruel is abandoning a six-year-old boy
in the halls of the British Art Museum for two hours
while his father engages in a game of 'Hide the
Wienerschnitzel' with a young RAF nurse in a
janitorial closet. That, madam, is cruel!"

"Oh … kay."

Spencer took a long, deep breath, calming
himself. "My God, where did that come from? Don't
know why I regurgitated that old steak bone. I
suppose some things in our past are meant to remain
buried."

Nancy's eyes welled up with tears.

"Oh, dear, what have I done?"

"It's not you," she said, biting her lip. "My father
… on his death bed—he apologized for doing
something to me … revealing a secret he never
intended to tell me."

"Sweet Jesus, not another instance of sexual abuse."

"God, no. He apologized for leaving more money to my sister, Lana. He said it was done ... because she was *his*."

"I don't understand?"

"He was inadvertently telling me I was adopted. My parents never told me. I'm not even sure my sister knows. We're only a few years apart."

Spencer gathered her in his arms, holding her close as she sobbed against his chest. "A horrible way to find out. Still, it doesn't change anything."

Sam heard her from the backyard and started barking. "It changes everything, unless I keep it to myself. Ugh, listen to that stupid dog!"

"Clearly, he's attached to you. Even though you weren't his first owner, it doesn't matter. He still loves you just the same, as I'm sure your father did."

Nancy broke into fresh tears as she hugged him again.

"All right, enough. You're mussing my shirt up with snot."

She laughed. "Sorry. You're the only person I've ever told."

"And you're the first person I ever told about my father's adultery, excluding my wife and three therapists."

"You've been a good friend, Spencer Botchin."

"And you've been a wonderful surrogate daughter, Nancy Beach." He looked up as Sam's barking reached a frenzied state. "What say we go around back and teach your dog a few manners?"

❊ ❊ ❊

"I'm telling you, Helen, I've never seen Sam so responsive. By the third shock he was heeling at my side like a show dog."

"He didn't try to pull off the collar?"

"Spencer said the shock is instantaneous through-out the entire central nervous system. There's no way for the dog to pinpoint the source."

"Too bad we can't invent something like that for my husband."

"Why? I thought things were better." Nancy turned into the restaurant parking lot, waiting in line to valet.

"Vinnie treated a new patient the other day, a twenty-two-year-old platinum blonde named Tonja Davidson. Tonja, who happens to be a cheerleader with the Miami Dolphins, just loved her Gynnie Gusher so much that she recommended it to all her cheerleader friends—every fucking one of them. Vincent is like a horny teenager with a subscription to *Penthouse*, and all of Wanda's wicked love toys

335

won't get him to even look at me."

Nancy inched her car forward in the valet line. "Helen, I'm sure it's just a passing phase."

"Yeah, so is middle age. What's the ungrateful son of a bitch need with me when he's got naked centerfolds parading around his office like he was Hugh Hefner."

Nancy looked to her right as the valet approached, her eyes catching sight of a lighted billboard. As the man reached for her door, she accelerated out of line.

"What are you doing?"

"Let's skip lunch. I just had a crazy idea."

"Tell me. I like crazy."

She exited onto Glades road, pointing to the billboard:

CUSTOM ELECTRONICS
You design it—We build it!

The women entered the store an hour later, having bought two electronic dog training collars at the local pet supermarket. They were greeted at the jewelry counter by a short, gray-haired Israeli man in his sixties, who gazed lazily at them from behind coke bottle–thick glasses.

"Can I help you ladies?" he said, his accent heavy.

From a brown plastic shopping bag Nancy removed the two still-packaged electronic dog collars. "We'd like you to rig these electrical devices to a man's watch."

"Why? Are you teaching your doggy to tell time?"

"Can you do it or not?" Helen asked.

"Pay me enough, I can do anything. Where are the watches?"

Nancy and Helen looked at one another then searched the glass display case.

Nancy pointed to a large-faced watch. "That one for me."

The manager removed the watch from the case. "That's a dive master watch. Does your doggy like to scuba dive too?"

"The watch isn't for my dog. It's for my boyfriend."

"And you're training him to tell time? It's a little cruel, don't you think? You should try bribing him with treats."

"Get me one just like hers," Helen said.

"Two dive watches it is."

"When do you think they'll be ready?" Nancy asked.

"I don't know. I never designed a watch with a shocker before. A *faggala* once paid me to rig a spiked neck ring for his gerbil. Is your boyfriend a *faggala*?"

337

"No. Look, is there any way we could get the watches by Thursday? I have an important seminar that I'd like to bring mine to as show-and-tell. It could lead to a lot more business for you."

"What a blessing," the Israeli man said, the sarcasm dripping. "Okay, Wednesday it is. But you have to pay for the watches now."

Nancy reached for her purse, only Helen stopped her. "This one's on Vincent." She handed the manager a credit card.

He glanced at the name. "You're a doctor?"

"It's my husband's card."

"Your husband's a doctor, and he can't tell time? No offense, but I hope he's not the same *schmendrik* scheduled to remove my prostate next week."

50

Ruby Tuesday

JACOB WAS EN ROUTE to his second service call of the day when his iPhone reverberated in his shirt pocket. "Ruby, I can't talk now."

"Then just listen. I spoke to the booking agent who handles the Improv at City Place. If she likes you, she said she'll commit to two Tuesday nights a month beginning next week."

"Wow. That's excellent."

"She wants to see your act right away. Did you bring the Bush dummy with you like I advised you to do last week?"

"Yes, but—"

"Good. I'm going to text you the address."

"No need. I know where the Improv is."

"The tryout's not at the Improv. It's at a private home in Lake Worth. I'll meet you there in an hour."

"An hour? Ruby, I'm en route to a service call."

"That's a job; this is your career. See you in an hour."

Maybe it was the positive vibes coming from his meeting with Zev, but Jacob felt like his luck was improving. The private home was located in a gated community less than three miles from Jacob's second service call. Having fixed the client's computer in record time, he arrived only a few minutes late.

The driveway and adjacent curbs were lined with vehicles. Locating a parking spot, he gargled the remains of his bottled water to lubricate his throat then grabbed the case with the Bush dummy and hustled up the driveway.

At least I'll be performing to a real audience this time. He rang the bell.

The door opened, revealing Ruby Kleinhenz—who was wearing a squirrel outfit—her long gray wig adorned with cute squirrel ears, her arms and legs in furry gray sleeves, paws and boots. What was not concealed was her bare mid-section and buttocks, the revealing gray thong undergarment quite sexy.

Jacob stared at her, baffled and strangely aroused. "Ruby?"

"You're late. Hurry up. We need to get you

dressed."

"What are you talking about? What is all this?"

She dragged him inside, where he caught a glimpse down the hall of a dozen guests—all wearing furry animal costumes.

"It's a furry party," Ruby explained, dragging him inside a guest bedroom. "We need to get you onstage before the furry festivities begin."

"What the heck is a furry?"

She pushed him down onto the bed, tearing off his shoes and socks. "Furries are people who dress up like anthropomorphic animals. It's part fetish, part hidden persona. They're quite a creative bunch. Just go with the flow. And they like to throw parties, so take this seriously." She unbuckled his belt, pulling off his dress pants.

"Hey!"

From an open closet she removed a brown and white puppy suit hanging on a hook. "Put this on."

Jacob slid his legs into the suit. "Wow, it's soft inside."

"You need a cute furry name."

"Rock-a-Poochie."

Ruby smiled. "Where did that come from?"

"It was my favorite stuffed animal when I was growing up. What's your name?"

"I don't have one. I'm just dressing like this to

341

help you get the gig."

"Come on, you need a name. How about Nutcracker Jones."

"Fine. Now stick your head on, grab Bush and kick some furry ass."

There were fifteen of them seated around the living room and lying in colorful clusters on the floor. Most were in full costume (fur-suitors), a few of the more provocative entries revealing thong underwear or jock straps. There were tigers and a sexy Siamese cat, a bear named Snuffy, a red fox and his lamb, a pink pony, a black and white cow (complete with udder), a purple beaver and an assortment of dogs, each furry evoking the noises of their particular species.

Men and women, gays and straights … *who could tell?* All Jacob knew is that it was his most receptive audience ever.

Feeling giddy, he decided to end with an animal joke. "Mr. President, what's the most frightening experience you ever faced? Was it 9/11? The shock and awe of the Iraqi invasion?"

"There were two experiences that stand out, Rock-a-Poochie. The first was when I choked on that damn pretzel. Saw my life flash before my eyes

… frightening. But the scariest experience had to be when I was lost in the woods back when I was governor of Texas."

"What happened?"

"Gave a speech on illegal immigrants, got lost on the drive back to the mansion, and ran out of gas. Had to walk. Figured I'd take a shortcut and ended up in the woods. I was lost for three days—hungry, exhausted. In the middle of a dark and stormy night I came upon a farmhouse. I knocked on the door and a farmer and his wife answered. 'Please,' I said, 'I've been lost in the woods for days. I haven't rested. I haven't eaten. If I could just rest in your barn for the night …'

"The farmer said, 'Nonsense. We're good Christians. You'll sleep in our guest room tonight.' Well, they took me in, fed me and then I fell asleep in their guest room. When I woke up the next morning, the farmer's wife cooked me a great breakfast. Good people. Solid Republicans."

"You must have been very grateful. How did you thank them? Money? Political favors?"

"Better. See, a lot of people don't know this about me, Rock-a-Poochie, but I can talk to animals, and they talk to me. Just like God."

The furries went crazy.

"See that? Anyway, I told the farmer and his wife

about my gift, and then I went outside to talk to the animals—you know, to get the inside scoop. First I spoke with the horse." The woman in the pink pony outfit applauded. "Then I had a few words with the cow." The man in the cow suit stood and bowed. "Last, I spoke with the sheep." The woman in the lamb furry high-fived her boyfriend, the fox. "When I was done I came back inside to deliver the news.

"'Folks,' I said, 'I spoke to your animals. There's good news and bad news. I spoke to the horse, and the horse really likes you, only you recently switched from a round bit to a square bit, and its hurting his gums. So you need to switch back.' The farmer looked at me, amazed.

"'Next, I spoke to your cow. The cow likes you, too, but she needs to be milked twice a day, not once.'

"'Amazing,' the farmer said.

"'Now, I spoke with the sheep—'

"'Hey, those sheep are liars!'"

The group burst into laughter and baaing sounds, clapping with their fur-covered paws.

Jacob bowed, the Bush dummy waved good-bye and then he hurried off to change in the guest bedroom.

Ruby was waiting in her squirrel outfit, her thong undergarment gone. She slammed the door behind him, locking the door.

"Ruby, wait—"

"I'm tired of waiting. I want to feel your furry groin pushing up inside me."

"Really? This costume has a fly?"

"Let me show you." She reached for his dog suit.

"Ruby, I can't."

"Why not? Don't you find me attractive?"

"I do, but I have a serious girlfriend."

"You're not listening. I don't want to have sex with Jacob. I want to do it doggy style with Rock-a-Poochie."

"Oh. I guess that's okay."

She reached for his furry groin. Locating the Velcro flap, she was interrupted by a knock on the bedroom door. "Ruby, you need to move your car. The mayor can't get out."

"Move it for me. I'm busy!"

"Where's your keys?"

"Find my purse. Never mind—I hid it. Just wait a second. I'll be right out." She located the thong undergarment and snapped it around her waist and buttocks then turned back to Jacob. "Stay."

🐾 🐾 🐾

Kneeling to his groin, she reached beneath the bed, gathered up his black dress pants, socks and shoes, then exited the bedroom.

"Jesus, Jakester, what the hell are you doing?"

Jacob turned to face the Bush dummy, which was leaning back against a pillow. "It's okay, sir. Rock-a-Poochie will give her a quickie, and then we can be on our way."

"Shit-for-brains, there is no Rock-a-Poochie. There's just you and your hard-on. Now make like a dog and flee before she comes back and squirrel-fucks you to death."

Suddenly in a full-blown panic, Jacob stuffed the Bush dummy in its case and opened the door, only to see Ruby hurrying back through the crowded hallway.

He shut the door and locked it.

Ruby tried the knob. "Rock-a-Poochie, open the door. It's Nutcracker Jones, come to lick your nuts."

"Ruby, it's me, Jacob. I have to get back to work. Can I please have my pants?"

"Not until you handle our unfinished business. Now open the door or I'll claw my way in."

He backed away and searched the room. Hearing her work the lock, Jacob unlocked and opened the window. He grabbed the Bush dummy and began to climb out only to lose his balance in the fur shoes and fall out the open first-floor window onto a hedge, taking the screen with him.

Gathering himself, still dressed in full costume, he hurried to the company van. But then he realized

the keys were in his pants. "Shit, shit, shit, shit. …
Wait—there's a spare key in the glove box!"

He tried the doors—locked.

Contemplating the passenger window, he
punched it, his furry paw offering nothing more than
a glancing blow. Looking around, he located a white-
painted round curb stone.

"Mr. President?"

*"Smash it, Fido! You can fix the window a lot easier
than you can fix this with Nancy."*

Gripping the rock, he heaved it at the window,
shattering it and setting off the alarm.

"Oh hell." He reached inside to unlock the
passenger door as a dozen costumed figures ventured
out the front of the house to check on their vehicles
and then scurried back inside as a police car accelerated down the street, screeching to a halt behind
the van.

Two armed cops leaped out of the squad car,
aiming their weapons.

"Freeze, fur-ball!"

"Paws in the air!"

"Don't shoot! It's my vehicle. I locked my keys
in the glove box."

"Let's see a license and registration."

"The registration's in the glove box with the
keys. My license is in my wallet, which is in my

347

pants, which is in that house. The squirrel has it and won't give it back unless I fuck her."

The two cops looked at one another and laughed. "This is better than the guy we arrested last month for murdering his Yoko Ono sex doll."

"Yeah, that was me."

"Jacob?" One of the cops pulled the dog head off, revealing the familiar sweat-laced, bearded face.

"Son, I don't know whether to arrest you or party with you."

"Please guys, can you just get my wallet and clothes back from the squirrel."

They turned as Ruby approached. She had dressed into her street clothes and was carrying his clothing. "Jacob, you bad dog, you left this inside.

She handed him his stuff, kissed him on the lips, then climbed inside a black Porsche 911 parked across the street and drove away.

51

Dry Hump Wednesday

OLIVIA CABOT VALET PARKED her silver Mercedes SLR McLaren at West Boca hospital, grabbed the ticket from the attendant and marched into the visitor's lobby.

A uniformed older black man greeted her with a smile. "Morning ma'am."

"It's afternoon. The patient's name is Cabot."

The security guard scanned his computer monitor. "I have a Truman Cabot. Room 316, bed B."

"That's him. Any chance he died over the last hour?"

"Excuse me?"

"Never mind." She handed him her driver's license.

The guard typed in her information and snapped her picture, which spewed out of the side of his machine as a guest pass sticker.

349

"Take the elevators on the left and—"

Olivia pushed past him before he could finish.

❧ ❧ ❧

She had gotten the phone call two hours earlier. When the man had identified himself as the physician treating her father at West Boca hospital, her heart had raced with adrenaline.

"Ma'am, we need you to come down to the hospital and sign a few papers."

"If it's a 'To Not Resuscitate' order, I can give you a fax number to expedite matters."

"That won't be necessary."

"You mean he's already dead?"

"What? God, no. I'm calling because he listed you as an emergency contact."

"The emergency—was it a stroke? A heart attack?"

"It was a circumcision."

"Sorry, I didn't hear you. It sounded like you said circumcision."

"Yes ma'am."

"Is this a joke?"

"You weren't aware your father was admitted Sunday morning to have his foreskin removed?"

"You must have the wrong Cabot. My father's name is Truman. He'll be eighty-three years old on Friday."

"Truman Cabot. Born March 7, 1933."

"This is insane. Why the hell would he be getting his dick flap removed at his age?"

"Comfort, cleanliness, a religious conversion—it's really none of my business. But we need you to come down as soon as possible."

Olivia Cabot stepped off the elevator onto the third floor, quickly finding her way to Room 316. The first bed was occupied by an older gentleman with a thick Italian accent who was receiving instructions from a Jamaican nurse from behind a partially enclosed curtain.

"Mr. Coglioni, your colonoscopy is scheduled for 3:00 p.m. You need to finish your prep."

"*Mi fa cagare!*" (It makes me poop.)

"I'm setting this bedpan by your bed so it'll be close. Do you know how to use it?"

"*Va fungool.*" (Fuck off.)

Olivia walked past the closed curtain to the next bed. Her father was sitting up, arguing with a male nurse.

"Sir, I can't discharge you until I change your bandage."

"And I told you, I don't want another man touching my Johnson! Olivia, tell him."

351

"I'm his step-daughter. Would you give us a few minutes?" She waited until the male nurse left. "Truman, what the hell? Have you lost your mind?"

"Ah, here we go. I told the doctor not to call you, that I already had a ride home. But did the son-of-a-bitch listen to me? Hell no."

"Why on earth would you get a circumcision?"

"What do you care?"

"You're eighty-two years old. What's next? Tattoos? A tongue piercing?"

"If it makes my bride-to-be happy."

"Your bride? You're getting married again?"

An explosion of diarrhea echoed from behind the drawn curtain, followed by a gag-inducing smell as Mr. Coglioni emptied his bowels into the bedpan.

"Hey, Luigi, do that in the goddam bathroom!"

"Shaddup and go fuck your *goomah*!"

"She's my daughter, not my girlfriend, you dumb guinea wop."

"*Finocchio*! I hope your new Jew-dick falls off."

"And I pray to my lord and savior that you shit out your lower intestines."

"Hey Truman, I'm'a gonna come over there and'a bare ass'a your pillow."

Cabot cracked up laughing. "I love this guy."

"Truman, who's the woman?" Olive asked.

"Her name's Carmella, and she stole my heart."

"Jesus, not another clone of mom."

"And what if she is? I miss your mother. God took her from me too soon."

"How long have you two been seeing one another?"

"We haven't dated yet. I had to get circumcised first."

"Truman, you are not marrying this woman. I forbid it."

"Try and stop me."

"I'll do one better: As CEO of Cabot Enterprises, I'll cut off your money before I allow you to will it to this gold digger."

"Ah, horseshit. As long as I'm alive I still own 51 percent of the corporation."

"Unless I have a doctor declare you incompetent. Getting circumcised at your age without telling anyone sure qualifies."

"She's a Jew. They liked the fat trimmed!"

Luigi let loose with another bowel movement. "Hey, Truman, that one was'a for your Jew *goomah*."

"You son of a bitch!" Truman Cabot leaped out of bed, yanking out his IV line as he pushed his way through the curtained partition and attacked his roommate, knocking him off the bedpan.

Nancy exited the hospital elevator. Seeing Cabot's physician speaking to a police officer, she joined him at the third-floor nurses' station. "Dr. Maharaj, how's Mr. Cabot doing?"

The Indian surgeon turned. "He's gone."

"What?" Nancy's heart skipped a beat. "When? How?"

"About two hours ago. I tried to reach you."

"I was in the middle of a live radio show. You told me the procedure was safe!"

"It is."

"Then how did he die? Did you hit a vein?"

"No, no—he's not dead. I meant he already left the hospital."

"Oh God, thank you. Wait, who drove him home?"

"His step-daughter."

The tension headache announced itself behind Nancy's right eyeball. "Was she in a good mood when she left?"

"Actually, she was quite furious. She left without signing the discharge forms."

"Oh, shit."

"Yes. How did you know?"

"How did I know what?"

"That her dress was covered in diarrhea."

"Why was she covered in diarrhea?"

"Mr. Cabot got into a fight with another patient. The nurse said it reminded her of two angry monkeys at the zoo tossing feces at one another. Here, you need to give this to your friend." He handed her several pages of papers.

"What's this?"

"A prescription for pain medication, along with his postsurgical instructions. It's important he wait at least a week before taking any more Viagra, or he'll tear loose his stitches. Ms. Beach, where are you going?"

Nancy ignored the Indian physician, rushing to catch the elevator.

🐾 🐾 🐾

It was four o'clock by the time Truman Cabot stepped out of his apartment. Freshly showered, he was dressed in loose-fitting cream-colored dress pants and a black golf shirt.

The bandage around his penis had been removed, his trimmed "unit" feeling airy and only a touch sore. It didn't matter. This evening was just a tease to let his goddess know that he had transformed himself for her—that he had staked his claim in her future.

He pressed the button to summon the elevator, checking his watch. Having taken the Viagra fifteen minutes earlier, he calculated the arrival time of his anticipated four-hour "woody," wondering if his lack of foreskin would increase its perceived length.

Carmella Cope was enjoying the cool, late-afternoon seventy-three-degree temperatures outside with her "entourage." The four women were dressed in their standard recreational attire (tennis skirts, sweaters, hats and sunglasses), competing in a heated game of two-on-two horseshoes.

Sylvia Krawitz underhand-tossed her horseshoe to the opposite pit, knocking loose Carmella Cope's leaner, rendering it dead. "Take that, C.C."

"Kiss my ass, you old bitch."

Sylvia tempered her laugh as she spotted Truman Cabot crossing the putting green, making a beeline for them. "Don't look now, but here comes Richie Rich. Did you hear why he checked into the hospital?"

"I heard."

"He looks like he means business."

"Follow my lead, Sil. Let's screw with the horny old fart's mind."

"Afternoon, ladies."

Carmella offered a Cheshire cat smile. "Well, if it isn't little Lord Fauntleroy. I hear you were in the hospital getting castrated."

"Yes—wait, no. The balls are still there. I was circumcised. I did it for you, Carmella."

"How thoughtful. Wasn't that thoughtful, Sylvia?"

"Very thoughtful. Naturally, you had it done by a mohel."

"Of course. Wait, what's a mohel?"

"A mohel is a Jewish man specifically trained to remove the male foreskin."

"I, uh … am sure he was Jewish. Absolutely."

"What's his last name?"

"Mah … stein. Abraham Mahstein. That Jew enough for you?"

"Sylvia, your late husband was a mohel. Isn't a mohel required to suck on the wound until it stops bleeding?"

"According to Talmudic law."

"No man sucked on my wound!"

"How do you know?" Carmella asked. "Didn't they put you to sleep?"

"Yes, but it wasn't a religious procedure. The surgeon stitched the wound."

Carmella shrugged. "If you didn't get snipped by a mohel, it doesn't count, does it, Sylvia?"

"Not in our book. Of course, it's not too late. If you could find a Jewish man willing to perform the ceremony …"

Cabot looked pale. "But the wound's almost healed."

Carmella shook her head. "According to Jewish law, it's not officially healed until the stitches are removed. Thank God it's not too late, eh, Syl?"

"Thank God," Sylvia said, turning her head while biting her lip to keep from laughing.

"Just what are you ladies suggesting? That I allow a man to—to suck on my Johnson?"

"Of course not," Carmella said. "It has to be a Jewish man. Syl, who could we get to suck Truman's Johnson?"

"What about Sol?"

"Wouldn't work. Truman's Catholic. Sol keeps Kosher."

"Is Bruce Jewish?"

"Why, yes he is. And he's experienced."

"The fag from New York?" Cabot felt ill. "No … no way, I couldn't—"

Sylvia winked at him. "Not even for a hot date with C.C. Rider?"

Carmella shot her friend a look to kill.

Cabot's eyes widened. "Friday night on my yacht. It's my birthday."

Sylvia nudged her friend. "Come on, C.C., one date for Truman's circumcision cleansing."

"How will we know if he actually went through

with it?"

"Truman can take a video."

"Oh no. No videos!"

"All right. How about Carm and I watch the ceremony?"

"Two of you, huh? Been a while since I did a—uhhh!" Truman Cabot doubled over in pain as a burning, stabbing sensation lanced at his enlarging penis.

"Is that a yes?"

"*Ahhh! Ahh!*"

"What's wrong with him?"

"Hurts … bad!"

Sylvia pointed. "Look, Carm. He's pitching tent."

Carmella inspected the kneeling man's crotch closer. "Is that blood? Hey Truman, I think your dick's bleeding."

Sylvia shook her head. "This is what happens when you don't use a mohel."

The ladies' two teammates approached from the opposite horseshoe pit, the fallen senior attracting a small crowd.

"Jesus God, my dick's on fire!"

"What did he say?" squawked Esther Rabinowitz.

"He said his *schmeckle's* on fire," her husband, Sol, yelled back.

"He's on fire? Quickly, everyone—get him into the pool!"

Seven senior citizens (two with walkers) grabbed Truman Cabot by his arms and legs and half-carried, half-dragged the screaming millionaire across two shuffleboard courts before tossing him into the shallow end of the pool.

52

Shocking Thursday

NANCY BEACH STOOD at the podium and looked out at a multitude of women, the small auditorium filled to capacity.

"Good afternoon ladies … and gentleman," she nodded to Pete Soderblom, who was seated next to Olivia Cabot in the third row, "and welcome to this special afternoon edition of W.O.M.B.—Women Overcoming Male Bondage. Before we begin, let's stand in unity and recite our pledge."

Five hundred and seventeen women stood. "Knowledge is power. With power I enlighten my soul. With knowledge I begin my rebirth, emancipating myself from my male bondage." Palms over their faces, the women slowly pushed their noses through their separating hands, their heads birthed from their imaginary vaginas.

"And we are reborn in unity, leaning forward out

of society's womb—excellent. Ladies, today's agenda is packed with excitement, including the debut of a new line of Y training apparel from Wanda Jackson, owner of the Sex Emporium. But before we begin, I'd like to discuss a hormone responsible for every conflict since Cain slew his brother Abel, a hormone that has led to our near financial collapse, drug wars, political corruption, gang violence, the poisoning of the environment, the energy crises, a hormone called *testosterone*. It's testosterone that fuels the male ego; it's what caused Neanderthals to club their mates and the sole reason the Catholic Church and Congress are nothing but old boys' clubs reeking in scandal.

"Ladies, it's not enough that our gender 'lean in' when it comes to opportunities at the workplace. In order to truly change society, we must become masters of testosterone, not by being more aggressive but by reconditioning the male ego by redirecting testosterone the way a judo wrestler uses his opponent's force against him. This afternoon, I'm going to provide you with a few tools to become judo masters, but before I do, I'd like to introduce you to someone who is very important to the success of my radio show, our station's programming director, Mr. Peter Soderblom."

The crowd applauded politely. Pete waved from

his seat.

"Pete, can you join me at the dais for a moment? I have a small gift of appreciation I'd like to present to you."

Pete glanced at Olivia, who shrugged. With a hop in his step, he joined Nancy at her podium. "Morning, ladies. By the way, I never clubbed my wife. Slipped her a roofie—just kidding."

Pete snorted a laugh and then stopped when he saw the women's expressions of disgust.

"Peter, for being such an inspiring Y in my life, I'd like to give you this specially handcrafted dive watch, with my gratitude." She handed her programming director the watch.

"Thanks. I don't really dive, but—"

"Go on, put it on."

Pete adjusted the watch to fit his left wrist. "It's nice. Got some weight to it." He waved to the crowd and then headed back to his seat.

"Pete, before you go, I need a volunteer to play the role of my significant Y in a quick W.O.M.B. exercise. Since you're the only male present—"

"What about Juan Carlos?" Lynnie yelled out from the first row, pointing to the slight five-foot-four Mexican. "And here's some good news, ladies: this baby-making machine is still on the market. Check out the size of his fingers."

Nancy ground her teeth. "Thanks, Lynnie, but for this exercise I really wanted Pete."

"Ah, go on; let the little guy handle it." Pete headed back to his seat.

"Stay!"

As if struck by an invisible bolt of lightning, Peter Soderblom flailed wildly in the aisle, his blonde hair standing on end.

The female audience gasped, confused yet engrossed.

"What … the … hell?"

Nancy feigned innocence, the palm control concealed in her left hand. "My goodness, are you all right?"

"Felt like I stepped on a live wire."

"Well, thank you for agreeing to help us out. Ladies, can we give our volunteer a warm round of applause?"

The audience clapped. Pete waved, unsure.

Nancy pointed to Trish, who was supervising the setup of a small round table, checkered table cloth and chairs. Two chairs, side by side, had already been placed to the left of the podium. "Ladies, in this first exercise, Peter will play my husband, the two of us en route to a local restaurant for dinner. First we'll pretend to be in the car." She pointed to the two chairs facing the audience. "Then we'll enter the restaurant, the outside door represented by those two orange cones, at which time we'll seat ourselves at the table. Ready, Pete?"

"Seems kind of stupid, but whatever."

Nancy led him to the two side-by-side chairs. "Here's our family car. Pete, you're driving, so you sit in this seat on the left. Go on, sit down. Now I'll sit next to you, and you pretend to drive."

The programming director rolled his eyes, his hands maneuvering an invisible steering wheel. "Do I need to make engine noises? *Rrrm rrrm.*"

"And we've arrived. My husband parks the car. He shuts off the engine—shut it off—and we exit the vehicle to walk to the entrance of the restaurant."

Pete stood. He pretended to close the car door then walked over to the orange cones, leaving Nancy seated in the vehicle.

ZAP!

Pete's limbs flailed wildly as he fell backward on his buttocks.

The women whooped and hollered.

"What the hell was that?"

"Honey, you forgot to open my car door for me. Can you do that now, please?"

"Huh?"

"The car door." She nodded to her invisible passenger door.

Still a bit woozy, Peter pretended to open the door for Nancy while his eyes searched the floor by the podium for a loose wire.

"Thank you, honey. Shall we go inside and eat?" Nancy led him to the orange cones, waiting for him to open the invisible door.

Feeling ridiculous, Pete feigned opening the door, the audience applauding.

He nodded, a stupid half-grin creasing his face.

"Oh look, honey, there's an open table." Nancy walked ahead of him to the table and then waited by her chair.

Pete pulled his own chair out and sat.

ZAP!

He went down again, moaning on the floor in pain.

"What did my husband forget to do, ladies?"

"*Pull out your wife's chair*!"

Pete looked up, bewildered.

Nancy removed his dive watch and held it up to the audience. "Introducing the Y training device, a combination electrical dog collar and men's dive watch. As you can see, the controls are easily concealed in the palm of my hand, and the electrical charge can't be traced back to the watch. I had the intensity set on high, but there are two lower settings. I'm also hoping to have a reward setting that stimulates the Y's genitalia."

The women stood and applauded, many yelling out, "Where can I buy one?"

"Sorry, ladies, this is just a prototype. I have to speak with someone about mass-producing them."

Wanda Jackson took over the lecture twenty minutes later, her five college-age female employees modeling a line of sexy lingerie, corsets and bustiers. No longer in pain, Peter Soderblom watched from the third row, thoroughly enjoying the show.

Olivia Cabot joined Nancy in the corridor outside the lecture hall. "Very impressive, Dr. Beach. You're original, creative and your audience loves you. I'm renewing your show for two years, with a 30 percent bump in salary. We'll include a syndication clause. I think we can open markets in New York, Philly and LA."

"Oh my God." Nancy teared up.

"I also want to talk to you about setting up a partnership to manufacture those watches, along with an exclusive line of Y training items."

"That would be amazing."

"The dive watch—may I?"

"Huh? Oh yes, of course." She handed Olivia the dive watch and its palm control.

"Simple yet effective. We'll have to refine the design of course, make the watches more fashionable."

"Of course."

"I'm hosting a party tomorrow night on our yacht. Why don't you join me as my guest?"

"That would be amazing."

"Be at the Bridge Hotel dock in Boca at eight o'clock. It's black tie."

"I'll be there. Thank you so much."

"Oh, would you mind if I borrowed the watch for the weekend?" Olivia winked. "I have a new young stud that needs to be corralled."

Nancy smiled. "Keep it. It's yours. Give the young stud a jolt from me."

🐾 🐾 🐾

Helen Cope entered her husband's workplace, disturbed to find a pair of long-legged, well-endowed, Miami Dolphin cheerleaders occupying the waiting room—a peroxide-blonde and an auburn-haired black girl, both with bare midriffs and short skirts.

Two twits twittering away on their iPhones.

Nurse Kim opened the door separating the waiting area from the exam rooms. "Tina Owens?"

The black cheerleader stood. "That's me. Only I'm just here for my Vanilla Swirl."

"Before you get your Gynnie Gusher, Dr. Cope needs to examine you. Wait in Exam Room 3." The nurse held the door open for the patient and then spotted Helen. "Hi Mrs. C. Are you here socially or for an exam?"

"Exams I get at home. I brought the Muffin King his dinner. Tonight's his late night." She held up the deli take-out bag.

"He's pretty busy. I can take that for you."

"That's all right. I'll just put it in his office fridge and be on my way." Helen entered the treatment area, pausing at the receptionist desk to say hi to the staff.

An elderly woman entered the waiting room and signed in at the front desk. "Edna Dombrowski. I have the 4:15."

The receptionist broke from her conversation with Helen. "I need your insurance card and a photo ID."

The sixty-three-year-old divorcée from New York extracted the items from her purse. "Nurse, how long do you think Dr. Cope will be? I have a dinner date in an hour—a realtor I met on JDate."

"There are two patients ahead of you. Go on and have a seat. We'll call you back as soon as we can."

Helen finished her conversation with the receptionist and then headed down the corridor for Vincent's office. She walked past several closed exam room doors, pausing as she heard a girl giggling inside Exam Room 4, followed by her husband's voice.

"We never had cheerleaders who looked like you when I played college ball. If we had, I probably would have turned pro."

The door opened, and Dr. Cope exited, leaving a gorgeous wavy-haired brunette on the table, her hiked-up dressing gown exposing a tan, hairless vagina.

"Vincent Thaddeus Cope!"

Vin clutched his heart, dropping the patient file. "Jesus, Helen. Are you trying to give me a heart attack?"

"You were flirting."

"No, I was speaking to one of my patients."

"Then why are you so nervous?"

"I'm not nervous. I wasn't expecting you … standing there, lurking in the hallway."

They turned as Nurse Kim led the peroxide blonde into Exam Room 6, the twenty-three-year-old cheerleader winking at the red-faced gynecologist as she sauntered by.

Vin casually turned back to his wife, his mind racing for something to say that might diffuse the situation. "What's in the bag? Dinner? Smells great. You smell great."

"Office. Now!"

He followed her into his private office and closed the door behind him. "Don't get mad."

"Why should I be mad?"

"You shouldn't be mad."

"I'm not mad."

"Then why are we in my office?"

"I just wanted a moment alone with my husband to give the man I love an early birthday present."

"Birthday present?" *My birthday's not for five months. Probably tickets to a show she wants to see, or a cyanide capsule.*

Helen reached into her handbag and removed a small jeweler's box, the second-hand velvet packaging scuffed. "Happy birthday, honey."

Vin checked the box for a trip wire before opening it. "Wow, a dive watch." *Jesus, what the hell am I supposed to do with this cheap piece of shit? Looks like she bought it in a Vegas pawn shop.* "Honey ... this is awesome."

"Try it on."

"Absolutely. Are you kidding?" He removed his $19,000 titanium Piaget Polo timepiece with the luminescent hour markers and sapphire back and strapped on the $159 plastic and rubber dive watch.

"It's a beauty. Thanks, hon. What, no card?" Vin forced a laugh, giving her a quick hug as he rolled his eyes behind her back.

Nurse Kim opened the door. "Sorry to interrupt. I've got you in Room 4 next. Get this: the blonde in Room 6 wants to discuss whether she needs birth control for anal sex."

Sweat beads broke out across Vinnie's upper lip. "Jesus, Kim, can't you see my wife and I are sharing an intimate moment?" He leaned over and French-kissed Helen, who pushed him off her, gagging. "Go. Examine your cheerleader. I'll see you at home."

Helen left Vincent's office, pausing outside Exam Room 4. The door was ajar, revealing the black cheerleader's nude body. The exhibitionist had her back to the door, completely oblivious, as she casually turned her dressing gown inside-out, confused over which opening to place her arms.

Helen slammed the door shut. Ignoring good-byes from the check-out nurse and receptionist, she exited to the waiting room as Nurse Kim called out, "Edna Dombrowski?"

"Right here."

"Exam Room 2." Nurse Kim waved to Helen and shut the door.

Instead of leaving, Helen selected a magazine

from a rack, found a vacant seat close to the door and pretended to read—her left hand searching her handbag for the watch's control device.

🐾 🐾 🐾

Vince left his office, his heart still racing from "Warden Helen's" surprise inspection. Deciding it best to settle his nerves before moving on to the highlights of his day, he bypassed the Nubian cheerleader in Room 4, grabbing the chart off the door of Exam Room 2.

He knocked and entered. "Mrs. Dombrowski, what brings you by this afternoon?"

"Wow that was fast. I have a date tonight, Dr. Cope, and I thought—just in case—I better make sure the yeast infection's completely cleared up."

"Sounds like somebody might get lucky. Let's get your feet up in the stirrups, and I'll take a quick look."

"Dr. Cope, may I ask you a personal question?"

"Ask away."

"Do you think I'm a lesbo?"

"I'm sorry?"

"I've been sexually active for forty-six years, and I've yet to meet a man who can bring me to," she whispered, "orgasm."

"How many men have you been with?"

"Three. The last forty-two years with the ex. But I'm available again, and I'd like to … you know—"

"Date women?"

"Why would I date a woman?"

"Well, you just asked. … Never mind. Ever use a vibrator?"

"You mean one of those electrical devices? Oh my, no. I'm afraid of putting something mechanical down there."

"They're perfectly safe. My nurse, Wanda, sells them. It might be a more private way to get the juices flowing."

"Walter, my ex—he was all thumbs down there. The man couldn't find my clitoris if I painted it blue and gave him a coal miner's hat with a light on top."

Vincent laughed. "Well don't give up on us yet. Sometimes a man just needs a little instruction. Okay, I'm going to put two fingers inside to feel around."

ZAP!

The neurological shock hit Vin like an invisible wave, turning his muscles to mush and taking his feet out from under him. He collapsed face-first onto the table between Edna Dombrowski's spread legs, his two fingers still buried three inches deep inside his patient's vagina, her clitoris tingling from the electrical charge.

"Oh my goodness. Oh my God. Dr. Cope, what

was that?"

Still seeing purple flashing lights, Vince opened his mouth to answer.

ZAP!

"Unhhhh!"

"Wow!" Edna retracted both legs from the stirrups and crossed her heels, sandwiching Dr. Cope's left arm between her clenched thighs in a wrestling hold, pinning his hand inside her quivering orifice.

"Mrs. Dombrowski, let go—"

ZAP!

"Oh my God! Oh my God!"

Back in the waiting room, Helen Cope was in a state of panic. Hearing the dueling screams of her husband and the older woman, she had accidentally dropped the control switch, and now the red light refused to power off. Flipping the jammed device over, she tried to remove the batteries only to discover the back panel was screwed into place.

"Ahhhh!" Every three seconds a surge of electricity coursed through Vincent Cope's frayed nervous system, stimulating Edna Dombrowski's genitalia, her orgasm building into a forty-six-year-old towering wave of frustration nearly ready to burst.

"Edna, let go!"

Lost in the moment, Edna panted like an overheated dog, her eyelids fluttering. "Deeper to the right—more to the right! Oh, God. Oh my God … yes! YES!" She grabbed the gynecologist by the hair. "Don't you dare move, you bastard!"

Helen stomped on the device, smashed it against the arm of her chair, and still it wouldn't power off.

The receptionist and Nurse Kim listened outside the door of Exam Room 2. Down the hall, the cheerleaders stood outside their respective exam rooms in their dressing gowns.

"I don't know what's going on in there, Dawn, but I'm gettin' me some of that."

Edna Dombrowski bucked like a wild bronco, screaming in ecstasy—each contortion pile-driving Vinnie's face into the paper-sheeted table cushion as she climaxed for a second and third time.

Helen raced out the front entrance to her car and placed the jammed device beneath the left front tire. She opened the door, started the engine, shifted into reverse and backed over the cursed controller.

The screaming coming from Exam Room 2 stopped, dying into moans of delightful giggles. After a minute, the door swung open, revealing Edna Dombrowski, her graying hair down and wavy, her cherub cheeks bright pink balls on her smiling face.

"Book me again for next week ladies—same Bat-time, same Bat-channel."

Vinnie pushed past her, his hair resembling Don King's, the smoldering dive watch dangling from his singed left wrist. Blinded by purple spots, he never saw the scantily clad women waiting for him at the end of the hall. Instead, he staggered past them, entered his office and collapsed in his desk chair.

The venue of Zev's free seminar was located on Palmetto Park Road, less than a mile from Vin's office. As Jacob turned into the parking lot, he realized that he must have driven by the domed single-story building at least fifty times in the last three months without giving it a second thought.

There were more than a hundred new students attending the free introductory seminar—men and women, old and young, black and white and every shade in between. Jacob was greeted by a volunteer who seated him at one of a dozen tables inside a conference room.

The lecture began at 8:00 p.m. sharp, led by a man in his forties, his dark beard as thick as Jacob's, his hairline receding.

"Good evening. My name is Solomon Jian, and I am one of the teachers at the center. Tonight our goal is to give you a basic introduction to an ancient knowledge that hopefully you can take home and make use of in your daily lives. The word Kabbalah means 'to receive.' The question is to receive what? What do you feel you need in your life? On your tables are paper and pens; I want you to write down five things that you want to receive in this lifetime."

Jacob wrote, "Love, success, happiness, money and health."

The teacher continued. "Now I want you to circle the one you want the most."

Jacob hesitated. *What good is money or fame without health? What good is health without love?* He circled love, then crossed it out and circled happiness.

"Okay, what we're going to do is list on the blackboard the most important things within each group. Just call out from each table."

"Health."

"Love."

"Peace."

"Happiness."

"Money."

"Prosperity."

"Success."

Solomon Jian wrote each item on the blackboard, adding check marks when an answer was duplicated. "Very good. Believe it or not, throughout the world, people always want the same things. There is a reason for that. As emotional creatures, we want to feel. As for money, we aren't really interested in accumulating physical dollars; we want what these physical dollars can bring us. Maybe being rich means having security. Maybe it means less stress. A nice home, a new car—we want money for things we are lacking.

"Religious people love to use words like, 'I hope.' The big difference between a religious person and a spiritual person is that religious people pray to God for help, while spiritual people already know God is in the equation but recognize that they have to do something from within themselves in order to get what they want.

"To achieve what you desire out of your lives,

you have to accept certain rules. In the game of life, you need to learn these rules. Without rules, there is chaos. You can take the ten best basketball players in the world and put them all on a basketball court with a ball, but if they have no idea how to play the game, there can be no fulfillment. You can't win in the game of life without knowing the rules. Kabbalah is all about learning the rules.

"The first rule we must learn is that what we truly desire in our lives is lasting, endless fulfillment. Physical things will never make you happy. They may be fun for a while, but the happiness won't last. You can buy a new car or home, but it won't make you happy. You could go out tonight and buy a red Ferrari, and for a while you'd be happier, but after a while you'd lose interest in that too. Am I telling you not to be rich? No. Just don't expect it to make you happy. Happiness is not a physical feeling. It can't be bought.

"We make decisions in our life by using our five senses. Our senses give us information that we've come to accept as reality. We recognize things in our life through our five senses. We see, touch, smell, taste and hear. Do our senses ever mislead us? The next rule we need to understand is that we can't trust our five senses. We see a blackboard, and it appears solid to us. But if we examine the atoms that make up the blackboard, we would see great expanses as vast as space itself. We meet someone special. Our senses tell us it's the right person. We get married, but the marriage ends in divorce. What happened? In life, it's not about the senses; it's about our consciousness.

"Kabbalah teaches us that there are actually two realities, two universes. There is the *1 percent* universe, which is the physical world of the five senses, and the *99 percent* universe, which we call *the endless world.* Creativity comes from the endless world. Mozart wrote his symphonies by tapping into the 99 percent. This is where miracles come from. Remaining stuck in the physical world is like being stuck in the mud. To get out of the mud you need to tap into the 99 percent. Are we training you to be psychics? No. But we are going to teach you how to access the energy of abundance found in the 99 percent—the creator's energy—what we call *the light.*

"There is a very easy way to tap into the 99 percent—it will sound easy, but it's tough to do. The 1 percent world deals with blame. The 99 percent means taking full responsibility for whatever happens in your life. Nothing happens suddenly; everything follows the laws of cause and effect. Blame is the cause. Responsibility is being the effect. When you take full responsibility, you are now in control of your life. And yet nothing is more painful. My marriage isn't working; my wife doesn't make love to me; she's always yelling at me to pick up my clothes—blah, blah, blah. Stop blaming. Take full responsibility for fixing it. It's not about blaming the other person. It's not about being right. You hate your job? Don't blame your boss; do something about it. If you are always blaming someone else for your misery, you'll always be in the darkness. You want a life full of love? Don't blame the other person; give love. And stop with the guilt. It only brings you down. Guilt is nothing more than self-blame. Stop doing it. It's not about being right; it's about being happy. You can have all the money in the world. It won't make you happy. I've met billionaires who were miserable, blaming their ex-wives for taking a hundred million dollars in the divorce, blaming their kids for not loving them—blame, blame, blame. At the end of the day, you have to take responsibility for your life. The area that you blame the most—that is where your potential lies"

"You have a choice—do you want to be happy or do you want to be right? Some people spend their entire lives wanting justice against the people they blame for their troubles. These individuals will never be happy. The change must come from you.

"Before you leave, I want to give you an assignment. I want you to figure out who annoys you the most and do something nice for that person."

53

Freakout Friday

NANCY AWOKE TO THE DOG barking at the birds. She rolled over, checking the alarm clock—7:12 a.m. "Jacob, wake up. Your dog needs to go out. Jacob!"

"Whaa?"

"Let your dog out and get ready for work."

"My dog? You're the one training him. How about training him to use the toilet?"

"I'm sure he'd get less pee on the seat. Come on, get up!" Jacob rolled out of bed. He staggered out of the bedroom only to be bull-rushed by the hyperactive German shepherd as he attempted to escape into the hall bathroom to empty his own aching bladder. "Easy boy … watch my toes—oww! Okay, okay—outside."

The spinning tan and black dervish of fur-covered muscle leaped at the glass door until Jacob could unbolt the lock and release him.

Unable to hold his own urine any longer, Jacob stepped outside and peed on a shrub.

"Jacob!"

"Sorry. Must have been the asparagus." He finished then tossed Sam his ball for ten minutes, hoping to wear the dog out before they returned inside.

"Hey, boy, what's that around your neck?" Jacob unhooked the collar, inspecting the two metal prods. "Nancy, what's with Sam's new collar? Is this some kind of tracking device?"

She emerged from the bedroom, already dressed for work. "It's a shock collar."

"Shock collar? You're shocking my dog? Why are you shocking my dog?"

"It's for his advanced training."

"How advanced does he need to be? Are we sending him to college?"

"Relax. Spencer said it doesn't hurt; it just hits Sam with an uncomfortable jolt, which deters the negative behavior."

"Where's the control?"

"Hanging from the key hook. Jacob, I trust Spencer. If he says it doesn't hurt the dog, then— what are you doing?"

"Testing it." Jacob snapped Sam's collar around

his own neck then retrieved the palm controls. "Is it this red button—Ahhhhhhh … ahhh! Ahhh!"

"Stop pushing it!" She knocked the controller from his hand, a slight buzz running down her arm. "Are you all right?"

"I don't know."

"Why didn't you stop?"

"I couldn't let go. The charge kept my fingers squeezing the button. Gosh, maybe I really am Friedrich Riesfeldt's kid."

"Who? Oh, right … the zookeeper."

Nancy tossed the shock collar on the counter. "Where were you last night?"

"I went to a self-help seminar. It was pretty cool. You were asleep when I got home."

"I went to bed early; I was exhausted. But I have some amazing news. The station's renewing my contract for two years with a 30 percent raise in salary."

"Nancy, that's great."

"I know. It's like a dream come true. And I didn't tell you the best part. They want to syndicate the show and add a product line."

"What kind of product line?"

"You know … women's stuff. Nothing you'd be interested in. The owner of the station invited me to a private party tonight to discuss business."

Jacob's smile faded. "Old Man Cabot invited you to his party?"

"Cabot's retired. His daughter, Olivia—she owns the station—it's her party."

"Olivia Cabot's his daughter?"

"I thought you knew that."

"How would I know that? You never told me Cabot's daughter was your boss. You never told me her name was Olivia!"

"Calm down. Say, isn't Ruby's big gig tonight?"

"Is it? I nearly forgot. I think it's at a comedy club."

"You told me it was a private party."

"A private party at a comedy club. I have to check my text messages for the address."

"Take it easy. I think that shock collar made you hyper."

"Hyper? I'm not hyper. And what if I was? Would you cut off my balls like you did Sam's?"

She kissed him quickly on the lips then patted his hairy left cheek. "Only if you cheated on me. Maybe it's time to trim the beard. I have a rash on my thighs from the other day."

Jacob drove east out to the beach, ignoring the calls from his dispatcher. *Nancy's going to be at the party. She'll*

see Ruby and Olivia chasing after me in their sexy outfits. The moment Nancy flips out, Olivia will know she's my girlfriend. That'll give her leverage. She could force me to sleep with her by threatening to cancel Nancy's contract. She might even lie to Nancy and say I already slept with her just to get Nancy to leave me.

"Suck balls!"

He recalled a John Lennon quote: *"The postman wants an autograph. The cab driver wants a picture. The waitress wants a handshake. Everyone wants a piece of you."*

He arrived at the high-rise beach condominium ten minutes later, parking in the vendor's lot. Using a Federal Express delivery as cover, he snuck past the twelve-dollar-an-hour guard working the security desk and followed an older woman and her miniature toy poodle onto a waiting elevator.

The dog sniffed Jacob's pants.

"Little fella probably smells my German shepherd. Sam likes to rub his ass against me so I'll scratch his butt."

The woman offered a polite smile and then quickly exited on the fifth floor.

Jacob pushed the button for eleven.

Enough is enough. I'm tired of being manipulated by these two rich menopausal horndogs. Ruby and Olivia will need to back off, or I won't do the show.

Stepping off the elevator, he stormed across the

carpeted corridor to the double oak door at the end of the hall and rang the bell to suite 1101.

The door opened, revealing Ruby in a bathrobe and silk pajamas. She wasn't wearing make-up, and her hair was twisted in a loose ball atop her head as if she had just woken up.

"Jacob? What are you doing here?"

"We need to talk."

"Can we talk later? I don't feel well."

"No. It has to be now."

"Fine." She stepped aside, allowing him entrée into the three-bedroom condo. He followed her through the living room, its white marble floors ending at a balcony overlooking the Atlantic Ocean.

Ruby shuffled barefooted over to a U-shaped beige leather sofa, where she laid down, curling herself in a ball. "You trimmed your beard. It looks better."

"Thanks." He noticed the assortment of medication on the coffee table. "What's wrong?"

"It's a female thing. Are you ready for tonight?"

"I suppose."

"Don't *suppose*. You need to be good tonight. I'm running out of influential friends."

"I'd be more confident if I knew you and your friends weren't in a contest to see who could have sex with me first."

"Who told you that? Cyril?"

"Is it true?"

"No. Well, yes. It was Olivia's idea, but it was just a tease. We didn't think you'd mind."

"Normally I wouldn't, but I have a girlfriend … someone I really care about."

She winced in pain. "So I'll back off."

"What about Olivia?"

"I'll call her."

Jacob breathed a sigh of relief. "Thank you. And don't think for a minute it's not because I don't find you attractive—I do. It's just—"

"I'm happy you found someone special in your life."

"Thanks. You know, John Lennon once said—" he paused, his cell phone reverberating with a 911 text from his boss at I-Guru. He typed a response and then thought better of it. "Ruby, is there a land-line I can use?"

"Down the hall, my home office." She rolled over, covering herself with a wool blanket.

Jacob found his way to the converted bedroom and sat at the desk. Using Ruby's house phone, he dialed Mr. Patel's number, his eyes wandering to the cluster of framed photos situated on the glass table top: Ruby with her two kids, some taken as babies and teens, the more recent photos taken in their

390

mid-twenties. One with her parents. A family Christmas photo, taken long ago. A graduation photo with her son.

Missing in action, her husband of thirty years.

"I'm happy you found someone special in your life." Ruby had found someone special, and he had cheated on her, tossing her life into disarray.

Jacob recalled his brother's words: *"Ruby's not insane; she's in pain. Her ex hurt her pretty badly. Now she's trying to bury the last thirty years by reinventing herself."*

Thirty years. … How do you erase thirty years of marriage? Thirty years of memories? How do you trust another man after your spouse cheated on you?

Vince was wrong. Ruby wasn't trying to reinvent herself; right now she was just trying to survive a tsunami of hurt by numbing herself with sex until her heart could form scars.

"This is Patel."

"Mr. Patel, it's Jacob. I dropped my iPhone this morning, and it's not working. Can you transfer me to dispatch for my first appointment?"

"What took you so long to call in?"

"I had to stop at a friend's house to use his phone."

"Very well. But you had better not go missing again, or you are fired. I do not care what Ganesha says."

"Yes sir." Jacob waited for the dispatcher, who

read him an address in West Palm Beach. He wrote the information on a scrap of paper, listening to Ruby moaning in pain in the living room.

Completing the call, he stood to leave, hesitated, then texted his brother.

The iPhone rang a minute later. "This better be an emergency."

"Vin, I'm with Ruby. She's in a lot of pain."

"What did you do to her?"

"Nothing. She says it's female pain, but it seems pretty bad."

"Put her on the phone."

Jacob left the office and then knelt by the sofa. "Ruby, my brother wants to speak with you."

Ruby opened her eyes and took the phone. "Hello?"

"Ruby, it's Dr. Cope. What's wrong, sweetheart?"

"I hurt inside. Really bad."

"When did the pain start?"

"This morning."

"Are you spotting?"

"Yes."

"I'll have Wanda expedite the results from your last pap smear. Can you get to my office?"

"I don't think I can drive. I'll have to call a friend."

Jacob took the phone. "It's okay, Vin. I'll drive her."

❧ ❧ ❧

"You teased him, Carmella. Then you and your witch's coven tossed him into the pool."

"I did nothing of the sort, whore." Carmella Cope left her lounge chair and headed for the steps leading into the shallow end of the pool to claim a good spot for the morning water aerobics class.

Nancy followed her across the deck. "After all Truman did for you, would it have killed you to be nice to him?"

"I never asked him to get snipped. That was your idea, whore."

"Stop calling me a whore!"

"Why? That's what you are. Money, money, money—that's all that matters to you. The only reason you care about Cabot is because he bribed you. One whore bribing another."

"Okay, you're right. I was desperate. For a while I had no idea if I was going to keep my job. Forget about the money—I don't want the money. But Truman, he really likes you. He says you remind him of his deceased wife."

"Blah, blah, blah." Carmella pushed past Nancy to access the pool steps. "You're just afraid Richie Rich will tell his Richie Bitch daughter whose idea it was to get clipped and you'll be fired."

"Is that what you want, Carmella? To see me fired? Do you think that's what Jacob would want?"

Carmella ignored her, focusing on her warm-up exercises.

Infuriated, Nancy took off her shoes and followed the older woman into the waist-deep water, soaking her skirt and blouse in the process. "Why do you have to be so nasty?"

"Go away."

"From the first moment we met, you treated me like dirt. I want to know why."

"You're the hotshot radio whore psychiatrist. Why don't you tell me?"

"Okay. For starters, you've been hurt. You probably loved Jacob's father very much. After what happened, no one could blame you for being bitter."

"Bitter?"

"Angry then. It's a natural response when a loved one commits suicide. But after twenty years—"

Carmella shoved Nancy backward so hard she slipped underwater. "You think you know what that man put me through? You don't know nothing! I had to clean blood stains out of the bedroom carpet on my hands and knees because I couldn't afford to replace it. I had to use a screwdriver to pick skull fragments out of the drywall before I could repaint the bedroom walls. For months I had nightmares. I had to sleep in the living room. The boys begged me to move. Only I couldn't afford to because the military cut off my husband's benefits. Think I'm mean and nasty now? For years I resented my kids for being around because they forced me to stay sober. Instead of checking out on my family, I chain-smoked my way through double shifts driving a cab just so my oldest son could go to med school. But instead of becoming a brain surgeon, the stupid schmuck got his girlfriend pregnant and had to marry her."

"And then your youngest son moved in with a radio whore who ... what? Just wanted his money? For a long time I was just like you, Carmella: stuck in the blame game, feeling sorry for myself—poor me. Know what I learned? Everyone has problems. Mine may not be nearly as bad as yours were, but I learned something recently. Being bitter about the past doesn't help me today. So go on, keep calling me a whore and see where that gets you with Jacob."

Carmella removed her sunglasses, her squinting hazel eyes filled with rage. "*Love's a Beach with Nancy Beach.* I used to listen to your show. I got a kick out of all the hecklers who'd tease you about offering relationship advice when you couldn't stay in a relationship yourself. So you tell me, Doctor Beach. Why did you really move in with my Jacob? Was it because you loved him? Or was it because you were using him, trying to prove to your listening audience that you could actually hang on to a guy?"

"To be honest, Carmella, a little of both. Before I met Jacob I had serious trust issues—I still do. But your son was kind and sincere, and even though I was mad at him for bringing home that dog from the pound, I realize now why he did it—because he has a big heart. I love that about him, and I love that he'd rather make people laugh than earn the big bucks on Wall Street. And yes, while his phobias can drive me crazy, I also know that he's loyal, that he'd never hurt me and that has helped me get over my own trust issues. I'd like to think I've done the same for him."

🐾 🐾 🐾

Cyril was waiting outside the tuxedo shop when Jacob arrived at ten minutes after six. "You're late, Mr. Jacob."

"Sorry, been behind schedule all day. Ruby's sick. I had to take her to my brother's office."

"Your brother's a doctor?"

"Gynecologist."

"Really? Is he single?"

"He's married—to a woman. Geez, dude, I thought you had a boyfriend."

"We split. Come on, we need to get your tux and be at the dock before the yacht leaves."

The color drained from Jacob's face. "The yacht's going out to sea? At night? Nobody told me that."

"Relax. We're taking a three-hour tour around the Intracoastal. I seriously doubt you'll be in any danger."

"Gilligan took a three-hour tour—look what happened to him!" Jacob followed Cyril inside the rental store. "How deep is the Intracoastal? Does it get rough? Maybe I can do my act early, while we're still docked. Do you think we can convince Olivia to let me go on early?"

"I doubt it. It was hard enough to convince her we were lovers."

"Wait, what?"

The store manager greeted them. "Can I help you gentlemen?"

Cyril smiled sweetly. "We're picking up two rentals. It's under the names Mr. and Mr. Ben Dover." He handed the man a ticket.

"Give me a few minutes."

Jacob waited until the manager left. "You think this is funny?"

"Hey, don't get snippity. I did this for you. You told me you have a serious girlfriend, yes?"

"So?"

"By telling Olivia we were lovers, she agreed to back off. That is what you wanted."

Jacob grinned. "That was a good idea. Thanks, Cyril. But dude, seriously—if you try something tonight like you did back at your house, I'm going to beat you to death with my Lisa Simpson dummy."

"Is that supposed to be a dumb-blonde joke?"

"No. But there is a blonde. Her name's Nancy, and I just found out she's going to be on board tonight."

"Your girlfriend's coming to the party? Does Olivia know?"

"She's the one who invited her. Olivia's Nancy's boss, only she doesn't know Nancy and I live together. We need to keep that a secret."

Cyril clapped his hands. "And here I thought this was going to be a boring party."

54

Dog Training the American Male
Lesson Thirteen:
Obedience Training

THE BOCA RATON INLET is located in South Palm Beach County. Its 150-foot-wide channel is one of several local access points connecting the Intracoastal Waterway with the Atlantic Ocean. The inlet's southern jetty bordered the Bridge Hotel and South Inlet Beach Park, the northern jetty securing the Boca Raton Beach Resort. Along this scenic stretch of converging waterways rose beach condominiums and some of the most expensive properties in Florida.

Occupying the Bridge Hotel's length of dock was the *Cabot-II*, a sleek white fiberglass 116-foot Lazzara motor yacht. The three-deck Mecca of entertainment was powered by two 1,015 horsepower engines. In addition to the crews' quarters, there were five guest staterooms, a movie theater, a Jacuzzi, a dining room and three salons featuring wall-size LCD flat-screen televisions wired to the ship's satellite dishes.

Jacob and Cyril arrived at the dock at 7:20 only to wait in line at the pier while security guards checked in each boarding guest. The setting sun splattered golden sparks across the dark blue waters of the inlet, the humidity causing the back of Jacob's dress shirt to accumulate sweat beneath his rented tux as he searched the crowd for Nancy.

To his relief, she was not among the cluster of passengers waiting to board.

Jacob's plan was simple: get on board and hide from Nancy until his stand-up routine was over. If Nancy saw him before the gig, she'd demand to know why he didn't tell her that Olivia had hired him. She'd want details—like how they met, why a gay man was hanging on his arm, or, God forbid, why her boss was coming on to him. Once he got paid the five grand (he had insisted Olivia pay him in cash), he could pull Nancy aside and give her enough of an explanation to keep her from blurting out that they lived together.

Testifying before Congress was easier.

His eyes caught Nancy's car as it arrived at the hotel's valet parking.

His heart beat faster as Nancy made her way down the sidewalk that led to the wharf, his girlfriend looking hot in a black low-cut cocktail dress and matching pumps. He ducked his head while a crewman verified Jacob's and Cyril's names on the guest list and a police officer inspected the interior of the suitcase carrying the Lisa Simpson dummy.

"They're okay."

"All right, gentlemen, you can board. Have a good evening." Jacob darted up a short gangway to the mid-deck, leading Cyril onto the yacht, the air-conditioning helping to settle his frayed nerves.

The deck, walls and laminated built-ins in the main salon were finished in cherry wood. The furniture consisted of a cream leather wraparound sofa and matching recliners situated before a forty-two-inch LCD television screen. A dozen guests mingled in the lavish surroundings.

Squeezing through the crowd, Jacob and Cyril headed forward, entering the dining room, its mirrored bulkhead reflecting a cherry wood oval dining table with seating for eight. Trays of hors d'oeuvres covered the table, attracting a crowd.

"There they are—my favorite man couple!"

Olivia swept in from the galley entrance. The millionairess was dressed in a scarlet Tony Bowls evening gown, its deep V-cut neckline accentuating her bulging, tan breasts, the tiered draped skirt opening up in a side split that revealed her bare left leg and spiked high-heeled shoe.

She kissed Jacob full on the lips and then turned her attention to Cyril. "I could scratch your eyes out for snagging this baby grizzly from me, but fair is fair. Be a dear and fetch us something to drink."

Cyril turned to Jacob. "Bourbon, darling?"

Jacob's eyes flashed a warning. "Ginger ale, dear."

"You two are adorable. Seven and seven for me, Cyril."

Jacob watched the gay man squeeze his way through the crowd to get outside to the bar. "Olivia, have you spoken to Ruby? I dropped her off at the doctor's this morning and haven't heard a thing."

"She texted me earlier and said she was still waiting to get her test results. Don't worry about her. I'm sure she's fine. Before I forget, I have something I want you to wear tonight." Fishing through her purse, she removed the dive watch and handed it to him. "Consider it a good-luck charm."

"A dive watch? You know, I don't really dive. Wait, is there something wrong with the yacht? Do you think we could sink? Is that why you're giving me this? So I can find my way back to shore?"

"Don't be ridiculous."

"It's not ridiculous when you suffer from extreme

hydrophobia like I do. Sometimes I have to take a Dramamine just to take a shower."

"You're hysterical. Save it for the show."

"The show—Olivia, is there any way you'd let me do my stand-up while we're still docked? I'd be much more relaxed."

"Sorry, pet, but the cruise is the best part of the night—except for those lucky guests rocking the boat from their staterooms." She winked. "Go on, try it on."

Removing his old watch, Jacob secured the bulkier dive watch to his left wrist. "Feels kind of heavy."

"You'll get used to it."

"Drinks!" Cyril pushed his way through the crowd. He handed Olivia one of the two drinks in his right hand, handing the ecstasy-laced soda in his left hand to Jacob. "A toast to the wild evening ahead."

"I'll drink to that." Olivia clinked her glass.

Jacob gulped down the flat soda, glancing out the tinted window in time to see Nancy ascending a spiral staircase that led to the upper deck.

🐾 🐾 🐾

Nancy climbed the aluminum steps, seeking to avoid the mid-deck crowd. Occupying the open upper deck were sixty folding chairs arranged in rows facing a small stage situated beneath a banner: "Happy

Birthday Truman." She located the guest of honor seated alone in the bow and nursing a beer.

Nancy accepted a glass of champagne from a waitress and joined him. "How are you feeling?"

"Old." He looked up. "You? What are you doing here?"

"Your daughter invited me. Truman, I'm so sorry about what happened. I don't want your money, but I still want to help you get together with Carmella."

"She hates me."

"She doesn't hate you. Me she hates."

"I could make her happy if she'd let me."

"Not everyone wants to be happy." She looked around. Night had taken the Intracoastal, tempering the South Florida heat. A few couples were standing by the starboard rail. The upper deck was otherwise deserted. "Where are all your friends?"

"Dead. Just like this party."

Thunder rattled the air as the yacht's powerful engines came to life. A horn sounded its warning.

Looking down, she saw a familiar figure hustle past security to make her way on board. Ruby— what's she doing here?

The blades engaged, churning up the bottom, and they lurched ahead, moving steadily through the Intracoastal Waterway, heading out to sea. Nancy inhaled the briny air, the wind tossing strands of blonde hair across her forehead. "Truman, are you cold?"

"I'm eighty-three. That old enough for you?"

"No, no. Are you cold? Can I get you a sweater?"

"Nah. Maybe I'll get lucky and die of pneumonia."

"I need to warm up. Be back in a bit." She headed for the pilothouse, pushing open the steel door of the ship's command center. The captain nodded from behind the wheel, his eyes lingering on her breasts.

"Excuse me, why are we headed out to sea?"

"Only way to get to Fort Lauderdale. Why don't you sit on my lap, and I'll let you steer the boat."

"Why don't you sit on the throttle and go fuck yourself." She pushed past him, heading below.

Jacob felt woozy and a bit warm. He found himself staring at the pretty lights, which seemed to be dancing as they melded together in his vision.

Cyril touched his arm, and it felt good. "Somebody need a hug?"

"Yeah."

Ruby pushed her way between them. Her purple strapless chiffon dress was topped by an ivory jacket, the fabric stretched tight over her breasts.

Jacob stared at the swollen bouncing mounds of flesh, his heart racing. "Ruby Tuesday."

"Hi, Jacob. Thanks for earlier."

"Earlier what?"

Cyril winked. "He's a little buzzed."

"Jacob, are you drinking? I need you on you're a game. I invited a booking agent from *The Tonight Show*."

"Honey, that's so exciting." Cyril leaned in and kissed Jacob on the lips.

From across the crowded stateroom, Nancy spotted her boyfriend seconds before a man in a white tuxedo jacket kissed him passionately. *What the hell?*

"Cyril, I need to speak with Jacob … in private." Ruby grabbed Jacob by the wrist and dragged the giddy man through the galley and down the grand stairwell that led to the lower deck sleeping quarters.

Nancy pushed through the crowd after them but was intercepted by Olivia Cabot.

"Dr. Beach, I'm so glad you made it." She fake kissed Nancy cheek to cheek. "Come with me. I want to introduce you to a dear friend of mine who can get you syndicated in New York and LA."

Olivia worked her way aft through the crowded stateroom.

Nancy hesitated, glancing toward the stairs. *Screw him. I'm not going to allow another man to cheat on me and ruin my career.*

Squeezing through the crowd, she followed her boss to the stern.

Ruby led Jacob down the carpeted stairwell to a foyer that flowed into a starboard study. A forward corridor separated two VIP suites, the aft corridor leading to three smaller staterooms and the crews' quarters.

She opened the cabin door to the suite on the starboard side, flipping on the lights. The chamber was decorated in the same cherry wood motif as the rest of the yacht. A king-size bed faced a large flatscreen LCD television. The starboard wall was a tinted oval window looking out to sea. A connecting door led to the master bath, which was all marble with wood trim.

"Must be enough cherry wood on board this ship to fill a Pennsylvania forest." Jacob said, lying back on the bed, his dress pants stretching beneath his hard-on. "Speaking of wood." Unbuckling his belt, he pulled his trousers down to his knees, exposing his SpongeBob SquarePants boxer shorts, which were now animating.

"Jacob, what are you doing?"

"What do you think?"

"Jacob, I didn't bring you down here to have sex. Did you forget our conversation this morning?"

"No. Yeah. Is it getting brighter in here?"

"I brought you down here to talk. Your brother got the test results back from my pap smear."

"Are you pregnant?"

"What? No." Her eyes welled up with tears. "I have uterine cancer."

"Oh shit." Jacob sat up, his suddenly flaccid penis flopping inside his shorts. "How bad is it?"

"Pretty bad."

🐾 🐾 🐾

Nancy followed Olivia through the stateroom and outside to the aft deck bar. Seated on a sofa shaped like a giant lifesaver was a couple in their late thirties. The man was Venezuelan, possessing an athletic physique beneath his ivory suit, his dark hair slicked back into a ponytail. The woman was his equal, her long platinum-blonde hair pulled into a stylistic weave atop her head, exposing her well-defined shoulders and upper back.

"Dr. Beach, I want you to meet Mercedes Duggan, the producer I told you about, and this is her fiancé, Sebastian Bastidas."

"Nancy?"

Nancy's eyes widened in the dim light. "Sebastian?"

Mercedes smiled nervously. "Darling, do you know this woman?"

"You might say that," Nancy interjected. "Your fiancé and I were engaged two years ago when I found out he was fucking my roommate."

Instead of reacting, the platinum blonde playfully tugged on Sebastian's earlobe. "You are such a bastard, aren't you?"

"Guilty as charged."

Nancy's blood boiled. "Yeah? Well he not only fucked her; he got her pregnant!"

"Really?" Olivia said. "Boy or girl?"

"A boy. Little bastard has my eyes."

Sebastian's sheepish grin poured gasoline on the fire flowing through Nancy's veins. "Let's hope he doesn't have your dick!"

"Dr. Beach—"

"No, I'm sorry Olivia, but this creep ruined my life. Asshole!"

"Is your life really ruined?" Mercedes asked.

"Yes. No. Not anymore."

"Would it have been better if you had married Sebastian?"

"No, definitely not."

"Then his cheating with your roommate turned out to be a blessing, yes?"

Nancy felt her cheeks flush. "I suppose."

Sebastian nodded. "You're welcome."

Nancy stomped on his right shoe as hard as she could, the heel of her pump crushing his big toe through the Italian leather.

Jacob hugged Ruby, his skin tingling against hers. "When's the surgery?"

"Monday morning. I'm scared, Jacob."

"Listen to me. You know how it seems like everyone has that one thing they do very well. Surgery is what my brother does really well. The guy was on track to become a great brain surgeon when he switched to women's plumbing after Helen's mother died of breast cancer. But she didn't have a surgeon as good as Vince. So don't be scared, okay?"

"Okay."

He massaged her shoulders, his hands becoming two spider-like creatures working their way toward Ruby's—

"Sweetie, what are you doing?"

"Feeling fig newtonie."

"What?"

"Remember that old commercial jingle? Ooey

gooey, rich and chewy inside. Golden flaky-bakey on the outside …"

Ruby pushed him away. "That little shit, Cyril—I bet he slipped something in your drink."

"I need to suck on something. Can I suck on your lips? They look ewwie gooey." Jacob tried to kiss her, but Ruby ducked away. She didn't get far. Jacob's watch caught on her strapless dress, causing her left breast to flop out just as the cabin door opened.

Nancy covered her mouth. "Oh my God."

Jacob smiled stupidly. "Nancy, hi. This is Ruby, and this is Ruby's tit. We had an itty bitty titty of a wardrobe malfunction."

Disgusted, Nancy backed away, slamming the door shut.

"Your girlfriend?"

"She was."

Ruby repositioned her breast and then slapped Jacob hard across his face. "Sober yet?"

"No, but my face hurts … ow."

"Go after her!"

"And say what?"

"Apologize, Jacob."

"For what? Never mind." Jacob ran out of the stateroom.

ZAP!

He collapsed in a heap, his legs twitching.

Olivia helped him up. "Darling, are you all right?"

"What happened?"

"You must have tripped. Come with me. Your head is bleeding." She led him across the passage to the portside master stateroom, a gaudy bedroom with ropes around the bedposts and sexual devices adorning the walls.

Olivia hit a switch, causing music to play, the cabin darkening with mood lighting.

The music pulsated in Jacob's veins, the lights melding into pools of colors in his eyes. "I … I should go."

Olivia shut the door, the dress slipping off her shoulders.

Jacob glanced out the tinted window. He saw Nancy by the guardrail hailing a water taxi. "I have to go." He struggled to rise off the bed.

ZAP! He went down again, the colors in his vision sizzling like fireworks.

Olivia straddled him. "Cyril thinks he's so clever. I knew you weren't gay."

Jacob flung her off his waist onto the floor. He made it to the door.

ZAP! He was suddenly on the floor, his legs rubber.

"Stud muffin, I'm gonna ride you until the sun

comes up over Santa Monica Boulevard."

The cabin door was forcibly opened, smashing him in the head.

It was Truman.

"Another rabbit caught in your trap, eh Olivia?" Reaching down, he grabbed Jacob by his jacket collar and dragged him to his feet. "Go find your girlfriend before you lose her."

Jacob nodded then rushed out of the cabin and up the stairs in time to see Nancy speed away in a water taxi. Distraught, he glanced across the dark waterway.

They were back in the Intracoastal, cruising at ten knots past the private docks and yards of luxury homes—land a good hundred yards away across a forbidding, dark chop.

Cyril joined him, holding an inflatable life vest. "Sorry about the ecstasy, but you'll need it to overcome your fear."

"You think I'm swimming at night? In that?"

"I don't know. I guess it depends on how much you like the girl."

Still a bit high, Jacob removed his tuxedo jacket, his heart pounding as he slipped his arms through the vest, securing it around his waist.

Cyril yanked on the cord, inflating the vest. He leaned in, pursing his lips. "For luck."

Jacob punched him in the mouth. "Thanks for a wonderful evening." Climbing over the rail, he jumped from the moving vessel.

He sank into thundering blackness. For a frightening moment he was caught in the suction of the passing yacht, dragged deep underwater.

Somewhere in this maelstrom of panic his consciousness latched onto a memory.

"Fears actually create what we're afraid of. It's always the guy who's afraid of amputees that runs into a VA hospital. The people who are afraid of flying—those are the ones who always find themselves on the planes experiencing turbulence. Fear manifests a negative energy field that brings the actual situation to life. When you panic, you've shut yourself off from God. Instead of drowning in fear, focus your mind on swimming to the solution."

Swim asshole!

Jacob kicked and paddled against the current, his head breaking the surface in time to be washed over by the yacht's wake. He gagged and fought his way to another breath even as he looked around frantically to make sure there were no other boats bearing down on him.

Sharks—Olivia said my head was bleeding!

Shut up and swim!

He targeted the pier of a restaurant and started swimming, no longer afraid.

55

Dog Training the American Male
Lesson Fourteen:
Unconditional Love

THE WATER TAXI had taken Nancy to a restaurant where she had caught a cab back to the Bridge Hotel to get her car, burning through an entire Adele CD on the drive home.

It was after ten by the time she entered her house, only to be bulldozed by Sam. Enraged, she dragged the dog into the kitchen by its cinch collar, tossing the German shepherd out back. "I don't need you in my life anymore either!"

Entering the bedroom, she stripped off the cocktail dress and donned her running clothes.

The dog leaped at the sliding glass door, demanding to go with her.

"Forget it!"

She grabbed her house key and stormed out the front door, her mind replaying the events of the past two hours. After a minute sprint, she settled into a steady pace, her jog fueled by anger.

How did I allow the dog up on the couch this time, Lana? I held the leash tight, kept Jacob in total control, gave him wild sex, and he still cheated on me!

Rounding the block, she continued on a second lap.

Lean in. Be in control. Bullshit! There is no control—who we're born to, who raises us, who lies to us, who gets cancer. Tears welled in her eyes as she thought about her father.

Nancy slowed. It was late, the night quiet. She reached the end of the block and continued running.

Push through the pain. The only thing we can control is ourselves. Like you have any control … big hypocrite. Ratings, job, boyfriends, birth parents—it's all bullshit. Life is bullshit.

Two blocks west, an unmarked police car drove slowly through the neighborhood, its lights off. The cop riding shotgun signaled his partner to pull over to the curb behind a 2005 Buick LeSabre. "This vehicle wasn't here ten minutes ago. Let's run the plates."

In the backyard, Sam whined, pacing nervously by the fence. The dog was agitated by a familiar smell in the air.

Nancy approached the end of another block, the sidewalk disappearing behind a seven-foot hedge. Still moving at a brisk pace, she followed the path and was startled by a cat that jumped out from behind the row of shrubs. Her heart beating wildly, she stopped and bent over, smiling at her own fear, her hair suddenly tearing from her scalp as she was forcibly dragged backward through the bushes, her skull bludgeoned by an object that flooded her vision with blinking purple lights.

Nancy opened her eyes, confused. She was on her back in the wet grass, the night sky spinning, her skull throbbing.

She felt her assailant before she saw him. He was straddling her hips, his weight pressing down on top of her, his red buzz-cut familiar beneath the dark hood of his running suit.

The jogger … the one Sam was growling at!

Oh, Jesus—he's out to rape me!

She screamed then abruptly stopped as he pressed the edge of a sharp knife to her throat. "Do that again and I'll open a vein."

She laid her head back, fighting the nausea rising up her esophagus. She heard Sam barking a million miles away. She felt her body trembling uncontrollably as the sociopath leaned in closer and whispered in her ear, "This is going to happen, do you understand? Lay back and enjoy it. Make noise and you die."

She stifled a cry as he yanked hard on her jogging pants.

Sam repeatedly attempted to leap the fence, but it was far too high. Circling the yard past the training circuit, the German shepherd suddenly broke for the doghouse and leaped onto its A-frame roof, using it to hurdle the fence.

The dog landed hard on the other side of the fence. It regained its feet and raced across the street as it picked up its master's scent—cutting off the unmarked police car. The vehicle braked hard, its driver executing a sharp U-turn to follow the loose canine.

The touch of alien flesh to her naked thighs was too much. Nancy opened her mouth to cry out. Her breath was taken away as a brown blur smashed into

418

her assailant, the suddenly clear night air rent with terrifying growls and a man's screams.

Somewhere in the insanity Nancy crawled away, her mind still shattered. She managed to hike her pants over her exposed hips and buttocks and curl into a ball of sniffling paralysis beneath the shrub, the chaos of screams interrupted by piercing red and blue strobe lights.

The unmarked cop car screeched to a halt. The two officers moved quickly, their guns drawn. Their car's searchlight revealed the German shepherd, its teeth tearing into the jogger's blood-soaked sleeve.

"Help!"

"Partner, I've got a clear shot."

Nancy snapped awake.

The two police officers were about to open fire when a woman staggered from the bushes, her clothing torn, her neck bleeding.

"Sam, heel!"

The dog halted its attack and rushed to the woman's side, sitting docilely by her right foot.

Sobbing hysterically, Nancy dropped to her knees, hugging the dog around its neck.

The cops holstered their weapons.

Twelve minutes, three police cars and an ambulance

later, two dozen neighbors watched as a bloodied man in a jogging outfit was handcuffed to a gurney.

Nancy was seated in the back of one of the squad cars, an EMT tending to the cut along the side of her neck, the dog never leaving her side.

"It's just a superficial cut where he had the blade pressing against your neck. You'll be okay."

One of the officers from the unmarked car joined them. "We called your friend. She's on her way."

"Thank you."

"You're lucky. We've been after this guy for quite a while." He knelt by Sam and gave the dog a big hug, allowing Sam to lick his face. "Good boy. You're a good doggy."

Tears flowed down Nancy's cheeks. "He saved me. And after I was so mean to him."

"That's the great thing about dogs: unconditional love."

A Lexus screeched to a halt by the curb. Helen and Vincent pushed through the crowd and ducked under the yellow police tape, hurrying over to Nancy.

Helen freaked. "Oh my God, are you alright? Did he … ?"

"No. Sam saved me."

"The dog … oh, thank God." Helen pet Sam

then turned to Vin, her emotions chaotic, and smacked him upside the head. "Why can't you buy me a big dog?"

At precisely 12:14 in the morning, the 1976 Volkswagen van with the two-tone white and tangerine-orange paint turned into the driveway and parked, expelling its driver—a bearded man wearing a soaking-wet floral shirt and tuxedo pants. He paused to remove something from the glove box then slogged to the front door and keyed in.

Jacob found Nancy on the sofa, cuddled next to Sam. "Vin called. He told me what happened. Are you okay?"

She nodded then stood and sobbed against his chest.

The whimpering dog nuzzled his legs.

"Nance, I swear to God, nothing happened with me and Ruby. Not tonight, not ever."

"I know. She called. She told me about the cancer. Why are you all wet?"

"I saw you speed off in the water taxi, so I leaped in after you."

"You leaped into the Intracoastal from a moving boat? You, Mr. Hydrophobia?"

"I had to catch you. Plus, I needed to get away

from that crazy bitch, Olivia."

"Olivia Cabot?"

"She hired me to do her father's birthday party. I was going to tell you, but I figured we'd see each other aboard her yacht. Only this gay pet dude spiked my ginger ale with ecstasy. Then Olivia tried to jump my bones."

"Wait, my boss was trying to sleep with you too?"

"What can I tell you—I'm a gray-pussy magnet. Only, it was the craziest thing. Every time I tried to get away from her, I kept getting shocked, like I was wearing Sam's collar."

She looked at his wrist. Seeing the dive watch, she tore it loose and tossed it. "How strange. Maybe you shouldn't do her gigs anymore."

"I only agreed to take it because I needed the money … for this." He reached into his pocket and removed the small box he had kept in the Volkswagen's glove box the last two weeks. "For you."

She opened it, revealing a one-carat diamond ring. "Jacob?"

"They say the third time's the charm. Marry me, Nancy, and I promise to put away my smelly shoes and wipe the toilet seat. I'll even buy you a white foofie dog."

She wiped back tears then leaned in and kissed him. "Thanks, but I already have a dog."

56

Dog Training the American Husband
Lesson One: Becoming A Family

SEVERAL DOZEN WEDDING guests filed into the sanctuary, the wedding ceremony minutes from starting. Helen located the maid of honor by the women's dressing room. Lana was dressed in a pink floral. "How's it going with the bride?"

"Nancy needs fifteen more minutes. Where's the best man?"

"In the men's room getting Cabot ready for my mother-in-law."

Dr. Vincent Cope was in a bathroom stall, seated on a toilet and facing Truman Cabot. The old man's back was pressed against the stall door, his dress pants unraveled in a pile around his ankles, exposing his silk boxer shorts.

Peeling the paper from the back of the colostomy bag's doughnut-shaped rubber housing, Vin applied a small amount of paste and then pressed the adhesive in place against the exposed flesh of Truman's lower-left belly.

The retired millionaire fidgeted. "Are you sure your father had a colostomy bag?"

"Yes, along with the rest of Ma's lovers. Now hold still while I snap the colostomy bag in place. Jesus, Truman, did you have to fill it with so much urine?"

"How the hell else will she see it when I walk Nancy down the aisle?"

Spencer entered the bathroom. The dog trainer washed his hands then checked his breath again, readying himself for his next kiss. "Ruby Kleinhenz, best in show. God, I feel like a teen again."

Suddenly Spencer realized he was not alone.

"Slow down! You're hurting me!"

"Damn thing's hard as a rock. I need to drain it if you expect me to slip it back inside your pants."

"Don't jerk it! It'll explode all over your face."

Glancing in the mirror, Spencer saw the old man's head bouncing against the inside of the stall door.

Dog Training the American Male

The dog trainer gagged and then hurried out.

Sandra Beach sat in the cramped dressing room drying her own tears as she listened to her youngest daughter. "We wanted to tell you, but what was the point? We adopted you when you were only eight weeks old. Lana was only two. How did you find out?"

"Dad told me on his death bed. He apologized for leaving Lana a larger inheritance. He said it was done … because she was his."

"Yes, you received less money, but that was because we paid back all your college loans, not to mention the down payments your father and I forfeited from two cancelled wedding ceremonies. As far as Lana being his, your father was delirious. They had him on heavy doses of morphine. He loved you just as much as your sister and was so proud when you earned all your degrees. He was your father, Nancy. Look at your face—you ruined your make-up."

Nancy dried her eyes. "I love you, Mom. I guess this wasn't the best place to bring all this up."

"I should say not. Thank God Jacob's a stable man, or I'd really be worried about you. Now when can I expect some grandbabies?"

Rabbi Solomon Jian stood at the pulpit, the groom and best man to his left.

The music began.

As maid of honor, Lana walked down the aisle first, followed by Helen, a bridesmaid. Rabbi Jian's eyes widened as he witnessed a second bridesmaid stride down the aisle in pumps, her dress barely containing her 230-pound muscular frame.

Next up was the flower girl. An inebriated Carmella Cope puttered slowly down the aisle in her motorized wheelchair, dropping rose petals from a basket as she veered drunkenly from side to side, ramming guests and knocking over flower arrangements on both sides of the aisle.

Vincent guided her into her parking space in the first row, taking the keys.

The music changed, announcing the bride. The crowd stood.

Nancy was escorted slowly down the aisle by Mr. Cabot, the old man's pants bulging on his left side from the fake colostomy bag.

Jacob leaned over to whisper in his brother's ear. "Vin, have you got the ring?"

"On the way."

Sam followed the bride down the aisle, carrying a pillow in his mouth, the ring held in place by a white ribbon.

"Nicely played, sir."

"Thank you. Have you have got your vows?"

Jacob's expression dropped. "Vows?"

The guests on the left side of the aisle shrieked as they were doused by a fountain of urine, Mr. Cabot's colostomy bag having sprung a leak.

From the front row, Carmella Cope eyeballed Truman like a bee to honey.

"Your wedding vows, Jacob! You and Nancy agreed to make up your own vows."

"Shh, it's okay. I'll just quote her some John Lennon. I'll open with, 'A dream you dream alone is only a dream. A dream you dream together is reality.' Then I'll hit her with, 'Love is like a flower; you've got to let it grow.' I'll end with, 'And we all shine on … like the moon and the stars and the sun,' or do you prefer, 'I'm not going to change the way I look or the way I feel to conform to anything. I've always been a freak'?"

"You are a freak." Vin searched his tuxedo jacket pocket and extracted a wedding card. Turning his back to the crowd, he tore open the envelope, pocketed the check, and then shoved the "sentiment" in Jacob's pants pocket without reading it.

"Wanda picked it out for me. I'm sure it's bleeding sentiment."

Having finished his Rabbinical duties, Solomon Jian turned to the young couple. "And now Nancy and Jacob would like to exchange vows they've written especially for this blessed occasion. Nancy?"

Nancy removed a slip of paper from her cleavage. "To my best friend and partner: Today we continue a journey that began only a short time ago. You are the man of my dreams, my one true soul mate. I eagerly anticipate the chance for us to grow together, getting to know the husband you will become, falling in love a little bit more each and every day. You are the Y who empowers me."

"Lovely. Jacob?"

Jacob removed the wedding card his brother had slipped in his pocket fifteen minutes earlier. "Hickory Dickory Doc, we hope she likes your cock. If she likes to screw, congrats to you. Hickory Dickory Doc."

The Rabbi's jaw dropped.

Nancy smiled. "Well, I would have preferred a John Lennon quote, but I do like your cock."

"That's what I told Vin, but he insisted I take the card."

Helen shot her husband a look to kill.

Vin snatched back the card. "Beautiful sentiment. Empowering, don't you think? Rabbi, you, uh, want to finish the ceremony."

"Uh, yes. I now pronounce you man and wife. You may kiss the bride."

The guests were seated at tables situated around a small dance floor. The band played a hokey rendition of Adele's "Someone Like You" as Jacob and Nancy Cope took their first dance together as husband and wife.

Nancy glanced at the table on her left where Truman Cabot was seated next to her mother-in-law, the millionaire offering her a thumbs-up. Spencer was seated at the next table over holding hands with Ruby.

"Jacob, I need to ask you a question. The whole time I was training Sam, did you know I was using the dog training techniques on you?"

"Not at first."

"When did you start to get suspicious? Was it the sex? The walks in the park? The exercise routine?"

"I think it was just before you had Sam neutered, the time you hired the mobile dog groomer to come over and bathe the dog. For days my eyes were tearing at work. That's when I realized you paid them to fumigate my van for fleas."

"Sorry."

"It's okay."

"It needed it."

"It was still sneaky."

"How 'bout I blow you on the drive to the airport to make up for it."

"Cool."

Nancy stopped dancing, her right shoe sliding in white icing. "Jacob, where's the dog?"

"The dog?" He searched the room, his eyes settling on the dessert spread. Sam's front paws were on the table, the German shepherd was eating the wedding cake. "Aw, hell, it's ruined. Vin's kids were supposed to be watching him."

"It's okay."

"Stupid dog's gonna shit his brains out. Remind me to tell Vin to keep him chained outside tonight."

Nancy kissed her husband. "Don't tell him. He'll figure it out in the morning."

L.A. Knight was the first pup born to a litter of four. Managing to escape from several disobedient schools in Philadelphia and a failed mating with a Shih Tzu from New York, L.A. relocated to South Florida and quickly went in heat over a gorgeous poodle who was still nursing two pups from a prior breeding. The couple had produced two pups of their own when L.A. penned DOG TRAINING THE AMERICAN MALE. To reach the author, contact L.A. at: lknightentertain@aol.com